DEATH UN

Dennis Casley

Constable · London

First published in Great Britain 1995
by Constable & Company Ltd
3 The Lanchesters, 162 Fulham Palace Road
London W6 9ER
Copyright © 1995 by Dennis Casley
The right of Dennis Casley to be
identified as the author of this work
has been asserted by him in accordance
with the Copyright, Designs and Patents Act 1988
ISBN 0 09 475130 7
Set in Linotron Palatino 10 pt by
Pure Tech India Ltd, Pondicherry
Printed and bound in Great Britain
by Hartnolls Ltd., Bodmin, Cornwall

A CIP catalogue record for this book
is available from the British Library

1

Cari Odhiambo looked at her husband over the rim of her glass. Despite his protestations to the contrary he was adapting to American beer and was now showing every sign of enjoyment as he quaffed deeply from his second glass. Cari was concerned about her husband's mental state, rather than his physical. He was recovering well from his head injury and the rest of him had healed almost as good as new. But he was edgy, nervous and tense. He seemed uncomfortable in her parents' Virginia home, and even when they were alone together his normal openness and easiness with her were missing. It was understandable, of course. He had survived a series of horrific times in Cornwall – enough to make any man a nervous wreck – but Cari knew it was something else that was troubling him. Ah well, she would get him to open up in time.

Meanwhile the sun, although it was late in the fall, was warm and they were sitting on the verandah of a fish restaurant beside the Potomac, on the outskirts of the attractive old town of Alexandria. Cari put down her wineglass.

'Penny for them, big guy.'

Chief Inspector James Odhiambo looked at his wife appraisingly. Actually, he was feeling more relaxed than he had since arriving in America. The beer, the attractive and restful scene as a few small boats pottered about on the water, and the mildly warming sun had achieved a restful state in his troubled mind. Pulled back now to his quandary by his wife's casual question, he prevaricated.

'Just day-dreaming, Cari. Letting the world go by.' He smiled. 'Somehow I imagined Washington to be a frenetic place. Seems peaceful enough here.'

Cari looked across the water towards the nation's capital.

'There's plenty of problems over there, believe me. But none of them anything to do with you, thank God. It's great you're finding it restful.' She looked back at the large dark man opposite. 'You've got some way to go yet. You're not your old self. But as long as you're getting there.'

Again she sensed the shutter behind the eyes. There was something he was holding back, something related to his recent experiences. Well, she was confident he would tell her in his own good time. They had always had a completely open relationship and James was not the type of man to hold things inside him, to bottle things up. It was his attempt to do so now that was so evidently causing him great difficulty. Tonight, perhaps, she would get him to bed early and establish close contact in every sense. Then she remembered, damn, her parents were giving a cocktail party tonight; a party in honour of their son-in-law to welcome him to Washington. That meant a late night and, probably, a tipsy and exhausted husband. Ah well, another time. Once more she allowed her eyes to turn towards the river.

What a fine-looking woman he had, James Odhiambo thought, as he watched his wife turn back to look at the riverside scene. With a model's face, but with more than a model's curves, she roused his sexual feeling merely by sitting there. On top of that she possessed a fine mind (getting a little too heavily into feminism and other trendy causes, he was discovering) and held a well-paid job. What more could a man ask? Well, attributes like loyalty and sympathy – she gave him these too. What could he have been thinking of, back there on the Cornish coast? But even as his mind asked the question, he could see an image of the woman who had shared with him the horrors of those days and into whose bed he had invited himself. Guilt lay on his soul. Betrayal was bad enough, but concealing his secret was betrayal perpetuated. Should he confess? He knew what his old Luo friends would say over a beer in the bars of Kisumu: a man is entitled to a little fun when he's away from home. But one of the reasons Odhiambo had not maintained old friendships was his desire to break away from old habits and customs and, yes, crassness.

'Don't forget you've got to be on your best behaviour tonight.' His wife's words were tossed back over her shoulder. 'Mum and Dad's party for you.'

Odhiambo groaned, but inwardly.

'Ah, yes. Who's coming? Or did you tell me already? Don't suppose it makes any difference. I wouldn't know anyone.'

'One or two from the University.' Cari's father was a professor at

6

a local Virginia campus. 'One or two, I think, from the Embassy. Sally Eves. You should have heard of her if you were up in current social affairs. She's a friend of mine. I mentioned her already. She wrote *Women on the Cross*. A major piece of feminist writing. Or as one of the male critics wrote, "She advances feminism to a new intensity of bile against her perceived oppression of her sex by man." ' Cari laughed, to show she didn't take her friend's work too seriously. 'And my boss, of course, Glen Hills. I want to show you off to him.'

Cari had turned to face her husband again and laid a long-nailed hand on his leg. This time Odhiambo groaned audibly.

'Jeez, Cari. Academics, diplomats and your boss. What a prospect. What did you say this woman wrote? *Women on the Cross*. My God!'

'No pun intended, I assume. You'll enjoy . . .' Cari broke off as she saw her husband stiffen and narrow his eyes. She turned to look along his line of sight. A man was jogging along the towpath by the river. As she looked, Cari thought the figure was vaguely familiar, but couldn't place him. 'You recognise that guy? James! I'm talking, feller. You recognise him?'

Odhiambo refocused on to his wife's face. He had once heard a statistician debunking the constant amazement of people at the "it's a small world" coincidences that seem to occur with regularity. 'Usually,' the statistician had said, 'there's a hidden correlation, a link. Like they're all shuttling around the same international circuit on business. The actual number is quite small in relative terms, they're bound to bump into each other occasionally.' Odhiambo had thought at the time that there was something in this and his recent experiences confirmed it. Now it had happened again.

'You remember the Nairobi business. The girl in Hawk's Nest. Well, one of the men in her circle was called Fulton. I'm pretty sure that was him that just jogged past.'

Memories flooded back to Cari. Waiting for the murderer to call in that house with that bastard Price-Allen outside. How could she forget?

'Fulton? I'm not sure I met him. But you spoke of him. Badly as I remember. Wasn't he a banker?'

'Yeah. With some international outfit. I guess that explains it.'

'Oh. IBID. It's just up the river, in Rosslyn on Wilson Boulevard. He's probably taking a run during his lunch break.'

'Well, I'll be dammed. Fulton. Never thought I'd see him again.

Never wanted to see him again if I tell the truth. It's a respectable outfit is it, this IBID?'

'Nearly as blue chip as the World Bank. Big loans to companies in countries like Kenya. OK as long as you don't mind environmental damage. Most of these development deals involve harm to the environment.'

'Yes, it comes back now. He was putting together a loan for some shady operation in Mombasa. A man of dubious morals, Mr Fulton.'

'Well, when you meet Sally Eves tonight, you can join her new organisation, SEND. Then you can do Mr Fulton down.'

Odhiambo gazed at his wife, who seemed determinedly cheerful. He allowed himself to capture a little of her mood. His mouth widened in the beginning of a smile.

'SEND. What the hell's that?'

'Stop Environmental Degradation. Sally wants me to join. Then we can picket IBID's offices.'

Odhiambo laughed, genuine laughter.

'You join a woolly group like that? You work for Metroarcs, remember? In Kenya, Metroarcs is seen as the sort of multinational that your friend should be lobbying against.'

Cari tossed her head and got up, ready to leave.

'That's what impresses her. I'm an employee of Metroarcs and I believe in the environment and rights for minorities. Actually Metroarcs has an enlightened attitude. I think.'

As his wife disappeared towards the toilets, Odhiambo signalled to the waiter for his bill. His Luo superstitions told him that seeing Fulton again was an omen – a bad omen. If he had known how bad, he would have driven Cari to Dulles Airport and booked his passage back to Kenya.

2

The seven men and one woman seated around the polished oak table chatted desultorily, but kept one eye on the double doors at the opposite end of the room from the smaller door through which they had entered ten minutes earlier. They had no expectation of escaping their Managing Director's sarcasm, but it didn't help if he noticed your attention was elsewhere when he made his entrance. William Chivers, the only non-director in the room, was amused at the atmosphere of, yes, nervousness – there was no other word for it. These were powerful people, highly paid, each controlling loans running into hundreds of millions, some of them bullies in their own right, but, awaiting the arrival of Giles Faucon, they emitted the tension of boys sitting outside the headmaster's study expecting retribution for some misdemeanour.

Suddenly the double doors opened and there framed in the opening to his personal office stood a small, slender man with greying hair brushed tight to his scalp, piercing almost translucent blue eyes above a sharp nose, and a mouth that in repose seemed set in a wry grimace at the stupidity of his fellow men. He moved to his chair at the head of the table on which sat a file containing his papers for this morning's meeting, one of which was Chivers' paper summarising recent findings of his section within the Internal Audit Department.

Faucon's nod and good morning were greeted with the expectancy of an audience hearing the opening lines of *Richard III*. He sat, gazed for a moment or two at the closed file in front of him and then, without opening it, looked around the table.

'The first item this morning is the paper on recent evaluations of intra-country procurements. I see you're bottom of the league again, Paul.'

Paul Villiers looked up, startled. His briefing notes said nothing of any regional league table.

'I beg your pardon, Giles, what league exactly?'

Faucon smiled, an old trick had worked again.

'Annexe 2, man. The table showing the incidence of projects with concerns regarding improper practices within our clients' systems. I had assumed you had all read Mr . . . er . . . Mr Chivers' interesting piece.'

A brief flash of the eyes down the table acknowledged Chivers' presence. Around him hasty mutters of reassurance that the paper had been read, and anxious scanning of their briefing notes.

Villiers gathered his wits and attempted his riposte.

'East Asia has the fastest disbursement profile and the highest success rate of projects, Giles. Yes, there are problems associated with accelerating performance, but I am confident –'

'Your propensity to change the subject is as strong as ever, I see.'

Yes, thought Chivers, Faucon is well named. He looks like a bird, a bird of prey. 'I am discussing system leakages. If there are leaks, the faster the flow the more is lost. Are we all clear, regarding the subject of discussion?'

Mensat Khan knew that he would not avoid attention for long, so he might as well enter the lists early. He leaned back in his chair as he turned slightly towards Faucon. His high forehead gleamed as it reflected the light from above, for the room was windowless – no scene across the Potomac to the Lincoln Memorial and the Washington Monument was available as a distraction.

'It must be conceded, Giles, that attempts to short-circuit approved procurement procedures have been and are being made. In Nigeria, it is a constant concern, as this paper usefully quantifies.' Khan's manicured hands spread out, palms upwards, in the ancient gesture seeking understanding. 'But, in some countries, and Nigeria is notably one, such practices are inbuilt into company procedures. You might say they are institutionalised.'

Faucon fixed Khan with his almost hypnotic stare. He did not much like Mensat Khan. His patrician arrogance, stemming from his wealthy Pakistani family, his effortless air of superiority and his beautifully modulated voice – that of a former President of the Oxford Union – all irritated Faucon, who had come from humble French stock and spoke English flawlessly, but with a slight mid-Atlantic accent derived from his days at Harvard.

'You've used that excuse in many contexts, Mensat. It is as unacceptable today as on previous occasions.' He paused and then continued, speaking more slowly as if to a slightly retarded child. 'We exist to channel money through such companies and to insist on proper procedures to improve their performance and sustainability. That's why we have you and your large staff.'

Chivers relaxed in his comfortable leather chair. He was there in case elucidation of his paper was required. As usual, with Faucon in the chair, such backstopping was unnecessary. It seemed unlikely he would be asked to speak, nor indeed, as the discussion went on, was he.

Chivers left the building on Wilson Boulevard, in Rosslyn, Virginia, and inhaled the air with appreciation. It was a glorious autumnal day after what had been a hot, humid summer. His own office was a few hundred yards away in the direction of Key Bridge. He strolled leisurely down the sloping road towards it. He enjoyed his job with the International Bank for International Development. It was much smaller in staff and lending volumes than its big brother across the river – the World Bank. It had been set up to lend directly to companies, not governments, in countries where companies were trying to nurture the private industrial and rural development sectors, often despite, rather than with the assistance of, their own governments. Chivers worked within the Internal Audit Department, but he was not a financial accounts auditor. His task was to detect fraud in connection with the services or the products that the client company provided to their customers. IBID's money was to be used to purchase inputs that would lead to quantified outputs of a specified quality. It was not unknown for the company to sign all the legal agreements and then to use the loans for some other purpose or, and this is where Chivers came in, to procure an inferior input or produce a lower quality output, thus achieving substantial savings to be diverted for unauthorised purposes. Listening to Mensat Khan earlier reminded Chivers of his current investigation involving one of the largest projects in Nigeria. The data set he had acquired with some digging and a lot of persuasion was assembled on his computer and ready for statistical analysis. Chivers thought that Khan might well have cause for concern. Those more directly responsible were already showing agitation. Kraxma, the dour mid-European sector manager, would be smoking even more heavily, except that he chain-smoked already. And then there was Romaine Caradonna. Chivers was not so old that thoughts of the woman who supervised the Nigeria project could fail to conjure up her physical splendour. He had heard that she had needed an armed guard in Nigeria to keep the men away from her. Exaggerated perhaps, but Romaine was living proof that a Ph.D. in macroeconomics was not incompatible with a high-voltage sexual charge.

These thoughts occupied Chivers until he approached the entrance to the building in which his office was situated – a building leased to house the 'overflow' from IBID's new headquarters he had just left, mainly low-profile departments such as Internal Audit. Chivers had formulated a corollary to one of the old-established Parkinson Laws, namely, whatever its size, a new building on completion will be too small to house the staff for which it was designed.

As he went through the door and showed his pass to the security guard he saw, hovering in the background, the chief of security for

11

IBID, Simon Katawi, a Kenyan. This moved his thoughts on Africa abruptly from the West to the East, for it was Kenya that presented him with his other current problem, only this one was more personal, and, unlike his official concerns, it deeply upset him. It was not pleasant to be in his current dilemma. He had thought that putting pressure on an old friend, a man he liked and respected, was bad enough, but now he faced the prospect of putting himself up front as the key witness and he could guess the furore that would break out when he issued a statement. What was more, he could be in physical danger. His acute sense of the bizarre saw the ironic humour in that. He sighed, his spirits, which had risen in the crisp sunshine, deflated once more. Ah well, problems were designed to be tackled. Thrusting his shoulders back he strode towards what he had learnt to call the elevators.

Simon Katawi watched the man's back as he entered the elevator. He knew Chivers' history. He was one of those white Kenyans who had welcomed the end of the colonial era and who had stayed on, first in government, then in a successful business with Kenyan partners, and who remained discreet when it came to matters of Kenyan politics. The sort of white man that President Kenyatta had said was welcome and needed in Kenya. He should have stayed there, thought Katawi. He had taken the trouble to check Chivers' position in IBID – there were, he had heard, those who were deeply concerned about the investigation Chivers was currently conducting. Making enemies was not unusual for an auditor in an organisation like IBID containing powerful people with egos to match, but it left Chivers exposed. Was it plausible that work concerns could lead to anything, even murder?

3

Abbie Bito surveyed her dinner table on which a substantial buffet was laid out. The party was beginning to gather momentum as her husband dispensed drinks and the hubbub of conversation picked up. Her son-in-law was holding his end up, although she knew he was not in his element. His face when he emerged from his and Cari's rooms revealed his foreboding. He was a man, she thought, who was not happy when faced with a group of assorted people previously unknown to him. Abbie had taken various psychology courses at Georgetown University – she recognised in her son-in-law the profile of a man who was uneasy with strangers unless he was in control of the circumstances. In other words he needed to dominate his immediate environment. Cari, now, was a different character altogether. She was in her element here in Washington and in a typical Washington social scene. Abbie knew that Cari found life in her native country uncomfortable – she felt more at home here than in Nairobi. And why not – after all she had been raised here, when she and Sam had left Kenya for good and settled here in the early 1960s. Cari had been a small girl then and remembered little of her very first years in Kenya. Abbie suspected that an impending crisis in the Cari–James Odhiambo marriage would come soon, when it was time for Cari to return to Kenya with her husband.

But it was not her daughter's future that was troubling Abbie Bito. It was that of her husband, Samuel Bito. There he was, mingling with his guests, apologising for his late arrival at his own party, conveying the impression of a typical absent-minded professor. He was small in stature but, Abbie believed, still distinguished-looking – in fact, more so now his hair had turned a suitably academic grey. Abbie did not feel as if America was her home, despite the long years of residence and her liking for their life here. Samuel, she knew, did now regard himself as virtually American, although he had not taken the final step of applying for citizenship. He loved American football, basketball and hamburgers. Abbie still remembered the immediate pre-independence years in Kenya when her husband had participated in the political movements of the day, joining the Kenya African Democratic Union (KADU) party, the one that was foolhardy enough to run against Kenyatta's KANU. KADU's stronghold was the West – the Luos – and was doomed to lose the elections to the Kikuyu-based KANU. Samuel Bito never spoke of those days now. Even less, if such were possible, did he refer to the dramatic events that had led them to leave Kenya for ever. She could almost believe that he had banished the memories that still came to her on sleepless nights. But now the past was returning, she was sure of it. And Samuel Bito must face the agony of choice once again. Abbie Bito was fearful.

'A penny for your thoughts, Abbie, as Cari said to me earlier today.'

Abbie Bito looked around and up at her tall, powerfully built

13

son-in-law. They made a handsome pair, her daughter and this policeman. Abbie was proud of her daughter; her physical make-up had avoided the wide-hipped, big-bottomed inheritance that was the cause of Abbie's battles against further expansion now she was in middle age. Yet, pleased though they both were to have them here, she knew that James' presence acted as a visual amplification of the Kenya that had returned to haunt them.

'Oh, James. I guess everyone's here who's coming and had time for more than one drink. I was thinking – time to eat.'

Odhiambo nodded and smiled. But he had seen her face as she gazed blankly around the room. Ever since his first morning here he had sensed some trouble in what seemed an ideal middle-class American life. He had tried to probe Cari, but, sensitive though she was on some subjects, she seemed to have a blind spot when it came to insight regarding her parents.

'It was good of you to go to this trouble. Or do you entertain like this all the time?'

Abbie smiled.

'Not too often. Samuel is getting more anti-parties than ever as he gets older.'

'Good for him.' Odhiambo stopped, realising his endorsement of his father-in-law's aversion was rude, given his listener's efforts to make this party a success. 'I mean, er, a party like this is great, but . . . er . . . not all . . .'

He was saved from further embarrassment.

'Don't spiel me, James. I saw your expression when you faced the impending demand of being social. You're like Samuel. So have you met everyone?'

'Most, I think. But don't ask me to remember who they all were. I'm hopeless at this sort of thing.'

He saw, near the door to the hall, Cari gesturing at him to join her. With Cari was a tall man, white but with a well-tanned skin. His mother-in-law saw the summons also.

'Cari wants you, James. Her boss has just arrived, Glen Hills. Supposed to be one of the smartest lobbyists in DC. This is the only town where one of the best jobs is putting pressure on politicians.'

Odhiambo sighed.

'Well, I'd better obey. I'll be back for some of those prawns. And that *nyama*, what do you call them again?'

'Spare ribs.' Abbie laughed. 'I don't know the Swahili for that. Now get over there.'

14

*

Sally Eves surveyed her fellow guests from her vantage point on the step leading from the main living area to what was a small dining-room, not in use tonight for that purpose as the buffet was laid out along one wall of the larger room. A pretty dull crowd, she thought, which was what she had expected given that Bito, from what she knew of him at the University, was a pretty dull man. She had come because Cari had asked her and Cari was worth nurturing. An African who was rising within Metroarcs' hierarchy was worthy of note – but when that person was young, beautiful and female, Sally's interest was aroused. She sipped her glass of Californian Chardonnay, conscious that she was the object of some attention. She was the only well-known person in the room: her death's head face with skin stretched tight against a high cheekboned skull was a familiar sight gazing out of the cover of trendy and intellectual magazines. Her head guaranteed she would stand out in a throng, but with her tall, angular frame as well she was a distinctive presence indeed. Feminism was still her main source of a good living as a writer and lecturer, but she was growing bored and had a strong suspicion that she was seen by the new generation as being old-fashioned. She had wanted a new challenge and with SEND she believed she had found it.

She had arrived late – later than the normal thirty minutes after the time of the invitation – and was on her first drink whilst many had moved over to the buffet and were sampling the fare. One or two arrived even later than herself. She had just missed running into that bastard, Glen Hills; he had been a couple of minutes behind her. Later still she noticed the arrival of a squarely built black man – African, she thought – who looked vaguely familiar. Had she met him at Bito's campus? She thought not, but what did it matter? She noticed Cari Bito talking to her boss, the two joined by a tall, strong-looking, handsome man – another African, she thought. Then she realised, this must be the husband, the excuse for the party, but to Sally he was the threat that could deprive her of a useful contact in Metroarcs, if he dragged her back to Kenya.

'Good evening. It's Miss Eves, isn't it?'

Sally turned towards the speaker who had joined her on the higher level. He was the African she thought looked familiar. Close up she could see that his square build owed much to a chest and shoulder area of weightlifter proportions compared to which the

15

beer belly, although evident, was still subordinate. Middle-aged now, he was likely in the next few years, Sally thought, to become a tub of lard as the chest muscles lost their tone.

'Yes, that's me. Have we met?'

The cool hauteur seemed to pass by her companion.

'Yes, we have. I've seen you with Mr Faucon. I work for IBID, you see. Security.'

Sally looked at him appraisingly. Her relationship with the head of IBID was not a particularly public one. Both of them were sensitive to the fact that professionally they were an ill-matched pair. SEND and IBID were scarcely bed-fellows. And they were an ill-matched physical pair with her height and his lack of it. Sex was the magnetic force between them. The aura of power was what made Giles Faucon attractive to Sally – he exuded it more pungently than almost any man she had known.

'Are you Mr Faucon's bodyguard?'

Simon Katawi shook his head.

'No, no, not that. I'm in charge of security at IBID. Mr Faucon asked me to arrange for an extended visitor's pass for you. When you visited his office a month or two ago.'

'I see. Well, thank you for the pass, but I would prefer that a personal matter not be the subject of cocktail gossip.'

Katawi could recognise a rebuff. He had been about to drink from his glass of beer, but now lowered it without it reaching his lips.

'I'm sorry – I was only explaining how I recognised you. Good evening.'

Suddenly his companion's scowl gave way to a smile which seemed to stretch the already tight skin of her face to breaking point.

'No, wait. That was rude of me. Tell me, Mr . . . er . . . , are you from Kenya like Mr Bito? You are. I gather Miss Bito's husband is the guest of honour tonight. Is that him over there?'

She pointed at the group in question from which Cari had become detached.

'Katawi is my name. I'm a friend of Dr Bito, but I don't know Miss Bito well. But that's her husband. Another Kenyan. He's a policeman.'

'And wanting to take dear Cari back there, it seems. Such a pity. She would do so much better here. How long have you been here in the States?'

'A long time, ma'am, nearly as long as Dr Bito. He never goes back, but I like to get back home occasionally.'

16

'Did you know him when you were in Kenya?'

'Oh no.' The denial was delivered with emphasis. 'He's older than me, and he comes from a different tribe, a different part of Kenya.'

'I hear he left because of some scandal or other. Never struck me as the sort of man to be mixed up in any shady stuff.'

Katawi looked away; he was not prepared to proceed down this road.

'I don't know nothing about that, Miss Eves. Now if you'll excuse me . . .'

Sally Eves laughed, loud enough to turn a few heads in their direction.

'See no evil, hear no evil, speak no evil, eh, my security friend? Well, I'll tell you something, Mr Security. I hear that your government is looking into the death of one of your old politicos from way back. And Samuel Bito is wanted as a witness.'

'Yes, I believe so. A man called Omuto was shot at a railway station. It was a long time ago. Someone walked up and shot him twice and disappeared.'

'And now they want Samuel Bito as a witness.'

Her voice had risen and was audible to others around them. Simon Katawi backed away, looking for anonymity from the stares. He buried his face in his glass of beer. He made a mental note to steer clear of Miss Eves in the future. What on earth was a man like Faucon doing mixed up with a woman like that? Wasn't even as if she was good-looking. Scraggy sort of bird with that bony face. Wouldn't be his cup of tea if he had Faucon's money and power. He liked women with a bit of flesh on them.

Odhiambo had not expected to like Glen Hills, his wife's boss while she was working in Washington. He knew Hills was a lobbyist and in his mind's eye he equated lobbying with greasy palms and slimy deals over alcoholic lunches. He had been disturbed to discover that Cari was working, however temporarily, in this particular aspect of Metroarcs' business. She had pooh-poohed his qualms, saying her job was researching pending legislation and writing to Congressmen on aspects of such legislation where Metroarcs had a legitimate interest. He had dropped the matter but he remained doubtful.

Hills, however, turned out to be a man one could warm to. He

17

possessed the distinctly American male presence that combined widely set eyes, humorous mouth, firm jaw line, with the easy confidence acquired by a white, upper-class male with the backing of an expensive liberal education. About forty years of age, Odhiambo guessed, he had the air about him of an athlete who was keeping in good trim. Indeed, Hills, in appraising Odhiambo speculatively, revealed his athletic background.

'You know something, James, you should have got to this side of the water when you were college age. Like your lovely wife, here.' He looked to his right, but Cari had slipped away leaving the two men together. 'You've got the build for a good tight-end.'

'Tight-end?'

'Gee, I'm sorry. I guess you don't know much about our form of football. What do you play over there? Soccer, I guess. Yep? Sure. Well, a big guy like you, tall, good body strength – you could have got a football scholarship.'

'I wasn't very good at sports at school, in fact. And I doubt if I'd have been tough enough for your football. I never took much to being thumped about. What about you?'

'Yeah, I played a little. At college.'

'More than a little, I'd say.' A short portly man had joined them who, Odhiambo remembered, had been introduced as a working colleague of his father-in-law. 'More than a little, Glen.' He turned to Odhiambo. 'He was good, fast and strong with good hands. Could have made it in the pros. But he thought he was smart. Graduated well instead and decided to be a lawyer. We got plenty of lawyers. It's footballers we need.'

Hills laughed.

'No, James is right, Otto. I wasn't that keen on getting my brains scrambled either. And unless you were a quarter-back, the money wasn't so hot either. I reckon I'm better off on the Hill.' Hills turned back to Odhiambo. 'But you, James, you're in a tough business from what I hear. Otto, you know James here, right? Cari's husband.'

Odhiambo looked across to where Cari was chatting to another woman. She was looking marvellous as always in a cocktail dress, simple, sleek, black, that showed off her elegant figure and looked expensive. Probably cost more than his month's salary. He felt the familiar stirring of discomfort at finding himself an inferior being in his wife's world instead of the dominant force in his own. Yes, in

18

these surroundings Hills had summed him up perfectly, he was Cari's husband. He muttered the usual disclaimer.

'It's mainly routine. Can be boring, even.'

But Hills was persistent.

'Don't try and kid us, James. We were worried when Cari had to fly over the pond to go sit by your bedside. You had a rough time in peaceful old rural England from what little she told me. You all healed up again now?'

'Getting there, as Cari likes to say.'

'You know this guy, Otto. Attracts bodies, they say. Down in some sleepy old English scene he was piling them up at a rate of knots, what I hear.'

The third man smiled.

'Well, he should feel at home here – murder capital of the world, we're billed as now.'

Odhiambo was making the effort to be sociable.

'Why is that? I thought New York would hold that title.'

'No, siree. New York, the drugs are controlled by the Mafia. At least they keep others out. Here in Washington we're wide open and drug use is exploding. The Jamaicans have moved in and that upsets the Cubans and so on. They're knocking each other off at quite a lick. You'd never know uptown, but go down past 14th Street and you're in a different world.'

Hills grimaced and intervened.

'Don't go running us down to our guest of honour, Otto. If the drug gangs want to take each other out that's fine by me.'

'Oh, sure. Until one of these Jamaican guys becomes like Capone and starts buying politicians, if he isn't already.'

Suddenly, across their conversation, they heard the raised voice of a woman. They were too far away to pick up the words, but Odhiambo noted that heads closer to her turned as she posed on the raised area at the far end of the room. He saw Cari move across the room towards her, but the woman descended the step to meet her, laying her hand on Cari's arm as they met. Normal conversation broke out again; the incident, whatever it was, seemed over. As Odhiambo turned back to his companions he found that the man called Otto had moved away. Hills was frowning.

'Sally Eves wanting more attention as usual. Stupid bitch.'

'Sally Eves? Cari told me about her. She's well known, isn't she?' Odhiambo asked. 'A writer or something?'

Hills laughed sardonically.

'A goddam feminist is what she is, James. Yes, she puts all that "down with men" stuff in books and articles. Now she's into the environment, save the planet shit. Anti-development in countries like yours, James. As long as she's got her limo and pool you guys in Africa can stay in mud huts, but you must not cut down trees or build factories or dam rivers to improve your lot in life.'

There was genuine anger in the voice. Odhiambo remembered his conversation with Cari.

'I suppose she disapproves of Metroarcs?'

'Yep, she's on our case. That's where Cari is proving so valuable, James. She's good at handling women like Sally Eves as well as Congressmen who can't take their eyes off her.' There was a momentary pause, then Hills quickly added a rider. 'No offence, James. She can't help looking like a princess.'

Odhiambo was still concentrating on Sally Eves and her organisation – what was it again? He chose his words with some care.

'But Cari seems on very friendly terms with her. She mentioned a group Miss Eves runs. Seemed to think it was harmless.'

'Cari's a natural lobbyist, James. Get close to people, that's the idea. But she's new to the game. Don't buy the other guy's sales pitch. Get him to buy yours. She'll find out that Sally Eves is poison. Meanwhile it's good to have someone mixing with the Eves crowd. They bar the door to me.' He laughed with genuine merriment. 'Not that I fancy her. Face more like the wicked stepmother than Snow White.'

A few minutes later Odhiambo found himself next to his fellow Kenyan, whom he had seen talking to Sally Eves. Odhiambo re-introduced himself in order for the other man to reciprocate.

'Yes, that was it, Katawi. You're a long-time friend of Cari's father, I understand.'

'Yes, Samuel Bito and I have both been here a long time. Maybe too long.'

'I saw you talking to that writer woman. She seemed to get a bit loud. Has she had a glass too many?'

Katawi looked at Odhiambo for what seemed an undue time. Eventually he spoke, lowering his voice.

'She's a strange one, Odhiambo. But she seems to know something about the Omuto business. You know; the government has promised to hold an enquiry.'

Odhiambo was puzzled. Omuto was a prominent Luo politician in the years leading to independence in Kenya, who had joined Kenyatta and the mainly Kikuyu-based party, to the anger of others of his own tribe. His intentions had seemed honourable, he wanted to foster a genuine national unity, not have political parties split on tribal lines. It was widely assumed that after the elections that brought Kenyatta to power Omuto would have been offered a major Cabinet seat. However, getting out of the train at Nakuru for a political rally he was killed by a gunman who had never been caught. Each party blamed the other, but a lot of mud stuck to the leading Luo politicians. Odhiambo had heard that for some reason the matter had been reopened in his absence from Kenya, but what on earth had it to do with Sally Eves?

'The Omuto case? How does she know about that? And why should she care?'

Katawi hesitated again.

'Because she knows Samuel Bito, that is why. And just now when I was talking to her, she seemed to get . . . well sort of nasty, and that's when she got a bit loud. She said your father, I mean father-in-law, well, she said he knew something about it.'

Odhiambo stared in genuine bewilderment. What on earth was he, or rather this peculiar woman, on about?

'I don't understand. I –'

He was interrupted by the subject of Sally Eves' remarks. Samuel Bito had come up behind his son-in-law, but it was Odhiambo's companion he was seeking.

'Sorry, James, to interrupt. Katawi, there's a phone message. You're needed at the IBID building. The annexe on North Lynn Street. Someone's been found dead.'

Katawi's jaw dropped in an almost theatrical manner.

'Someone dead? Outside the building, you mean? An accident?'

Odhiambo could see the strain on Bito's face.

'No, in his office. A man called Chivers.'

As Odhiambo looked into his father-in-law's eyes, he could see not only concern but something else which seemed out of place. Samuel Bito was a very frightened man.

4

Odhiambo followed Katawi's instructions and drove the car down the ramp into the underground parking area. Many of the parking slots had designated users painted on the concrete wall and Katawi directed Odhiambo to one designated 'IBID Security'. Next to it, Odhiambo noticed, the sign said 'IBID Chief Security'. It was occupied. Katawi had told him he had taken a taxi to the party, intending to have a few beers and so not wishing to drive. Odhiambo, who had only consumed a glass and a half of beer, had volunteered to drive. Cari had looked at him questioningly, but he assured her he was sober. He was not reluctant to slip away and the name Chivers had struck a memory chord.

'He lived in Kenya, didn't he?' Odhiambo had asked Katawi as they drove down Washington Parkway towards Rosslyn. 'I remember meeting someone with that name. He did some analysis for us once. He was some sort of statistician or whatever.'

Katawi had been looking out across the Potomac glinting in the moonlight; he turned his head towards Odhiambo.

'Yeah, that's right. He lived in Nairobi. Came here a year or so back. I think he's a citizen. Of Kenya, I mean.'

Now, as he got out of the car, he hesitated and then bent to look back at his driver.

'You can go back to the party now. I can get home from here when I'm through. Or . . . or do you want to see him? Chivers, I mean.'

It was Odhiambo's turn to hesitate, but out of politeness more than real reluctance. 'OK. The party can wait. If I don't get in the way.'

The two men entered a small lift, almost filling it. Katawi pressed "Lobby" and they rose briefly, the doors opening on to a foyer.

'This is not our building,' Katawi said as he led Odhiambo out into the street. 'We rent parking space, there's not enough under this building.' He pointed across the street to a nondescript building and started to cross towards it. 'This is our annexe. Couldn't get everyone in our new building. Built it too small. I've got an office here though the main security area is around the corner on Wilson Boulevard.'

There were police cars parked outside the IBID building and a state policeman accosted them at the door. Katawi produced his identification, and, after a second officer consulted his two-way communication system, they were allowed to enter a much larger and smarter lift, or elevator as Katawi called it. When they emerged on the fifth floor the focus of action was immediately visible, with lights full on in the corridor on their left and men entering and leaving doors situated half-way down.

Katawi and Odhiambo were directed into an open-plan office area equipped with filing cabinets and computer terminals. There were no secretaries, but behind one desk sat a lean man chewing a pencil who watched them as they came to a halt in front of him. Extracting the pencil he waved it in an arc embracing the new arrivals.

'Which one of you is the security chief for this place?'

Katawi confirmed his identity. The policeman put the pencil back in the corner of his mouth.

'And who's he?'

'He's with me,' Katawi said, stating the obvious. 'He may know the victim. There is a victim?'

The skin of the pencil cracked as the teeth bit, but for the moment Odhiambo was let off with a suspicious look.

'Oh, yeah, there's a victim all right. A lulu of a victim. My name's Bolling. Lieutenant Bolling, Homicide. You're . . .' He looked down at a piece of paper on the desk. 'Katawi, right? Where you from, buddy?'

'Kenya originally, but I've resident status here, G-IV visa.'

Bolling nodded. There were enough international agencies in and around Arlington County for him to be familiar with the immigration status held by international non-diplomatic staff. He stood up.

'Right, let's go see the body. Cleaning woman found him. There's a name on the door – Chivers – but we aren't sure it's him. You know him, right?'

The three men rounded a partition consisting of bookshelves; Bolling continued on towards a door to one of the individual offices that led off from the open secretarial area. Katawi caught the detective up and asked:

'Hasn't he got his ID on him? His IBID card? Should have his photo on it.'

Bolling looked back and grinned. He stopped with his hand on the door.

'Yeah, he's got a card that says Chivers and that matches the name on this here door. But we'd still like a positive ID. You see, its kinda difficult to match the photo with the face. 'Cos he ain't got much face. You guys ready?'

Bolling pushed open the door. The office was smaller than Od-hiambo expected. He thought IBID executives might work in the sort of offices executives had in movies. There was a desk that was uncluttered except for papers in two metal trays. The right-hand side of the office consisted of a work area with a light wooden top. Papers lay haphazardly around the focal point of a computer termi-nal and the usual accompanying bits and pieces that meant nothing to Odhiambo.

There were only two chairs, one behind the desk and the second lying on its side beside the work area. And lying beside the over-turned chair was a body. Bolling was right: the face, or where the face should have been, was a stomach-turning mess of blood, bone and torn flesh.

'You see my problem?' Bolling perched himself on the corner of the desk. Katawi and Odhiambo were in the doorway because the office was already uncomfortably full with Bolling, the body and two scene of crime officers dusting and tagging. Bolling pointed at Odhiambo. 'You tagged along 'cos you're supposed to know Chi-vers. This him, can you tell?'

Odhiambo shook his head slightly in an expression of hopeless-ness rather than denial. He wasn't sure if he would have recognised Chivers anyway, but with this mangled head there was no chance. Katawi, however, spoke in his place.

'It's horrible. How could this have happened? I saw Mr Chivers earlier today. Coming back into the building. 'Bout eleven. He was wearing a light grey suit like that. And I'd say the body is the right size. I think it's him.'

Odhiambo couldn't stop himself asking the obvious question.
'Where's the weapon?'
Bolling looked at Odhiambo closely once more.
'Where you from, buddy? You didn't say.'
'I'm from Kenya, too. Odhiambo. I guess I'd better say: I'm a detective, too. In Kenya, I mean. No standing here, of course.'

Bolling nodded. 'I thought I could tell. Well, well. The murder weapon's missing but we think it's the twin of that one; cleaner said there were two.' He pointed to the wall opposite the work area. Fastened to the wall was a dark brown club. A handle gradually

24

expanded in thickness and culminated in an oblong and irregular head. 'Looks like some kinda African implement to me. What do you say, buddy?'

Odhiambo nodded. He looked at Bolling. He could sense the detective's thought processes.

'You're right. It's a tribal war club by the look of it. Chivers lived in Kenya, you see. Brought these with him as souvenirs, I expect.'

Bolling was standing again, clearly intending to usher the Kenyans out of Chivers' office.

'So we've got a corpse of a guy who lived in Kenya, gets knocked off by a tribal club, and I got me a couple of Kenyans claiming they're security and police. I guess we need to talk some more, guys.'

A new voice behind Odhiambo addressed Bolling.

'The medic's here, Lieutenant. Can she come in?'

'Right, fellows, make way for the ME. Hi, Miss Kasulski, how's it going?'

As Odhiambo made way for the grey-haired woman who pushed past, his eyes caught the computer terminal. On the screen was a set of figures. Underneath them Odhiambo saw the words 'Correlation 0.2: Not Significant'. The dead man had been working on some data when the murderer struck. But there was no sign of a struggle. Had he known his visitor? Had he turned back to his computer when his visitor snatched the club off the wall and dealt him the ghastly blow or blows?

Bolling stopped to speak briefly to the doctor and then rejoined the Kenyans. He was of only average height, five foot nine or ten, Odhiambo guessed, slimly built, but giving the impression of wiry, sinewy strength. Back at the desk he had commandeered, he waved them to chairs and started chewing again on his pencil, removing it only to speak.

'You can give full statements to one of my men when I've finished with you. I wanna know what's going on here – the Kenya connection and who you two are – particularly,' the pencil stabbed in the direction of Odhiambo, 'particularly you.'

Katawi explained his status simply enough, stressing that he knew the dead man by sight only. Odhiambo had to go into greater detail in explaining his presence and the coincidence that he had met Chivers, or thought he had, in Nairobi. Bolling looked sceptical, reasonably enough in Odhiambo's view; he could understand

Bolling finding the coincidences growing to a point where they were hard to swallow.

'And you guys were at a party given by yet another Kenyan when you got the news. That right?'

'Yes, my father-in-law, Bito, Samuel Bito.'

'And this was some sort of get-together, an old Kenyan reunion?'

'Not really, it was a mixed bunch of my in-laws' friends and my wife's company colleagues. She works for Metroarcs in their Washington office – until we return to Nairobi.'

'But there were other Kenyans there?'

'Sure. So what?'

'How come Mr Chivers here didn't get an invite? He's Kenyan, you tell me. Don't tell me he was ruled out because he's white?'

'Of course not, there were, are, all sorts there. The simple answer, which is probably correct, is that my father-in-law didn't know Chivers, or, even if they've met, they're not good friends.'

'And you say you only knew Chivers through a police connection in Nairobi?'

'Yes. Some years ago. He did some sort of analysis for us.'

'But he wasn't a forensic man, or chemist or whatever?'

'No. I seem to remember he was some sort of statistician. He analysed figures. Same as he seemed to be doing in there tonight.'

Bolling chewed his way around what he saw as the Kenya connection for a further few minutes, finally passing Katawi and Odhiambo over to a detective who started to record their full particulars and statements. Odhiambo, as he awaited his turn, regretted his impulse to accompany Katawi to the scene of the crime. What was it he had heard his father say back in Western Kenya? Do not go to the well unless you are thirsty. In other words don't butt into matters that are not your business. And yet ... Odhiambo could see his father-in-law's face as he broke the news of the summons to Katawi. Odhiambo was sure that the name Chivers was known to him. Bolling was no fool. Was there a connection between them?

He had almost completed his formal interview, while Katawi took his turn to wait, when Odhiambo saw Bolling reappear and cross the carpeted floor towards him. Bolling leaned over the detective taking down the statements and took the personal history form from the desk top. He looked at it and nodded to himself before turning to Odhiambo.

'I thought so. Your wife's parents – they're called Bito, right?'

Odhiambo's instincts told him that this was the moment when his passive involvement was over. He had tried to suppress what he instinctively knew, that somehow the IBID office murder would suck him in. He nodded.

'I said so. Yes. Samuel and Abbie Bito.'

'And you thought they didn't know the dead guy, right?'

'I didn't say that exactly. You wondered why he wasn't at the party. I said that was one plausible reason.'

'Sure, plausible, that's a good word, Mr Odhiambo. Enough to satisfy my curiosity, right? Well, it don't look too plausible now, feller.' Triumphantly, Bolling produced from his pocket a red pocket diary. He opened it at the page marked by the protruding red tapelet and thrust it under Odhiambo's nose. 'This here is Mr Chivers' diary. Still in his jacket, it was. See, today's date, Mr Odhiambo? And see his appointments for today? Starting nine thirty, 'Directors Meeting'. And ending on the bottom of the page, 'Bito' and next to that what looks like another name, African name like yours, 'Omuto'. You still think your relative Samuel Bito didn't know the stiff? Or are you ready to come clean with me?'

5

The last car doors had slammed, the last somewhat embarrassed goodbyes and thank yous had been shouted with strained heartiness, and the comfortable Bito residence with its lawn shelving down towards the waters of the Potomac was, at least to the casual observer, calm once again. Inside Samuel Bito's study, however, tensions were high. Odhiambo, in insisting on an urgent face-to-face with his father-in-law, had assumed at first that, in keeping with African traditions, it would be the two of them with the women of the family excluded. But the Bito women were contemptuous of tribal hierarchies and the family consultation included both Abbie and Cari. For all his adherence to modernity, Odhiambo felt uncomfortable with this – not because of his wife's presence; he felt constrained in speaking frankly in front of his mother-in-law.

The party, which had survived the temporary loss of its guest of honour, did not outlast the arrival of Lieutenant Bolling and colleagues. Samuel and Abbie Bito had been interviewed separately by Bolling, and his men had checked with guests their arrival times and their recollections of when they were greeted by their host. That Abbie had been present throughout was confirmed by many, but Samuel Bito had arrived late at his own party. It was with reluctance that Bolling took himself off without taking the Bito family into custody, but Odhiambo did not know how much time was available – one piece of tangible evidence and he felt Bolling would be back. Samuel Bito, however, was proving resistant. It was Cari's collapse into hysterical tears that finally broke his resistance.

'Cari, don't upset yourself. There's nothing to worry about, I tell you.'

His daughter beat her hands on her bare knees as she sat in an upright chair, looking down at her father who was in one of the two deep armchairs – although he was sitting erect with his bottom perched on the front portion of the cushion. She wiped her finger under her eyes.

'How can you say that? We're suspects in a murder case, for God's sake. Jeepers, I thought I was safe from this sort of nightmare here in the States. Kenya, yes. Who knows what happens there? But you've got to explain to me, Dad. You owe me that. What's going on? What's the connection between you, the dead man and Omuto?'

Abbie Bito had been sitting quietly, but her body was full of visible tension. She had seemed to be in a state of shock, but at her daughter's words she started to protest, only to be stopped by her husband's raised hand and peremptory tone.

'No, Abbie, she's right. I owe her.' He looked across at his son-in-law. 'This is a family meeting, James. That's understood?'

Odhiambo felt his frustration turning into anger. He struggled to keep his voice level in tone and pitch.

'Of course, Sam. Assuming that we're discussing the coincidental apparent link between you and Chivers that is causing the police to look at you, an innocent man.'

Bito nodded.

'Yes, I assure you of that, James. Now,' he turned back to face his daughter, 'let me tell you a bit of history, history that has resurfaced.'

'I was involved with politics in the pre-independence days. From our area in the Rift people mainly joined KANU and Jomo Kenyatta. I always wanted to swim against the tide in those days and I was linked with James' Luos in KADU. Omuto, of course, had gone the other way, a prominent Luo politician who joined KANU. He had tremendous credibility and was, therefore, a problem to certain KADU politicians. He was shot, as you know, as he arrived for a rally. KANU blamed KADU and most people believed it: Luos getting rid of a traitor to their cause, that was the line. But it wasn't quite like that and I knew it. By accident I had certain information that pointed the finger the other way. Never mind now the details. I heard I was next on the list to disappear – vanishment, some called it. I had the chance of a scholarship over here so I ran away and kept my mouth shut.' Bito paused and swallowed hard. His wife reached out and took his hand in hers. 'I'm not proud of it. I even left you and your mother behind at first. I didn't think there was any risk to you two, but I was a man and I ran away . . .' Another long pause. 'Since then I've stayed right away from Kenyan politics and Kenya. Not that I was afraid any more. Rather any reference to such matters brought back my shame. Now, Omuto is stirring in his grave. The government has promised an enquiry and I've been told I'm to be summoned as a witness.' Bito turned back to his son-in-law as if he saw him as representing the Kenya he had shunned so long. 'There's nothing to be gained, I tell you. Raking over the past. Only bad things can come of it.'

He fell silent, head bowed. Cari had been listening intently. She leaned forward.

'Dad, it's . . . it's OK. You did the best thing. But, but . . . where does tonight's killing come into it? Why did this *mzungu* have your name and Omuto's in his diary?'

Bito snorted.

'Chivers – the dead man – he was in Kenya in those days. The coincidence that meant I had some information involved him too. He was stationed near Nakuru. He knew I had certain information. When I met him here he didn't refer to it until this enquiry thing started up. He came to see me. "Now is the time, Bito," he said to me, "now you must go back and bring justice to bear." I told him no. Remember the old saying, I said – Only, the hyena and the vulture pick over the bones of the dead. He wasn't convinced. If I didn't respond, he said, he would have to consider releasing what he knew that would force my hand.'

Odhiambo closed his eyes and grimaced. Bito had provided a motive. It depended on how deeply Bito had been involved in the

Omuto affair; Odhiambo believed that there was a lot more that he had yet to hear. Now came the questions of means and opportunity. Cari was mouthing inconsequentialities of reassurance to her father. Odhiambo interrupted.

'Sorry, Cari. But we need to look at things from the police's perspective. Sam, where were you earlier this evening, before the party? I didn't see you until after the party started.'

Abbie Bito jumped in quickly.

'Now lookee here, boy. You're not the police here. Don't you start up questioning Samuel here.'

Her husband laid his hand on her arm.

'No, Abbie, don't get at James.' He faced his son-in-law, jaw pushed forward, a picture of determination in the face of adversity. 'I was on campus. I came from there to here . . . But . . . but I came home by way of Chivers' office. He called me this afternoon. Said we had to talk. I went by there, sometime after six. Told him I hadn't changed my mind. He was concerned. I made my excuses. That was it.'

And more than enough for Bolling, thought Odhiambo.

'Did you tell Bolling that?'

'Bolling . . .?'

'The policeman, Sam. The homicide lieutenant.'

'Oh, yes, Lieutenant Bolling. Well, er, no, I didn't go into detail – I said I came from the campus to here.'

'Did you deny seeing Chivers tonight?'

'Well, sort of. Yes. Yes I told him I came straight here.'

'Christ, Sam, you've been a damn fool. Your fingerprints are probably all over Chivers' office. Someone will have seen you. That's all Bolling is going to need to be straight back here.'

'James.' This was Cari. 'That's enough. Leave Dad alone. It was a natural thing to do. We'll have to straighten things out for him, that's all.'

'That's all! Yeah, that is all, but doing it isn't going to be so simple.'

'Don't be silly. Why should Dad harm this guy? Just because they didn't agree about Dad going back to Kenya. I don't know what business that is of Chivers or whatever his name is. But Dad says he told him to bug off. So that's that. If Chivers wants to tell what he knows, why should Dad worry?'

Ah, thought Odhiambo, there was the jackpot question. What had Chivers got on Sam Bito? He glanced at his father-in-law. He did not think Bito would go into more detail in front of his daughter – maybe later he would get him on his own.

Abbie Bito seemed to have come to the same conclusion as her son-in-law. She rose from the arm of the chair where her husband was sitting.

'Come on, let's start clearing up and I'll make some fresh coffee. Samuel didn't do anything so we've nothing to worry about.'

The others rose and dutifully followed Abbie's lead, but their faces revealed that worry was far from absent.

Sally Eves had wasted no time after she arrived back at her George-town apartment. Although there was an austere, almost ascetic, undercurrent in her writing, advocating a steely dedication in the cause of feminism and self-denial on behalf of the environment, she enjoyed, and believed she was entitled to, luxurious surroundings. Her waterfront apartment next to the famous Watergate building looked out across the Potomac River to Roosevelt Island, the small former plantation which had been allowed to return to natural swamp and woodland with no management other than that of the seasons and the elements. She never tired of looking out at night on the dark shadowy island surrounded by the lights of modern liv-ing. But she had other things to do this night.

'Giles, it's me, Sally. I've just come from a crummy party and heard about the murder at your offices. In fact, the police came to where the party was. Seems our host knew the dead man. You know about it?'

Giles Faucon had answered the telephone whilst continuing to read the papers on his desk in the study of his apartment some three miles from that of his caller. Now he took his eyes off the typed pages and gazed at the Gastin Lepage painting on his wall, but without seeing it.

'Sally, calm down. What on earth are you talking about? What murder?'

'Gee, don't they keep you informed? I thought you were sup-posed to be the boss-man of that outfit. One of your staff got himself knocked off tonight in his office.'

She went on to repeat what little she knew, but Faucon quickly stopped listening, and as soon as he dared made his excuses and severed the contact. It was not surprising he had not been told of the incident – after all, he had plenty of people to handle minor emergencies – but now his concern was aroused. If someone, Sally was unable to name the victim, was killed in his office could others in his organisation be involved? After all no one could just wander in off the street. Not any more, that is. He had found security to be almost non-existent when he took over at IBID, but he had done something about it. He looked at the little list of pre-recorded numbers on the side of his telephone and pressed a digit.

Sally Eves meanwhile, a little miffed at the unemotional – cold, even – response of her lover, had dialled another number.

'Sean? Sally. Are you alone?' Fat chance, she thought as she said the words. By now he was probably in bed with one of his pretty young actors from the Kennedy Center. 'Listen, Sean, some guy got himself murdered this evening in the IBID offices across the river in Rosslyn. See what you can find out about it, will you? You've got friends in the right places.'

Sean Gilbride looked at the naked body of the young man beside him. 'Hold on a moment,' he said into the telephone. Better move to the living-room even though his companion seemed to have no interests other than his stage parts and his body parts. He pulled on a dressing-gown and went out of the bedroom, leaving a pout on the face of his bed-mate behind him.

'Sally, what's got you so interested in our town's nightly murder rate?'

'Put your brains together, Sean. I'm sorry if I've disturbed you.' Sally grinned to herself. Serve the little sod right. 'I'm talking about someone with IBID. And I'm not talking about a janitor. I don't know who it is, but he's an executive.'

'So what, Sally? What's it to do with me? Or you, come to that?'

'You're on the executive of SEND, are you not, Sean? Didn't you get me involved? If IBID executives are knocking each other off, there might be something there we can embarrass them with.'

Sean clasped his forehead and kneaded it with his artist's fingers.

'Why not try asking your friend to tell you what you want to know? He runs the frigging place, that he does.'

'Look, Sean, if you listen instead of asking silly questions you'll be back with your playmate all the quicker. Giles doesn't know anything. That's why I want you to put out a few feelers. No, don't interrupt. I know what you're going to say. Look, the deal I have with Faucon is that nothing we hear on each other's pillow gets used, right? But nothing else is off limits. He knows that SEND is digging into some of his projects. He wouldn't try to head me off.

Maybe one day when we really go after them I'll have to show him the door. But they give out this image of being so squeaky clean, it pisses me off. If there's something going on in IBID I want to know about it.'

Two minutes later Gilbride put down the cordless phone. What a bitch she was. He was sure she was more concerned with notoriety and causing trouble than saving the environment. But she was useful to the cause. Well, the morning would do, meanwhile there were other more pleasant matters. He looked at the bedroom door and grinned to himself; he'd better get back or young Marco might be asleep.

Glen Hills had driven home in thoughtful mood. He lived in a house on Wisconsin Avenue that was far bigger than required for his bachelor needs, but it provided the space for entertaining, and entertaining was a major part of his life. He left his car outside the front door, entered his living-room and poured himself a malt whisky, a twelve-year-old Laphroig. He was caught in a rare mood of indecision. Cari's father had said a man called Chivers of IBID was dead – murdered. Hills knew he had heard the name before. Was he the one? And if so, what was the implication for the enterprise that was to provide him with his personal financial security package in the Bahamas? At last he crossed the handwoven Chinese rug to the telephone, hovered for one last moment of doubt and pressed the buttons.

'Kraxma.'

The voice was unmistakable, guttural with the rasp of a chain-smoker. Hills could picture him, short, stocky, stubby fingers clutching a cigarette, hair askew, his rumpled office suit still worn out of lack of motivation to change into casual clothes.

'Ernesto, this is Glen. Sorry to disturb you so late.'

'No problem. What is your problem, my friend?'

'I was at a party, to do with a colleague of mine. News came through that somebody had been killed in your building, in IBID.'

'Which building?'

Typical of the bloody man, thought Hills. A mid-European of pedantic stolidity. What did it matter which building? The exasperation showed in his voice.

'I don't know which building. You mean it might be where your office is? I hadn't thought of that. The point is, I believe the man is called Chivers. The dead man, I mean.' Hills added the last words to avoid having Kraxma ask him which man. There was silence. Hills waited a moment and added, 'Isn't he the man you told me about?'

'Ah. I see why you are concerned. Me, I am thinking. A murder on IBID property; this is not good. And Mr Chivers? You are sure?'

'Not a hundred per cent, no. I haven't been to see the body, for Chrissake. But that's the name, I think.'

'This is not good. You are correct, my friend. Chivers was the man. And his office is in the annexe, same as me. Why would he be killed in his office?'

Hills drained the last of his whisky while he summoned his reserves of patience.

'Don't be evasive with me, Ernesto. You know what I'm concerned about. If Chivers is dead where does it leave us? I mean, we were –'

'Do not talk too much on telephone, my friend. Not good practice.'

'That's all very well, Kraxma, but –'

'We didn't kill him so we remain free men.' Suddenly the voice got down to business as if, the matter having been thought through, a course had been decided. 'Chivers was one of team. Smarter than rest, maybe. But not alone. Another can do analysis of his data. If data gone, who knows, maybe we are what you say, off hook.'

'Exactly. That's what I'm getting at. Can't you go and have a look? You're a senior man there. Turn up, senior executive concerned, that sort of thing. Get into his office and give it the once over.'

The laugh was louder now and more derisive.

'Oh, my friend. You want me to interfere perhaps. I think you need to go to bed and think on it. I will make investigation, yes. But not in panic situation. Now you forget the name Chivers, you understand me, my friend?'

Kraxma turned back to the window and gazed at the dome of the Capitol across the lower roof-tops. He lived unpretentiously in a small apartment on the downtown side of the Capitol in a far less fashionable area of the capital than Hills. He lit another cigarette from the stub of the last and ground the stub into a loaded ashtray on the side table by the window. He had always had reservations about working with Metroarcs on the Nigeria project. Dealing with a conglomerate whose inner workings he knew not, so needing to rely on the insider's judgement and nerve, was not how he liked to operate. But he had no choice. And Hills was not, in his judgement, reliable. Now he was showing signs of panic, which was dangerous. Again he was distracted by the sound of the telephone. The beautifully modulated voice was instantly familiar.

'Kraxma? Mensat Khan here. There's been a death in the annexe building. Your building. A man called Chivers of Internal Audit. Strangely enough, he was at the directors' meeting today. He's one of the economic evaluation people. You know him?'

'A little.'

'Yes. You must have seen him about the place. Faucon is concerned, obviously. He's spoken to the police asking for a briefing. In the morning, of course. I don't know why he contacted me instead of Greene or somebody running that department. Had my number on his pad, I suppose. Anyway, I told him your office is in the same building. So to cut a long story short, get an internal review going tomorrow. To prepare a briefing note. Involve Greene, of course. Get the security chief. Inside details. The police will be responsible for how someone got in or out. Unless, God forbid, it was another staff member. What Giles wants from us is the man's record, current work, family and so on. Incidentally, the welfare office has been informed to look after next of kin and so forth.'

This is unbelievable, thought Kraxma. What was he supposed to be, a messenger boy?

'I don't understand what it has to do with us. Africa Projects, I mean. I'll ring Greene.'

Khan's voice became noticeably colder.

'Of course. I said involve Greene. He's directly responsible. But the MD asked me for whatever reason. That's good enough for me and, I trust, good enough for you. Goodnight.'

The Managing Director of IBID had called a regional director, who had called his senior manager. Luckily for Romaine Caradonna, Kraxma did not pass the buck further down the line. Her night of energetic sex with Senator Exelby was, therefore, undisturbed. Moreover, she was in blissful ignorance of the fact that her companion had voted against every bill to provide foreign aid or support to development agencies. If she had kown this, she might, as a loyal IBID employee, have been a little less impetuous in allowing him into her bed.

6

It was early, the light of morning only beginning to reveal the waters of the river as Odhiambo walked along the towpath. Yet he could hear, away to his right, the sound of traffic as commuters made their way towards Washington along the Washington Parkway. It had been a bad night. Cari's emotional state was all the more fraught because she believed she had been unobservant of and unsympathetic to the stresses affecting her parents. 'Why didn't I talk to them more?' was a reiterated self-accusation. Eventually she and her husband had drifted off to sleep, but James Odhiambo woke before dawn. He eased himself out of bed so as not to disturb the now peaceful Cari, felt for and secured his pullover and sat in the darkness on the little balcony outside their bedroom on the upper floor of the Bito house. The bulk of the accommodation, including the other bedrooms, was on the split-level lower floor. The Odhiambos had a mini-suite that afforded a considerable degree of privacy.

Odhiambo was not surprised when in the light from the lamp outside the front door he saw a short stubby figure emerge surreptitiously and set off across the lawn. Samuel Bito in sweater, slacks and old shoes was clearly intending a dawn walk and, no doubt, a dawn think. Odhiambo returned to the bedroom, retrieved his clothes from where he had placed them on a chair and dressed in the bathroom before quietly heading in his father-in-law's footsteps. Cari turned over and muttered something as he eased open the bedroom door, but seemed to settle back into slumber. As he walked, with the river on his left, along a path flanked by trees, Odhiambo experienced a momentary sense of physical displacement – back to that wood beside the dark lake and his own close brush with death. He felt a psychosomatic twinge of pain where the burns had seared his flesh, but more forcefully than that he saw again the red-haired woman standing on the cliffs framed against the background of the angry sea. And yet, for some reason, this morning the sense of guilt had subsided. As he thought about this, Odhiambo realised that what was pushing hang-ups of the past into the background was the excitement of the chase – the sense that once more his talents were needed, and this time in a family cause.

He walked on until around a bend the path veered closer to the river and there, sitting on a rock above the water, Odhiambo saw his quarry.

'Sam?' Then, as the figure turned, 'I guess we both needed some air this morning.'

Reluctantly, Samuel Bito rose from his private sanctuary and greeted his son-in-law. 'James! What brings you out so early?'

'Maybe I'm still adjusting to the time difference. It's mid-morning already in England. But maybe we're both thinking about the same thing, eh, Sam?'

'Not necessarily, James. Thinking isn't going to do much for my problem. Chivers is dead, I didn't do it and I have to rely on the police understanding that.'

The two men fell into step together as they retraced their path towards the house. Odhiambo shook his head impatiently.

'Sometimes the police need to be pointed in the right direction, Sam, and away from a false trail.'

It was the older man's turn to shake his head, but this was a gesture of helplessness.

'What can I do, James? I'll have to admit to the police I went to visit with Chivers. I can see that my denying it last night doesn't look good but . . .'

'We can assume that Bolling knows by now you were there. Did you have to sign in or anything?'

'Yes. The guard called Chivers' office and he authorised me to come through. There was a time log to sign people in and out.'

'So there's a record of the time you arrived and, more important, when you left?'

'Not when I left. When I came down the guard was on the phone – he didn't seem to notice me and I forgot to sign the book.'

Odhiambo felt light-headed. Here was a university professor who is witnessed going to see a man, signs himself as present and tells the police he was never there. Now it turned out the time of departure that might have exonerated him when the time of death was estimated was not recorded because of another oversight. Bito seemed to realise that he was not showing himself in an intelligent light. He looked crestfallen and helpless. Odhiambo searched for crumbs of comfort.

'We know you must have left by seven 'cos you were home by half-past.'

'I think it was a bit after. Abbie was cross I was late. Anyway, we shall see. No doubt that policeman, what did you call him? Bolling, that's right. No doubt he'll sort all that out.'

Odhiambo sighed. His father-in-law was becoming either fatalistic or passive. Either could be dangerous.

'Yeah. Well, maybe there's nothing to worry about. But suppose you're not ruled out on timing. Then a lot depends on motive. Bolling will be pursuing the Omuto angle. You've got to tell me, Sam. Just how deep were you in the Omuto business? Merely debating with Chivers the merits of giving evidence on minor matters is scarcely a motive. But if you were both more closely involved . . .'

Odhiambo left the implication dangling and silence fell for a while as the two men tramped on. Eventually, Bito sighed and spoke.

'I guess you have a right to ask, James. After all, you're family. You know, I'd almost succeeded in blotting those days out of my mind. Abbie and I, we never talk about it.' Bito stopped and brought his companion to a halt by laying his hand on Odhiambo's arm. He looked up into Odhiambo's face; his round face, although not chubby, normally gave evidence of a cheerful, jolly personality but now it was showing signs of strain. His cheeks seemed to have shrunk and bags under the eyes seemed dark. 'James, Cari doesn't know the details and I don't want her to know.'

Odhiambo leant forward slightly as he spoke with emphasis.

'Listen, Sam. The situation has changed. As of last night. To the extent that the Omuto business is relevant to motive, it's going to come out.' He paused. 'I know how Bolling's mind works. He'll have started digging already.' There was another pause. Odhiambo continued. 'At least give me a general picture, Sam. I want to help, but I'm in the dark.'

Bito looked away, staring back towards the river. At last, he seemed to make a decision. With a slight tug on Odhiambo's arm he resumed walking. Now as he talked the words came in a torrent.

'You know what happened to Omuto, James. An unknown gunman got him as he left the train in Nakuru. But it wasn't organised by your Luos, it wasn't KADU. It was Kiwonka, a leading KANU man. Kiwonka and I were old friends; we'd been to school together. He worked at the Research Centre near Nakuru. Chivers was the statistician there and a sort of manager as well. At least, Kiwonka worked there until he became a full-time politician. He asked me to let him know whether Omuto was coming to Nakuru by train or car. He knew I had close friends in the Omuto camp. I did know he was using the train – and I told Kiwonka. That was all he needed to get the killer there in good time. I, in the vernacular they use here, James, I put the finger on Omuto. One of the best hopes Kenya had. With Kenyatta gone now, someone like him could have been what Kenya needed to go forwards. But now . . . well, I don't know. How do you think it feels to have been part of the cause of his death?'

Odhiambo's mind started to race. No wonder Sam had kept the details from his daughter and, of course, himself.

'But you didn't know what Kiwonka was planning, Sam. It's no good blaming yourself. He could have just wanted to greet him. You couldn't have guessed. In fact, are you sure it was him?'

Bito stopped once more. They were nearing the house.

'That's not all, James. After it happened I went to see him. What else would I do? He brazened it out. More than that, he laughed and said I was a more likely suspect. After all, I knew Omuto was on the train and I favoured the other party. I remember he said, "You're both renegades, Bito. If a man deserts his own clan, anything can be expected of him." ' Bito paused as if seeing Kiwonka in front of him after all the years that had passed. Then his voice quickened again. 'I was frightened. I knew Chivers; he had let me stay in the guest house at the Centre. I went back there and did some thinking. I could almost see Kiwonka's mind working. I would be easy to set up and that would achieve his aim – KADU would get the blame. I decided to get out fast. I was due to come here on a scholarship. So I decided to go to Nairobi, get a message to Abbie and then get on a plane. Luckily I went to see Chivers to thank him. He saw I was upset and, yes, panicky. I realised he might think it was guilt, when Kiwonka started putting his story about, so I told him the politics were getting too hot. I was afraid of what the Nakuru people were up to, so I was going to stay away from it all. And I went. Now this is where my luck came in. That evening, Chivers went to the guest house to check it out. It was dark. He saw two men removing the glass strips from one of the windows. You know those slatted windows. He shouted and they ran away, dropping something. It was a gun. You can guess the rest. It was the gun used to kill Omuto. They were going to plant it on me. Maybe kill me and make it look like suicide and leave the incriminating gun behind. Chivers' intervention saved me. The incident got hushed up, of course, and Chivers was in no position to make a fuss.'

Odhiambo groaned, but internally. He pushed his father-in-law to the climax of the tale.

'And now the government is opening an enquiry into the Omuto affair, you are being summoned, you don't want to revisit the past, but Chivers could force you into it, because he knew of your involvement.'

'Yes. I'm afraid that's it. I told him, Chivers, I mean, I said I'm not interested in Kenyan politics any more. Who knows what's behind this enquiry? Is someone trying to stop Kiwonka's rise up the ladder? Or is it more complicated? Anyway, I don't want to know. But Chivers thought I should go back and testify. I don't know what his interest was.'

Odhiambo couldn't resist the slight barb.

'Perhaps he was just interested in justice, Sam. Perhaps he thought it was time Kiwonka got his deserts.'

Bito gave his son-in-law a sharp glance.

'OK. Point taken. And if you want to believe that, fine. But you should know Kenyan politics better than that. I'm not proud of myself, James, but I have to live with what happened and I don't want to be a party to more conspiracies. It's behind me; for ever.'

If life was only that simple, thought Odhiambo. You can't just walk away from some things. Life won't let you. Sam Bito thought he had built a wall around himself in his comfortable college campus. It must have been a shock to Bito when Chivers arrived in the Washington area and encountered his old temporary guest-house resident. But the enquiry was now of only indirect concern. The problem was that when Bolling got to hear the Bito story, the motive he was looking for would be there.

'Is that all, Sam? Have you told me everything?'

There was a long silence.

'Chivers may have known more than I thought he did. I can't say any more.'

Odhiambo pushed, but his companion shook his head. Odhiambo was sure Sam was still holding something back, but he could try again later.

'Come on, Sam, let's put some coffee on. We need to talk now about what you're going to say to Bolling.'

While Odhiambo listened to his father-in-law's story of the Kenyan political scene of the 1960s, life was already evident in the IBID annexe building in Rosslyn. Chivers' office area was sealed off with a Virginia State policeman ensconced in the open area guarding it. Three floors above, Kraxma was ensconced in his own office. He had made a trip down to Chivers' office, but had quickly realised the policeman *in situ* had no authority to let him pass so contented himself by asking for a message to be sent requesting the presence of the investigating officer. Chivers' boss, an American called Greene, had already responded to Kraxma's message and was in Kraxma's office. Greene was the Director of Internal Audit and nominally outranked Kraxma, a regional projects manager, but everyone in IBID knew that it was officers in positions like Kraxma's who held the real authority; they came up with new projects that allowed IBID to deploy its capital, they put pressure on unsupportive governments so that their projects were not unduly interfered with, and they put a gloss on the economic results so as to keep IBID's board happy. Sometimes Greene's people, viewing the results with a more jaundiced and unbiased eye, cast a damper on the prevailing mood of successful achievement, but Kraxma could take an occasional irritant as long as it didn't produce a lasting sore. Greene was a lean, elegantly dressed man with grey hair carefully styled. He contrasted with the rumpled, bag of potatoes shape of the man who, flicking ash into one of two ashtrays on his desk, now got to the point.

'So, Faucon wants a detailed report of what Chivers was working on, who in IBID he was currently dealing with, what his relations were with your staff in your department, and who else was working at the time Chivers was killed.'

Greene looked worried. He did not like problems like this one – problems that might reflect on his own managerial abilities.

'It must have been someone from outside, surely? I mean to say, Kraxma, we're not harbouring murderers in here.'

Kraxma grinned, stubbed out his cigarette and looked across the desk with an air that Greene, if he had not been too rattled to notice, could have regarded as condescending.

'Do not speak too easily, my friend. Was he a womaniser, this Chivers? Did he know something bad about someone? This is what you have to find out. And quickly.'

'The police will be doing this, won't they? Shouldn't an internal enquiry wait a while?'

'If you have a desire to tell Faucon that, OK.' Kraxma shrugged. 'But I would say you would be better giving him what he wants. He does not want to be, what you Americans say, blind-sided.'

Greene nodded, recognising the inevitable. Why did this have to happen to one of his people? As if he didn't have enough to worry about. He looked at Kraxma with growing irritation. Kraxma looked smug, as if he was enjoying himself.

'OK. I'll get Myerson on to it. I believe one of the things he was working on was your Nigerian project. The fertiliser distribution scheme.'

If he had hoped to jar his companion, he failed. There was no visible lessening of Kraxma's aura of control.

'Yes. That is correct. The project was good in first phase, but now there are questions. Always same problems in Africa. Why farmers do not do what we think they will do? Miss Caradonna is the PO. Chivers would deal with her.' Kraxma grinned again and pulled out another cigarette. Unfiltered French ones, Greene noted with distaste. 'If Chivers was fond of women, this Caradonna would excite him, no? She is plenty woman, I tell you. But no, this is not time for humour, no? I will tell Caradonna to speak to your man – what you say the name? Ah, Myerson, yes.' He scribbled on the pad in front of him. 'OK, we keep in touch, yes?'

Greene rose, following the lead of the other man. As they did so, the telephone rang. Kraxma seized it with his stubby, strong fingers, raised it to his ear and listened.

'Right. We come down.' He replaced the phone. 'That was the police. An officer called Bolling is below us in Chivers' office. You will come, no?'

After explaining to Bolling who they were, Kraxma and Greene were allowed into the death site, Bolling keeping close order behind them. They looked around much as Odhiambo and Katawi had done the night before, but now there was no body to place the scene in context. In response to Bolling's invitation the two IBID men spent some time looking at the papers on the desk and work area. Bolling watched their somewhat aimless scrutiny.

'Is there anything obviously missing?'

Kraxma shrugged and Greene sounded almost petulant as he replied.

42

'That's impossible to say. These are working sheets and a couple of files, project files, not ones from the central registry. We may be able to check them later.'

'Does it tell you anything about what he was doing when he was interrupted?'

'No.' This was Kraxma. 'He could have been reading one of these files. Or something else.'

Greene, however, was peering at the computer screen, which had been left on by the police.

'It looks like he was carrying out some statistical analysis. Testing the relationship between variables – that sort of thing.'

Bolling focused his gaze on Greene.

'Tell me, buddy. This is an audit department, right? The dead man, Chivers, he was some sort of financial expert, right? Auditor?'

Greene shook his head and spoke with greater confidence. He was on home ground now.

'No, Lieutenant, that's a common mistake. Most of my staff are not auditors in the financial sense. We are responsible for checking whether the projects this institution lends for are achieving their economic and social goals as well as being run soundly from the financial aspect. Mr Chivers was a statistician – an expert in analysing economic relationships. In his case, particularly in agriculture.'

Bolling grunted.

'Don't mean nothing to me. The point is, could what he was working on have had anything to do with his death?'

Greene looked suitably aggrieved, as if the idea was incomprehensible.

'I can't believe that this unfortunate business has any connection with his work. We will be looking . . .' He stopped as if realising he was about to say too much.

Bolling grinned sardonically.

'You leave the looking to us, Mr Greene. But we look for the full co-operation of you and your staff.'

'Of course.' Greene was anxious to demonstrate co-operation. 'Anything we can do.'

'We shall interview the staff in this section as they arrive. Meanwhile this area will be closed for normal work.'

Kraxma had seated himself at the desk. He looked up to Greene.

'One of the things to check is the data source if this policeman is interested. Look, there's no disc in the machine.' He pressed a series of keys on the console. 'And no data in the memory. Must have entered it manually.'

Greene waved a hand a little impatiently.

'Yes, yes, that will be easy enough. I'll get someone to sort through all the papers here.' He looked questioningly at Bolling. 'Assuming we can have access.'

Bolling nodded.

'Get your people to liaise with mine.'

Noises outside indicated the arrival of the first of the staff with offices in the same complex as Chivers. Bolling raised his chin as if sniffing the air like a gun dog who hears the flapping of a flight of wings. Grind away, grind away, he would constantly remind his men. It's the routine checking and cross-checking that breaks the cases. Although in this case he was already half persuaded that he was close to breaking it.

'One last thing, gentlemen.' Bolling produced Chivers' diary and showed Kraxma and Greene the page with the previous day's date. 'Do either of you know a Mr Bito? You see his name there in the evening section of the page?'

Kraxma shook his head and Greene frowned.

'I'm almost certain there's no one of that name in this department. I'll have it confirmed, of course.'

Bolling grinned.

'Do that. Just for the record. But I know the answer. Mr Bito was a visitor. And Mr Bito don't like to admit it.'

7

Romaine Caradonna arrived at her office later than her usual hour of nine. The Senator had given her a rough night and she had spent some time in a hot bubble bath rather than taking a hurried shower. In her tired state she was not keen-eyed and failed to notice the police presence in the foyer of the IBID annexe. She had collected a coffee and doughnut at the deli next door and it was while she was enjoying these that her secretary appeared at the door and told her of Chivers' death.

'Chivers? What, the man in Internal Audit? He was handling our

Nigeria fertiliser project. He was coming back with me to Nigeria this week. What happened? He have a heart attack?'

On being given the further details, Caradonna allowed her dimpled chin to drop in an unladylike way.

'Murdered? Here in this building? Who did it?'

Soon realising that her secretary possessed no further firm information, Caradonna waved her away and sought to force her brain to operate despite its resistance after a night of little sleep. Chivers murdered! Why? It surely couldn't be anything to do with her project, could it? The last time she had seen him was . . . when? Two days ago, that was it. They had met in the corridor and he asked her to stop by his office. He had been a bit mysterious – cagey was the word – but also concerned. She felt he was warning her. What had he said? She must try and remember. He had got some data from someone in Nigeria, it didn't make sense – that's what he had said. He was going to recheck. 'Are the farmers getting any response?' he had asked. 'Are they still buying?' She had given him only guarded replies. Kraxma had warned her to be polite and co-operative with the Internal Audit people but only up to a point. 'No need to make full confession,' he had said with that laugh that sounded more like a cough as he lit another of his interminable cigarettes. She told him there was a problem in farmer adoption of the inputs. 'Adoption', Chivers had said, 'or repeat adoption.' It was after this he had asked her if he could join her next supervision visit, for an unusual second visit during an audit.

She was uneasy. She wasn't trained in agriculture but in economics. And she had only joined the Nigeria section eight months ago. Kraxma had asked her to come over to his section. 'I want you to look after the biggest baby I have,' was how he'd put it. One, two years at the most and a promotion was almost a certainty, that had been the carrot. There was something seriously wrong, but she had not yet been able to pin-point it. Perhaps Chivers had.

Still, that couldn't be anything to do with him being murdered. Could it? She laughed at herself and finished the coffee, making a face as her palate sent the signal that it was cold. People didn't get murdered for discovering a bad project. No promotion, perhaps, but you didn't end up dead. Wonder who did it? Was it someone inside the building? Was there a murderer wandering about? In the elevator with her? Oh, pull yourself together, she said to herself sternly. Don't act like a nervous schoolgirl. It was probably a personal relationship thing. Jealousy. Sex or office politics.

The subdued double burr of her telephone brought her back to the here and now. Her secretary announced a Mr Gilbride on the line. She remembered meeting a Sean Gilbride. It was at the party her escort had taken her to after the premiere of a play at the Kennedy Center. He was attractive with the sunken-eyed, soulful look of a plaintive Irishman, but she quickly realised her sex appeal would be wasted on him. He was more interested in her escort.

'Yes, Mr Gilbride? Romaine Caradonna here.'

'Ah, my dear Miss Caradonna. Would you be remembering a poor artist you met just a few nights ago?'

'It was longer than that, Mr ... er ... Sean, wasn't it? Yes, I remember you.'

'Sean it is, it is. And Romaine as I remember. Sorry I am to trouble you this early but I heard there's been a tragedy in your office.'

'Not in my own department, or on my floor, no. But someone in the building, yes. Why? Do you know him?'

'A Mr Chivers, so I understand.' The lie followed fluently. 'Not a personal friend, no. But a friend of a friend, as it were. The mutual friend is away. I was wondering whether to contact him. What can you tell me, Romaine darling?'

Caradonna felt irritated. What cheek!

'What made you ring me?'

'Oh, Romaine. I know what you're thinking. This Sean fellow he ignores me until he wants something. What sort of friend is that? But you're wrong. I was asking after you the other day. You had disappeared, darling.'

His listener could not resist a smile. God, these artistic young men.

'OK. How can I help? A man called Chivers is dead. He worked in Internal Audit in this building. That's all I know. You should call that department. I can give you the number.'

'No, no. I can cope with that. It was a personal thing. My friend told me Chivers was working on a big Africa project that was under the wing of the most beautiful lady in international affairs. Was it sensitive, what he was doing? Or should I be minding my own business?'

'Yes, you should mind your own business.' Caradonna's suspicions were roused. 'Whatever that may be.'

'Ah, well, there's the rub, my darling. You see, as well as dabble in the arts, I give my humble talents to protecting the planet. I'm into the environment – aren't we all these days! Some of my friends, they want to make a noise about IBID and Nigeria. I told them, if Romaine is in charge I'm sure she's sensitive to these things. But they were interested in the work of Mr Chivers. I just wondered if you could set my mind at rest. I expect it was personal, don't you? His death, I mean.'

'This is really a ridiculous conversation.' Caradonna was almost befuddled by the man's casual impertinence. 'I can't help you. I know nothing about Mr Chivers' death. Yes, one of his many tasks involved a project I'm helping with – there's no secret about that. IBID is very open. I must go now, I'm sorry.'

After drumming her fingers on her desk a while, Caradonna reached for the telephone again, looked up a name in the internal directory and pressed the appropriate numbers. She didn't like the man much but she'd heard he knew everybody in the arts world.

'Fulton.'

'Ah, Guy, it's Romaine, Romaine Caradonna. This may seem odd, but do you know a man called Sean Gilbride? Something to do with the Kennedy Center.'

An almost feminine giggle came through the receiver at her ear.

'Sean, the campy Irishman. I'm not sure he's your type, if you know what I mean.'

She was becoming annoyed with men in general this morning.

'You'd be surprised. Anyway, is he involved with a group – a pressure group, I mean?'

A short silence.

'Yes, yes, he is. I was thinking of its name. SEND, that's it. One of the more aggressive of the environmental lot. Why, is he bothering you?'

'He seems interested in the man that was killed last night. Chivers. Audit.'

'Yes, I heard about that. Very sad. Very odd business. He was checking into Nigeria, wasn't he? If there's anything rum about the project, fertiliser plant polluting the river or something, that's the sort of thing SEND will make a big fuss about. Steer clear of Gilbride is my advice.'

'I don't know why we don't go on the attack. Some of these groups wouldn't bear much investigation.'

Again, the giggle.

'Don't get paranoid, dear lady. And if you're starting an anti-NGO compaign don't start with SEND. You see, the leading light of SEND is a certain Miss Sally Eves, the writer. And it is said on good authority that Miss Eves is, shall we say, a very close friend of our Managing Director.'

John Musoke waited at a table on the pavement near the corner of 20th and N Streets. The late fall sunshine was warm enough for customers to sit outside if they desired and Musoke felt, in some peculiar way, that he preferred to meet the policeman in the open air. He had checked his files and had telephoned Nairobi since he received the request from the Virginia Police Department. He had spoken to R. D. Price-Allen, the unofficial security chief there, who had reacted with much greater interest than Musoke had anticipated. Price-Allen authorised him to co-operate up to a point, so here he was. A waiter came and put his ordered coffee on the metal table. Musoke checked his watch; the policeman, Bolling, was late. His vigil was almost over; as he sipped his coffee an unmarked car pulled into the kerb and a wiry man got out of the passenger seat. Musoke knew instinctively that this was his man and so it proved.

'Mr Musoke? Bolling, Lieutenant Bolling, Virginia State Police. Thanks for coming. Didn't want to meet in your Embassy. More informal, if you get my meaning? Here in DC. I'm out of my territory.'

Musoke shrugged.

'Yeah, I understand. Do you want a coffee? No?' Bolling waved away the approaching waiter. 'How can I help you?'

Bolling sprawled at an angle in his chair. The air of nonchalance was, Musoke thought, a carefully cultivated one.

'Just a little information, Mr Musoke. My boss understood from your boss that you're concerned with intelligence, shall we say? My question may be right up your street.'

'I'm authorised to help you with information as long as it doesn't infringe diplomatic or security matters.'

Bolling looked at the Kenyan diplomat. Modest in height and build, conservatively dressed, impassive in demeanour, he seemed about what one would expect for an intelligence man.

'It's like this, Mr Musoke. A guy got killed last night. In his office across the river. IBID, international banking or whatever. Turns out he was Kenyan. White, but Kenyan. Chivers is his name. Your Embassy man said he knew him. We're checking into who he saw in his office early yesterday evening.'

Musoke knew this much already. He nodded impatiently.

'OK. Yes, I know he's dead. But how can I help?'

'Yeah. Right. In his diary for yesterday was the name Bito. Followed by a dash and the name Omuto.'

Musoke was not taken by surprise. He had been in touch with Katawi, the IBID security man. And one of the Embassy people had told him about the police arriving during Bito's party.

'I know of Mr Bito. Or rather Dr Bito.'

'Right. I've met Mr Bito. Another Kenyan, but he's been here many years. But who's Omuto? And how are they both connected with Mr Chivers?'

Musoke followed his brief and gave a short summary of the Omuto case, concluding with the forthcoming enquiry. He concluded, 'Dr Bito, it seems, was involved in some way. Not directly. It is said that he was being dragged into the investigation until he upped and left Kenya. He hasn't been back since. He has been approached to give evidence to the new enquiry.'

'When you say he was involved, you mean he was a suspect?'

Musoke hastened to qualify his remarks, stumbling slightly over his words in his haste to do so. 'No . . . er . . . no, no. I . . . I didn't say what you're saying. I didn't mean that. As far as I know, he wasn't. I don't know that anyone was really identified, if it comes to that.'

'So no suspects, no charges brought, new enquiry, Bito's name is still in the frame, right?'

'Well, I suppose so. I mean I'm not . . . I've not studied the matter.'

'And what about Chivers?'

'How do you mean?'

'Chivers and Omuto or Chivers and Bito. What's the connection?'

'I don't know. I mean, I don't know there is a connection.'

'Look, Mr Musoke, this is the key issue. Chivers is dead, right? Murdered in his office. He has the names Bito and Omuto linked in his diary against the date and approximate time when he met his death. Let's say Bito came to see Chivers last evening. The likelihood is it would be about Omuto, right? They're both from Kenya and Omuto's name is in this diary.'

Musoke shook his head.

'As far as I know, Chivers is not a witness. And Bito is refusing to go back and give evidence. So why would they be interested in the Omuto case?'

Bolling felt the tingle that came when he knew a witness was not being frank or honest. It would take some digging but he saw the picture. Chivers knew something that would tie Bito to the murder of the politician and was threatening to talk if Bito didn't do something Chivers wanted. So he had to be silenced. Get the IBID security guard to pick Bito out of an identity parade as the man who arrived asking for Chivers, check the signature in the visitors' book, and Bolling could leave the tidying up of loose ends to someone else. Meanwhile the diplomats were playing their usual game; polite but tell you nothing you didn't already know. He leaned forward.

'Tell me, Mr Musoke – were you at Bito's party last night?'

'Party? No. I don't know him. Not personally. He's not connected with the Embassy, although one or two of the Embassy people were there. As personal friends.'

'And what about Odhiambo? James Odhiambo. You know him?'

Musoke looked away, gazing up the street towards Dupont Circle. After a pause, he said, 'I've heard of him. He's a policeman, I think. He's here at the moment; on holiday.'

'Staying with Mr Bito, as a matter of fact. Small world, as they say.'

Bolling got up to go. He'd got enough. He was intrigued by the final little incident. Musoke had seemed relaxed and confident until the name Odhiambo was mentioned. Bolling was sure the link between Bito and Odhiambo had taken the Kenyan by surprise. Odhiambo would merit another look.

'I'll be in touch, Mr Musoke. And if you find out more about Mr Chivers, Mr Bito and Mr Omuto, you just let me know and I'll come running.'

Cari Odhiambo had finally made it to her office, but late. The trauma of the previous night and the worry that lingered had given her the intention of staying home. She had called Glen Hills, but his secretary said he had not come in either and had they both forgotten that Congresswoman Hives was coming to be briefed on the trade with Egypt issue. Metroarcs was anxious to strengthen its already growing business there. Cari cursed, checked that the secretary had failed to get her boss at his home, and sat undecided. Her mother guessed the reason for her daughter's gnawing of her lower lip and persuaded her forcibly to go to work if she was needed.

'You're doing no good here, moping about. Samuel's going to see the police and we agreed it was better if he went on his own. Then he insists he's going to college. James is here to look after me.'

As events turned out, Odhiambo too was called away. The Kenyan Embassy communicated an urgent summons so Cari drove her husband into the capital, dropped him at the Embassy and then made her way to her office just off the Mall. Glen Hills had now called in to say he was unavoidably detained so Cari greeted the Congresswoman, who arrived as Cari was collecting her thoughts. Luckily she had prepared the Metroarcs brief on the proposed Egypt trade deal so putting the middle-aged, stocky Congresswoman in the picture was well within her compass.

'I thought as much,' said Ms Hives contentedly, as she leaned back in her chair and lit a cheroot – the aroma from which Cari found distinctly unpleasant. 'It's another way of ripping off the American taxpayer to benefit you multinationals.' She held up a hand to prevent Cari's protest. 'No, no. I'm joking, my dear, but like all good jokes there's more than an element of truth in it. Now, in return for your information I've got a little warning for you.'

Cari brought her mind back from Port Said and the Suez Canal and focused on the square lined face across the desk.

'A warning? For me? Whatever do you mean?'

Hives waved away smoke that hung around her face. When she spoke, Cari thought at first she had changed the subject again.

'I know your father. I took a course on political development that he gave. I got to know him a little and I learned how proud he was of you. A high-flying career daughter was still a rarity in Kenya, he told me. So, here's my bit's worth in exchange for the help he gave me. Watch your ass with Sally Eves.'

'Sally! Why do you say that? She's been most kind to me.'

'Then pay double heed. Sally never did a good deed in her life unless she hoped to gain something from it. Sally, my dear, is pure poison.'

Cari felt uncomfortable.

'Sally is a friend. I really think –'

The other woman snorted.

'Don't come that hear no evil stuff with me. Sally has a voracious sexual appetite. Bisexual too. So that's something else to watch. But she made herself available to your boss, Hills, a year or so ago and he spurned her. She never forgives something like that. Now she's got some fringe outfit that's allowed her to take control and she's going to use it to go after your boss through Metroarcs. If you've chopped down trees somewhere, or dammed a valley with some tropical insect living in it, she'll come after you and she plays dirty.'

'SEND, you mean? She seems genuinely enthusiastic about the environment.'

The Congresswoman broke into a laugh that sounded like a witch's cackle.

'Genuinely enthusiastic – I must tell the boys that.' Hives sat up and her face became stern as she leaned across towards her listener. 'Listen to me, you silly little thing. I heard from one of Sally's henchmen about you. "Sally's little project", you were described as. Sally's eventual slave within Metroarcs. Now that's the truth and you think it over. I'm a rude old pol, dear, but my enemies don't accuse me of being duplicitous.'

With that the Congresswoman stumped out, leaving Cari in a confused mental state. As she collected her thoughts she realised that she was sure of one thing – Alice Hives had been very serious. I wonder what Sally did to upset her? Cari thought. And what do I do now?

Odhiambo walked down Connecticut Avenue intending to make his way to Cari's office close to the Mall. It was a nice day for walking and it seemed to be his day for it, starting early in the morning with Sam Bito. At least in Washington he knew where he was going. The system of numbered and lettered streets and regular-sized blocks made navigation simple, which was vital to Odhiambo who found a large urban environment disorienting. He had got himself into some hopelessly lost positions during his months in London.

Around him and past him went an urban mixture including business-suited men, attractive young business women, casually dressed late season tourists, mainly foreign, clutching maps and cameras, and a distinctive black young male type in expensive hip street clothes with flashes of gold on neck and wrist. Odhiambo remembered the conversation last night, of a dividing line in Washington only a few blocks from the White House – on one side tourists could walk in reasonable security, on the other the streets were dangerous to the casual walker, as the battle for drug distribution territory was waged with ruthless ferocity by Jamaican, Latin

American and local black gangs. Odhiambo was comfortably on the right side of the line and no one seemed threatened or worried.

The passing motley did not distract Odhiambo from his preoccupations for long. There was Sam Bito; he had agreed to voluntarily correct his statement to the police, but necessary though this was, Odhiambo believed Sam was deluding himself in thinking that he was not a prime suspect in Chivers' death. He might be right in hoping that Bolling would by now be on the track of the true reason for the murder, but Odhiambo was less optimistic. And now there was the Embassy visit, which had left Odhiambo even less easy in his mind. He had been interviewed by an official, position unspecified, which aroused Odhiambo's cautious instincts immediately. After enquiring about Odhiambo's intentions regarding returning to Kenya, the official had got around to the real reason why Odhiambo had been summoned.

'This man Chivers who was killed last night. You were there, I believe. You know he was a Kenyan citizen? Right. This gives us an interest, but there's something more that may make it our *shauri*. Chivers was an important point of contact for us.'

Odhiambo's concentration jumped to full volume. Oh no, he thought, this was all he needed to hear.

'Point of contact? What does that mean?'

The other Kenyan shrugged and turned his mouth down as if saying, Who can tell. The name plate on his desk said Amos Kasanga.

'He was well placed in IBID to keep us advised on matters affecting Kenya. Within the limits of his responsibilities to IBID, of course.'

'Of course.' Odhiambo did nothing to conceal the sarcasm. 'You mean he was your plant in there.'

'No. You're wrong, Odhiambo. We did nothing to secure him his post there. But he had been a civil servant, both before and after independence. We met him here at some cocktail party or other. That's the way it is in this town. He gave us information on the possibilities of loans, that sort of thing. Forthcoming tenders of interest to our companies. All clean stuff, bwana.'

Odhiambo shrugged.

'OK. I'll believe you.' He nearly added, 'but most wouldn't,' but held his tongue. 'So what can I do for you?'

The Embassy man probed Odhiambo on his connection with Chivers. The connection through his father-in-law seemed a surprise. Odhiambo did not mention that Sam Bito and Chivers had a common link with the Omuto affair. He waited for Kasanga to show his hand, but the face opposite seemed curious rather than scheming.

'I should be careful, Odhiambo. You and your relative. The police here might try and link you to this man's death.'

Odhiambo's smile was mirthless.

'Tell me something I don't know.'

'Yes. So, well . . . er, take care. We can't do much to help, you know. Still, you're the policeman. You must know how they operate. No, I didn't know you were involved. I thought as you were there you must be a friend. You see, he was helping us to get to the right people for a possible big loan for our horticultural export companies. You know – flowers, fruit and vegetables. Diversification is the name they give it. A third tusk for the elephant. Too dependent on coffee, the IMF says. If he was killed by someone inside we want to be sure it wasn't to do with our interests.'

Odhiambo snorted in disbelief.

'There's got to be more to it than that, man. What do you take me for? I'm not an empty vessel for you to play tunes on.'

Kasanga leaned back and seemed lost in contemplation. Odhiambo had come to the conclusion that he was not overly bright. Nor, probably, did he possess much authority. Finally, Kasanga shook his head as if coming to a decision.

'There's no more, Odhiambo. It's just we do not need a *shauri mkubwa* on this man Chivers. Better that it's treated low-key, *kitu kidogo*.'

After some further futile exchanges Odhiambo had left. His mind would not have been eased if he had been a party to the exchanges that followed his visit. Kasanga left the Embassy and placed a call from the back room of a nearby bar. He relayed the little information he had gleaned from Odhiambo. His listener seemed satisfied.

'So, you think he knows nothing about Chivers' death. That's good. But he was no help, either, eh?'

Kasanga shook his head, an instinctive but useless gesture for he was talking on the telephone.

'No, he didn't know Chivers. His connection is through his father-in-law, Bito. I didn't know he was Bito's son-in-law. Sounded to me as if the police thought they both might be suspects.'

54

'It would be good if the leopard takes the bait. Keep me informed.'

Almost simultaneously John Musoke was also talking to Nairobi from within the Embassy.

'Yes, I gave the police a brief outline as you said. Apparently, Omuto's name was in Chivers' diary, together with Bito's. I think Bolling, that's the local detective, sees Bito as his nominee for the job.'

The dry voice of the feared white man was clear enough but seemed almost a whisper.

'And you're sure Bito went to see Chivers? At about the right time?'

'Yes, bwana. The security man in IBID told me. Katawi. He spoke to his man who was on the reception desk last night. Bito was there.'

'With Chivers dead, Bito is the only other source. We have to make arrangements, just in case.'

Musoke listened to his instructions. The voice was emotionless and unthreatening and the orders were given in very guarded, elliptical language, but as he replaced the receiver Musoke shivered.

Half an hour later Musoke entered a bar on 12th Street. His entrance was watched with suspicion by hostile eyes. He was the right colour, but from the wrong part of the world. He waited for the barman to acknowledge his presence. As he approached with a glass of beer Musoke slid a five dollar note and the envelope across the dirty surface of the bartop. A slight nod and the transaction was completed. Musoke drained the small glass in two draughts and beat a hasty retreat. The barman slit open the envelope and read the message. 'Michael. Need to stand by for contract delivery. Tonight, 7 p.m.' He gestured towards a table. A dreadlocked young Jamaican came to the bar. The barman leaned across.

'Tell Michael the African wants to see him. Seven tonight.'

The messenger went off on his errand while the barman placed the note in an ashtray in the sink and burned it.

8

Odhiambo was thwarted on arrival at the Metroarcs office; Cari, it transpired, had left for a lunch engagement. He decided on a course of action but, as so often in the past, he knew not whether it was driven by foolish impulse or shrewd insight. Leaving a message that he would return in mid-afternoon, Odhiambo made his exit, hailed a cab and crossed the river to Rosslyn. He noticed crossing Roosevelt Bridge the strange overgrown small island below him. His driver, not one of the most recent immigrants, was able to satisfy his curiosity that it was Roosevelt Island.

'Sorta like a monument. But the Presidente, he wanted it left alone. Like the forests back home.'

Back home clearly meant somewhere in Latin America.

'Little rain forest in the middle of a city. Not bad.'

He had asked for the IBID office, but found himself at a different building to the one he had visited the previous night. However, the embossed logo on the wall and etched in the glass doors said IBID clearly enough. He paid off the informative cabman and mounted the steps.

His enquiry at the reception desk resulted in the security guard, an attractive black woman, looking up the name in her internal directory and scribbling a number on a slip which she passed to him.

'That's the number. There's phones behind you.'

She smiled, for the large man looking down at her was very good-looking.

Odhiambo smiled back and turned to the phone bank. Somewhat to his surprise, because he was inherently pessimistic about telephones, a familiar voice answered the tapped numbers.

'Fulton.'

Odhiambo hadn't given much thought to his next step. There seemed nothing for it but to come straight to the point. He introduced himself with reference to their Nairobi encounter. The returning voice was clearly taken aback.

'Odhiambo! Of course, I remember, not happily I may add. What on earth are you doing here?'

'On holiday with my in-laws. Who knew the man who was killed here last night. I wondered if I could see you for a few minutes.'

There was a pause before a reply came into Odhiambo's ear.

'You don't have any official standing, I presume.'

'None at all. It's just I'm concerned about my father-in-law.'

Another pause, then a grudging invitation and directions. Odhiambo a minute later found himself in what was becoming a familiar office layout: a large, open-plan, internal area with individual executive offices opening off it on the outer wall of the building. Executives got the windows and the daylight, support staff got artificial lighting and some leafy plants to give them an illusion of the outside. He was directed to a half-open door and found himself facing the lean, elegant man he had neither expected nor desired to meet again. Fulton, himself, was clearly not delighted at the reunion.

'So, Inspector Odhiambo. You made life unpleasant for me in Kenya. Why do you seek me out now?'

'I don't know. I suppose because I don't know anyone else in IBID. A man was killed in his office, my father-in-law saw him there shortly before – I needed someone to tell me what the chances are that it was someone inside the organisation who did it. What the man was like. Was he popular? Was his work sensitive?'

Fulton smiled, but not a smile of friendship.

'And what makes you think I would want to help you?'

Odhiambo cursed himself for his foolishness. What had possessed him to seek help from this man – a man he despised and who despised him in turn? He had to restrain an angry retort. Instead, he stepped up to the desk where Fulton sat and leaned forward over it.

'I don't suppose for a minute you want to help me. But I thought, mistakenly perhaps, you would be interested in the truth. The truth saved you in Nairobi.'

Fulton sneered. Then, looking up at the large figure looming over his desk, he spoke with a dismissive intonation.

'I hardly knew the man. He wasn't even in this building. Go and ask his staff if you want to interfere – or his boss, a man called Greene.'

'OK. I'm sorry to have bothered you, Fulton. I should have known better.'

Odhiambo turned to go. As he went through the door, Fulton chuckled as if to himself.

'Or if you fancy a more attractive appointment see a Miss Ca-radonna. Chivers was looking into one of her projects in Nigeria.'

Odhiambo swung around; Fulton's face gave him away – it was a picture of malicious mischief.

Cari sat on the terrace of the latest harbour development in George-town and watched her companion fidgeting with her glass of white wine. She could not help viewing Sally Eves somewhat differently since her encounter two hours ago with Congresswoman Hives. Sally had called, saying she needed to see Cari urgently, and here they were in this pleasant setting beside the Potomac sipping wine and waiting for their raisin and spinach salads. A sizeable yacht was being secured to the bollards with much jollity and badinage between the two men and two women involved. They were young, tanned and oozed that aura of easy money. What a strange place Washington is, thought Cari. Truly a cosmopolitan town. Even this uptown side contained such a variety: laid-back university under-graduates, young but hard-driving upwardly mobile lawyers and corporate people, hard-nosed politicians and their circle of preda-tors including the media, old-style money here in Georgetown mixed with brash new money springing up in the *laissez-faire* Rea-gan years. Somewhere she supposed she fitted into this spectrum – no, not spectrum, more kaleidoscope. Sally Eves straddled several of these characterisations – media personality, radical university activist, intimate associate of some of the political figures – and seemed to feel at home in each. Cari's musings were brought to an end as her companion leaned forward; the purpose of the meeting was about to be made clear.

'Such a shame your party was ruined last night by this IBID man's death. So upsetting, particularly to your parents.'

'Yes, it is. Upsetting, I mean. Particularly as Dad knew the man who was killed.'

'Most unlucky. And the police arriving and all. But I'm sure it will sort itself out. Do you have any theory as to the reason this man, Chivers, was killed?'

Cari thought about her words carefully as the bright young waiter put their low-calorie lunches in front of them. She nibbled a thin stick of celery as the waiter wished their appetites well and departed.

'No. At least not based on anything tangible. I assume it was some personal problem within the organisation. Jealousy, personal or office-related.'

'Perhaps, but I don't think so.' Sally's right hand was still twirling her half-empty wineglass almost as a form of twitch in her nervous system. She paused and then continued, her voice low but now more decisive. 'Look, Cari, I know your father is caught up in this in terms of police activity. The best way to get him off the hook is to get after the real motive for this business. And you may have the key to that.'

'Whatever do you mean?'

'You know about SEND, our little group. I've told you. I know you're sympathetic. Well, SEND has reason to believe that there is some scandal inside IBID to do with a major project and Chivers was looking into it. Suppose he was killed to keep the lid on. It's SEND's job to let the public know and it would help your father at the same time.'

'But what has this to do with me?'

'Not you personally: Metroarcs. Suppose IBID is financing a big project that involves great environmental damage or something similar and Metroarcs is a contractor.' She raised her hand, forestalling Cari's objection. The wineglass, released from her grip, swayed on the trellised metal table but stayed upright. 'No. Hear me out. I'm not asking you to compromise your duty to Metroarcs. I'm saying my interest and Metroarcs' are identical and, therefore, my aim and yours are compatible. Suppose my hypothesis is right and someone in IBID and, yes, someone in Metroarcs are concealing nefarious business of some sort. That's not in Metroarcs' interest. I'll go along with your belief that your outfit is environmentally more sympathetic these days. And we need people like you in large businesses to foster this awareness. But let's face facts, Cari, there are still dinosaurs in organisations like yours who couldn't care less what's done as long as the bottom line and their bonuses are healthy.'

Cari sat watchfully. Sally Eves had a commanding presence; her habit of assuming everyone identified with her objective and, therefore, it was only a matter of how to work together was remarkably persuasive. Faintly in her head, Cari could hear Ms Hives' snort of derision.

'So what are you getting at, Sally? Sure, Metroarcs is a contractor or supplier in lots of internationally financed projects, World Bank, UN, IBID, whatever. Some excellently conceived, some not so good. It's not Metroarcs who draws up these things or approves them for financing.'

'Absolutely. That's what I mean. There's no conflict of interest here. We've all got the interest of sound business combined with sound environmental management at heart. What I'm asking is whether you've heard of the IBID fertiliser project in Nigeria? Metroarcs is involved in a big way.'

Cari shook her head.

'No, I don't know it. But that doesn't mean anything. Dealing with individual contracts is not my area. In fact, it's not our Washington office's concern. We're here to watch over our interests in terms of Congressional legislation.'

Sally Eves curled her mouth into a sardonic smile.

'You don't have to define lobbying to me, Cari. I've met enough in my time. OK. The point is this, can you access information on Metroarcs contracts? Can you confirm what Metroarcs is doing exactly in Nigeria with IBID money? No breach of confidence. Information that is in the public domain. Contracts won in competitive tendering.'

'If it's public knowledge why do you need me?'

'Because I like you, Cari. You're one of us in attitude. I want you involved. Just suppose this particular case is being suppressed in some way. If you have a look at it you can make your own judgement as to whether there's something that needs investigating. You don't have to tell me anything that compromises your loyalty to Metroarcs. And remember it could help to get the pressure off your father.'

Cari now baited her hook.

'Glen. That's Glen Hills, my boss. He might know about it. And he has ready access to the computer files. I'll ask him if you like.'

Sally chewed on her salad for a while.

'Cari, dear. You're still relatively new here in DC. Take a word of advice from a seasoned campaigner. I'm not saying anything against Mr Hills, but it's best to keep the cards close to one's chest when making the first bid. Let's just keep this between ourselves while you see if there's anything worth following up. If so, we can bring your boss in then.'

'Do you know him?'

Sally seemed taken aback by the sudden direct question.

'Er . . . Hills . . . hm, well, yes, I've met him.' Assurance was re-established. 'There's not many people on the Hill I don't know.

Remember, I've been involved with women's issues long before I got involved with SEND.'

'OK. I'll see what there is. And I'll decide what if anything you should know that is of legitimate interest. But tell me this, Sally. I heard you have good contacts in IBID. Why can't you get what you want to know?'

Sally laughed, a genuine laugh, as if a certain tension had been relieved. 'Oh, the inside-Beltway gossip. You mean Giles. Yes, my dear, he's a friend of mine. But in relationships like that it's best to keep business and pleasure separate. In fact, that's why I cannot ferret about inside IBID. Giles would swing his considerable influence against me in a moment if I did.'

And that was as far as Cari got. But in the taxi on her way back to her office she had much to think about. On arrival she found an impatient and bad-tempered husband.

Across the river in the annexe to the Managing Director's office on the top floor of the main IBID building a group of men and one woman were seated around the ornately carved table – a gift from the head of a major company in Indonesia. The head of Personnel got up to leave: the MD, having been assured that all necessary was being done in terms of communications with Chivers' family, needed him no more. The others watched him go, realising the serious business was about to start.

Faucon sat well back in his chair, his hip wedged against the join of the chairback and the arm. He appeared relaxed, as befitted a man after a long day, but none of the other men, all sitting more upright, were deceived. Faucon's eyes fell on the chief of the Security Section; as the most junior man present, he had seated himself at the far end of the table.

'Now then.' The voice was soft but penetrating. 'Kindly summarise for us the facts regarding outsider entries last evening into the annexe building.'

Katawi swallowed once and then managed to get started in an even tone. He had already rehearsed his statement in his mind.

'There were two guards on duty after six in the evening in the annexe building. We have another four on duty here – one of them is available to strengthen the annexe monitoring if needed. There's much less coming and going there, of course.' He hurried on, Faucon immediately showing signs of impatience at redundant information. 'The guard, Montes is his name, has identified a Dr Bito who arrived around 6.30 p.m. and asked for Mr Chivers. He, Montes, called Chivers who instructed that Dr Bito be sent up. Bito signed the book. Montes remembers him leaving, but can't pinpoint the precise time because for some reason he slipped by without signing out. Montes was on the phone. No other visitor entered between six thirty and seven thirty, but some who were in the building from an earlier hour left, as did several staff members.'

'So.' The voice remained soft. 'Our security system still has deficiencies.'

Katawi shifted in his chair.

'Er . . . yes. But it works fairly well. You must remember until two years ago there was no controlled entry system at all. Montes should have called him back. But someone leaving isn't such a big deal as a stranger walking in. I have disc –'

But Katawi had come to the end of his hearing.

'Thank you Mr . . . er . . . Katawi; that will be all for now.'

Another pause while the discomfited security chief withdrew. Faucon surveyed the survivors with an acerbic eye.

'Well, we have all learned something. The system needs review.' He pointed at the occupant of the chair second on the right from his own. 'Remedy that without delay.'

The Senior Director of Administration and Services nodded weakly, his overall appearance, pale grey skin, grey hair, grey suit, coloured now by the flush in his face. Faucon moved on.

'No doubt the police will examine fully this Dr Bito's role in the affair – if any. I wish to be advised as to the other possible implications should Dr Bito not be involved. Yes, Greene?'

'Yes, sir. It does seem that Chivers' visitor is the most likely suspect. But, if not, there seems little or no motive. Chivers was competent, quiet, well liked by his colleagues. No indiscretions as far as we know.'

'Women?' Faucon sounded world-weary. 'Drugs? Alcohol? Homosexual?'

Greene was flustered.

'I don't think . . . I mean . . .' He paused and tried again. 'In terms of his office life there were no overt signs of problems. No complaints against him at all. He's only been with us a short time. Such family as he has is in Kenya. He was living alone here. Seemed to be settled.'

Faucon grunted. ' "No overt signs", "Seemed to be" – these are scarcely definitive assurances.' He raised a hand to prevent Greene embarking on a defence. 'Work? What was he working on? Any sensitivities there?'

Greene was glad to pass the inquisition on.

'He was currently reviewing the Nigeria fertiliser project. Mr Kraxma and Miss Caradonna here can fill you in.'

'Ah, yes, Africa Projects. Never the most trouble-free of our programmes. And Nigeria fertiliser's one of the biggest.'

Kraxma could feel the penetrating look of his boss, Mensat Khan, in addition to the interested gaze of the man at the head of the table.

'Yes. A mid-term evaluation, yes? Chivers was in charge of it. He made visit to Nigeria. Now he was working on report. Routine, I think. Big project like this, expect a careful evaluation.'

Faucon turned his head to gaze out at the lights of Washington. As if idly musing he spoke without looking at Kraxma.

'And questions have been asked. Farmers not supportive. Government concerned. I received a letter from the Prime Minister.'

Mensat Khan hastily intervened. This needed his touch; Kraxma was not exactly the diplomat.

'Ah, Giles. Yes, you're right, of course. A major initiative in Nigeria of this type – aid to small farmers – was never going to be trouble-free. I stressed this to the board at the time. That is why we made provision for a major review at this stage. We were anxious to have the Internal Audit report.'

Faucon's gaze was back in the room now.

'Thank you, Mensat. I'm sure the board will remember your cautions as well as your enthusiasms. But Mr Kraxma was telling us about Chivers' report.' He nodded at Kraxma. 'Tell us more.'

Kraxma glanced at Khan and then back at Faucon. He felt the need for a cigarette.

'Little more to tell. We wait for Chivers. Now Chivers gone. Someone else will have to take it on.'

'What contact had you with him?' The voice was suddenly sterner. 'He must have discussed it with you, man.'

Kraxma had decided attack was the best form of defence.

'Not so. Best to leave auditors alone until they ready. Any information he needed he get from Miss Caradonna. I spoke to him once at beginning. No more.'

'And in Nigeria? He was alone?'

'We had team there at time. But he worked independent of us.'

Faucon looked back at Greene.

'And the work can be completed?'

Greene cleared his throat noisily.

'That is what we would expect, yes. I have assigned another experienced officer.'

'But there's a problem.'

The voice was clear and confident: the men looked at the woman next to Kraxma. She was certainly the most eye-catching person in the room – amongst the mainly drab men her dark hair, Mediterranean skin, brightly coloured blouse and aura of sexuality blazed like a beacon.

Mensat Khan hurried to make the introduction.

'Giles, this is Miss Caradonna. Miss Caradonna is the project officer for the fertiliser project.'

Faucon's eyes glinted.

'Oh yes, Miss Caradonna is known to us all, I daresay. A problem?'

'Yes. I was allowed into Mr Chivers' office this afternoon. There were files on his desk to do with the project. But his working file with his notes and his data was not there. And there's no data on the computer and there's no floppy disc. Strange, if he was working on it when he was killed.'

Silence greeted this news. Faucon nodded to himself as if his anticipations had been justified. Kraxma cursed to himself. He had wanted Caradonna to be seen and not heard. He filled the vacuum.

'We will search more completely, no? There will be back-ups. Duplicate files. No big problem.'

Faucon's mouth stretched at one side. A small smile, if smile it was.

'You miss the point, Kraxma. The interesting question is why a file is missing.' He looked at Greene. 'You know he was working at the time of his death?'

Greene was on safe ground here. Or thought he was.

'Oh, yes. When Kraxma and I went to his office in the morning with the detective, the scattering of papers, the figures on the screen – it seems certain he was working.'

'And you noticed the absence of a file?'

'Well, no . . . no. There was no way of telling without an inventory. We're checking now, of course.'

Kraxma held no brief for Greene, but thought it expedient to add his voice.

'I did see that no data were in computer. He must have entered it manually. Remember, Greene, I say so.'

Greene nodded and was preparing to speak about commissioning an inventory of Chivers' office, but Faucon had moved on.

'Mensat – have you checked who was in the building last evening?'

'Yes, Giles. There are three departments housed there, or part of a department in my case. Internal Audit, Financial Systems and about half of my staff. Only two of Greene's staff say they were still there. One was on the same floor as Chivers. Both deny visiting Chivers. There were eleven others from Finance and Projects. Plus the security personnel, of course. No one saw anything suspicious.'

Faucon was silent, looking down at the papers in front of him, but without seeing them; the others waited. Finally, Faucon looked up; his eyes went around the table seeming to focus momentarily on each face.

'Right. Thank you. We shall, of course, co-operate fully with the police regarding this unfortunate matter. And I expect a full report without delay on Mr Chivers' work and the steps taken to complete it. Indeed,' he locked on to the uneasy Director of Internal Audit, 'I await at your earliest convenience your preliminary report on the fertiliser project.'

With that the meeting was over.

It had taken Cari and James Odhiambo some hours to find that each had been given the same lead independently during the day. They had driven home with Odhiambo brooding about when Bolling would strike in terms of Sam Bito. He tried to hide the reason for his depressed mood from Cari, but she knew him too well for his attempt to succeed. She finally broke him down.

'It's not looking good, Cari. Sam was there, he's got what looks like a motive and he lied to Bolling. I'm sure Bolling will be checking the Kenya end – the Omuto business; then we can expect trouble.'

'James, listen. Dad didn't do it. I assume you believe him. I do. He wouldn't harm a fly. There's got to be another motive. An internal one. Inside IBID, I mean.'

'I dunno, Cari. Whatever problems and rivalries there are in an office, how often does one party beat the other's brains out in his own office?'

'I'm looking into it.' The conversation broke off as Cari had to swerve when a car coming towards them drifted momentarily across the centre line towards their car. 'Watch what you're doing, you nitwit,' shouted Cari uselessly through the glass.

'The Kenya connection with Chivers is bigger than we thought.' Odhiambo was half talking to himself. 'Chivers was some sort of agent within IBID for the Kenyans. Kenya, Kenya, everywhere Bolling looks is the Kenya connection.'

It was later that evening after a domestic dinner eaten for the most part in strained silence that Cari returned to her task as enunciated by Sally Eves. Her parents were loading the dish-washer and tidying the kitchen, but had refused extra hands for these tasks. Cari sat on a sofa with her head resting lightly on her husband's shoulder. She gave him a potted version of her lunch with Sally Eves.

'So, she has this theory that Chivers, the dead man, was about to uncover a big scandal involving an IBID project. So someone killed him. What's more, she thinks Metroarcs may be involved – but from another source I hear that's because she's got it in for Glen.'

Odhiambo found it difficult to grasp Cari's story.

'What are you talking about? What does this Eves woman know? She doesn't work in IBID, does she? And where's your boss fit in?'

'How many questions is that?' Cari laughed. For some reason her spirits were rising, although the haggard face of her father was still fresh in mind. 'Sally's pressure group, SEND, I told you about it. Well, SEND believes there's some big problem in Nigeria that it could use to embarrass IBID. That in turn could mean someone gets fired. So Chivers gets bumped off. Sally wanted me to help dig up the dirt. Via Metroarcs files. Ow. What are you doing?'

Odhiambo had gripped her shoulder fiercely.

'Nigeria project? My God. Fulton, you remember Fulton, he told me today to look into a Nigeria project. What's going on?'

Cari sat up.

'Jeez, James. Do you think we're on to something? Sally said it would get Dad off the hook. What were you doing with Fulton?'

Further clarification was delayed because the door to the kitchen opened and Sam Bito rejoined them. By tacit consent, at least for this evening, the subject of Chivers' death was avoided in his presence.

9

The next morning – a Wednesday – the Odhiambos set out to implement the plan they had discussed in bed the night before. Cari had formulated it to override her somewhat sceptical partner.

'Look, James, if Chivers was killed by someone already inside the building, either it is someone carrying a personal grudge or it was because of something Chivers knew of through his work. There's nothing we can do to investigate his personal life – that's the police's job – but we are in a position to look into the second possibility.'

'How come you're so set on being a private investigator suddenly? You were only saying the other day that the best part of being here was that I couldn't possibly get involved in work.'

Even as he spoke, he knew that he had made a mistake. His wife sat up in bed, her profile and figure silhouetted against the faint light from the window.

'How can you say that? It's my father who's under suspicion. He might be arrested tomorrow.' The voice cracked and Cari bit her lip before continuing. 'We've got to do what we can. How can you suggest otherwise?'

'I want to do the best for your father, Cari.' He reached up to pull her down next to him once more, but the figure resisted. He sighed. 'But sometimes doing the best means doing nothing. Letting the police get on with their job.'

'I can't believe I'm hearing this. That man Bolling probably thinks his job is done when he arrests the first black man he can lay his hand on. Anyhow, I'm going to dig out what I can on that Nigeria project everyone keeps telling us about.'

'OK, Cari, I'm in. It's just I didn't want you rushing into something without thinking it through. And don't underestimate Bolling. I think he's pretty smart. So how do we go about investigating IBID?'

'If Metroarcs is a contractor, I can access our records. Then there's Glen Hills; he may know something, or know somebody who knows something. And if we're a major contractor I have an excuse to see whoever in IBID is running the show. Meanwhile, why don't you go and see that security man that you went with the other night? He might know what's going on.'

'You realise that if there's something in your theory a killer is out there who is likely to know you're getting too close?'

'Oh, stop being so namby-pamby. It's usually me that's trying to stop you from charging off. We're a long way from getting too close, as you put it. Get a lead, that's all. Then we can leave it to Bolling, if he's so smart.'

Finally, Cari had lain down once more and snuggled into her husband's side. Now she had decided on a course of action she was relaxed and soon the deeper breathing revealed to James that she was asleep. Sleep came much more slowly to him. He wasn't convinced by the project scandal theory. The memory that kept intruding on him was the Kenyan Embassy man skirting around Chivers' informant role. Was it credible that his death was not linked to Kenya in some way, given all the connections? But this line of reasoning kept bringing him back to Sam Bito and the Omuto enquiry. Finally he slept, to waken once in the night with a vivid image of a dream of watching television – he had been gazing at the screen intently, but the odd thing was that there was no picture on it, only a smudgy blur.

Now ensconced in her office, Cari wasted no time. Hills had still not put in a reappearance so there were some basic chores requiring attention, but by mid-morning she settled in front of her computer screen with an instruction guide to accessing the Metroarcs data base held on a main-frame in New York. Running the data file menu across the screen, and after a period of trial and error, Cari located a main file headed "IBID Project". Names of sub-files duly appeared on command but, perusing them, Cari could not find an acronym for Nigeria. She went through them again and there near the top of the list was a file headed "IBID. PR.AFR." Of course, Africa! Within the Africa file lay more sub-files, and one indeed had NIG as its suffix code. This file contained a list of six project titles with a project code, an indication of the total investment value, the amount involved in the Metroarcs sub-contract, and a brief paragraph of description. Cari typed in the project code for Nigeria: Fertilisers, but this time hit a security barrier. On the screen appeared: SECURED FILE. RESTRICTED ACCESS. INSERT USER CODE.

Returning to the Nigeria main file, Cari noted that the project was implemented through some company called Aginvest Holdings.

The total investment was two hundred million dollars with Metroarcs as a supplier of fertiliser handling a sixty million dollar sub-contract. Cari whistled – this was a big bucks project. She hadn't realised IBID dealt in these sorts of sums for a single project. She pressed the office intercom to access Hills' secretary.

'Hi, Cindy. Cari. I'm trying to put some analysis together here and I need access to details of our sub-contracts with IBID. Those details require a password. Do we have one in this office?'

'Do you just need a Read Only access? No manipulation of the contents?'

'Yeah, sure. Read Only will be fine.'

'Then all you do is enter 042, the code for this office, your staff number, full initials and today's date.'

'Great, thanks.'

Cari carefully typed in the code leaving a space between each segment. It worked. After a Please Wait sign the screen filled with an executive summary of a project called Nigeria-Fertilisers. It was not what Cari had assumed, namely construction of a fertiliser production plant, rather a one-off five-year project to import fertiliser for use by small farmers. Metroarcs supplied the fertiliser from one of its Mediterranean subsidiaries, Aginvest arranged the internal transport, storage and distribution to farmer advice centres, and the farmers received vouchers from the agricultural extension agents at a discount in exchange for contracts to grow a certain acreage of a specified cereal crop. Aginvest was reimbursed by IBID at the full commercial rate and Metroarcs got a satisfactory profit as the importer. It all looked orthodox enough, only the amounts involved were very large by African development programme standards.

The report ended with contact names and numbers. Aginvest had two staff named, one in England and one in Lagos; Deputy Secretary, Ministry of Agriculture was given as the government's contact; and the IBID contact was shown as E. N. Kraxma, IBID, Rosslyn. It was the top name that gave Cari pause; the Metroarcs contact was G. Hills! She contacted Hills' secretary once more.

'It's me again. Look, that worked fine. I got what I needed.'

'OK. That's good. Any time.'

'Sure. Thanks anyway. By the way, there was one entry that I noticed – it said our contact for one project in Africa was Glen. I didn't know we handled overseas contracts here.'

There was a silence that lasted for several seconds and seemed longer.

'We don't usually. Is this Nigeria-Fertilisers? Yeah, I thought so. It's Glen's baby. I don't know that he conceived it, but he sure acted as the midwife. He helped the Nigerians sell it to the bank in Rosslyn. Ever since, as I say, he thinks of it as his project. That's why he stays with it from here.'

'Right. Got you. Say, Cindy – if Glen calls in tell him I need to get in touch. And let me know.'

Cari sat back in her chair and thought. Then picking up the phone she asked her secretary to get her a Mr Kraxma in IBID.

Odhiambo had arranged to meet Simon Katawi when he took his mid-morning break. As instructed, when he announced himself at the main IBID entrance on Wilson Boulevard he was sent to the basement area, which provided the rest area as well as central control for Katawi and his security personnel. He was early and Katawi was late so the wait extended beyond Odhiambo's boredom threshold. One pair of guards left to take up duty at the entrance; the pair coming off duty entered and helped themselves to coffee from the large pot under the percolator.

'You still waiting for Mr Katawi?' The guard who had let Odhiambo in recognised him. 'You want a coffee?'

'No coffee, thanks. Yeah, I'm still here.'

'Everything's out of sync since the killing the other night.' This was the other guard, who then stopped, looking embarrassed, not knowing who Odhiambo was or what he knew.

'Yes, I can imagine. I was here with Katawi that night. When the police called.'

The guards looked at the large African with increased interest.

'You're not from around here, right? You a friend of Mr Katawi?'

'That's right. We're from the same country.'

'Yes, sir.' The second guard returned to his theme. 'Nothing's gone right since Monday night. And the police are still haunting the place down the road.'

'I hear Mr Faucon isn't too pleased with our system. Someone may have got in or out without being recorded.'

'How does he know that? System's pretty good but they keep the manpower down. Trying to save a few measly bucks. Can't do everything when you're on your own. I heard Montes saying he

70

was doing several things together. Not reasonable. Hope he don't get no hassle over this.'

'The chief's out of sorts too. Regular enough guy normally. Told him I couldn't lay my hands on my wet weather suit and he nigh bit my head off. "Don't see no rain outside," he said. "Get out in the car-park." Wasn't meaning it was raining right that minute. One or two things gone missing. Time we had a check.'

'Check for what, Jasper?' Katawi had come in behind the two chatting guards and caught the last words. 'You fussing again?'

'No, sir. Just saying wouldn't want to think we had a light-fingered guy with access here.'

'I still think it's carelessness. You lot can't remember half the time which building you left something in. Ah, Odhiambo. Sorry to keep you waiting. Things are still not back to normal. To be expected, of course.' He shook Odhiambo's hand. 'Let's go to the main canteen. I could do with some breakfast. I've been on since six.'

Odhiambo nursed his coffee as Katawi demolished a plate of scrambled eggs, sausage patties and hash browns. It looked good and he was tempted. He had had what Cari regarded as a sensible breakfast – orange juice, some tasteless brown flakes of cereal and a slice of toast – but he had a lunch date with her so he'd better keep his stomach waiting.

'I'm worried about Sam Bito, Katawi. Bolling may be closing in. This guy Chivers – he didn't have other visitors?'

Katawi briefed him on the lack of other outside suspects.

'So it would have to be an inside job?'

'If Dr Bito is in the clear, yes. Don't see any other choice.'

'Any chance it was work-related?'

Katawi shrugged.

'Anything's possible. You get jealousies, sex comes into it some-times, harassment, sexual harassment – that's the big thing to guard against these days. Some secretary accuses you and you're in trouble, man. Then someone gets overlooked for promotion. There's a lot of ambitious people in this building.'

'What about the work itself?'

'How d'you mean?'

'The guy was obviously working. Papers everywhere. Computer on. He was some sort of auditor. Could he have been a threat to someone?'

'You're outside my area now, Odhiambo.' Katawi chewed his last piece of sausage carefully, as if regretting its loss. 'Wouldn't know about Chivers' work. As for the computer being on – some of them leave them on all the time these days.'

'Do you know a Miss Caradonna?'

Katawi looked up with a smile.

'Hey, Odhiambo, you got yourself a beautiful smart wife. You don't need another.'

'I was told Chivers was working on a project she's in charge of. In Nigeria.'

'I know Miss Caradona by sight. Not easy to overlook.' Katawi made curving motions with his hands now free of knife and fork. 'No idea what she works on. Come to think of it, I've seen a Nigerian Airways tag on her briefcase.'

'You're an observant man, Katawi. Now I have one question and one favour to ask. For Sam's sake. To try and get Bolling off his back.'

Katawi looked doubtful.

'Look, Odhiambo, the police here aren't bad. Particularly this side of the river – in Virginia, I mean. But if you go sniffing about you may find you get the same reception the hyena gets when too close to a lion enjoying his kill.'

'Come on, Katawi. We're all Kenyans, right? You know Sam Bito. You were a guest in his house, dammit.' Katawi looked uncomfortable, but waited. Odhiambo continued. 'The question is, do you remember what was showing on the computer screen in Chivers' office? When we were there with Bolling.' Katawi's mouth fell open. He was clearly taken aback. Whatever he was expecting it was not this. He shook his head. Odhiambo pressed on. 'And the favour I want is an introduction to Miss Caradonna. Ring her. Imply without lying that I'm an industrialist and want to see her.'

Katawi protested.

'You're off base, Odhiambo, as they say here. There's all sorts of internal investigations going on as well as the police. You can't get away with it. And as for knowing what was on some damn computer, what do you think I am?'

'And before I see this Caradonna let me have a look at the file on her Nigeria project. I tell you what. Tell her you think I'm from Nigeria. After all, how can you be expected to know one African from another?' Katawi was looking at him with growing alarm. 'For Sam Bito, Katawi. Another Kenyan in a foreign land.'

Katawi sat as if stunned. Odhiambo decided to convey the impression that he had taken silence to signify assent and moved on.

'There's one thing that's been puzzling me since we saw the body, Katawi. It was a savage attack, blood everywhere. Whoever did it must have got blood splattered over his clothes. To walk out of the building without incurring great risk the murderer would need a change of clothes. This should rule Bito out. How could a visitor have a stash of clothes ready in the building? He arrived home in his normal clothes with not a bloodstain in sight.'

'Never mind about bloodstains, Odhiambo. I'm quite willing to accept Bito's innocence. What's worrying me is your wanting me to help with your digging into the bank's affairs. It's not your *shauri*, bwana.'

Ten minutes later, as he saw his guest out, Katawi was still shaking his head, but Odhiambo was smiling.

Bloodstains, or rather the lack of them, were also among the subjects of conversation between Lieutenant Bolling and his superior.

'I'll be ready to move on Bito when I get the information we've requested from Kenya. I need the full facts on this Omuto business – that's the only motive we have for Bito.'

'It's a bit thin, Pete. Some old murder, twenty years ago. What sort of motive is that? I can just see a good lawyer going after you on that.'

'The enquiry into this old case isn't old, it's current. And for someone that's a big danger. And that someone is almost certainly Bito. No, the facts on the Omuto case and a warrant to take the Bito house apart are what I need. The one problem I see is some tangible forensic evidence. Whoever killed Chivers must have got some blood or hair or brains or something over them. With the warrant we'll see what we can find.'

'But he arrived home to a party, for Chrissake. No one saw any blood on him. And you haven't found any discarded clothes in the area of the IBID building.'

'That's right. That's what I said. That's the hole I need to fill. It's likely he changed in the car or whatever. With a warrant we should find something, then we can charge him.'

'This could be a high profile case, Pete. Bankers, university professors, diplomats and all. Don't fumble the ball on this one. Cover your back every step of the way.'

'Sure, Cap'n. Don't worry. There's another little angle I'm watching. This guy Bito's son-in-law is a cop – a Kenyan cop. Chief

73

Inspector. Been involved in some high profile murder cases himself, it seems. And I get a sniff of something extra. He's supposed to be here on vacation, but the Embassy people seem to get shifty when his name is mentioned. I dunno whether he's intelligence or something. In which case we come back in all probability to this Omuto business.'

'OK, Pete. You're the quarter-back. Just make sure you don't throw an interception like that asshole in the stadium on Sunday.'

'That was the Giants, Cap'n. In and around this town you're supposed to celebrate when the 'Skins roll them over. Not reveal that you're a New York man at heart.'

It was twilight already in Nairobi, but R. D. Price-Allen sat at his unlit desk looking out over the city as the lights came on. The Chivers death was a major set-back, but more importantly it made Samuel Bito a crucial, critical figure. One way or another Bito had to be extracted from Washington. It was like a game of chess against an opponent he had never met. The detective in charge, Bolling – when would he make his next move and what would it be? Was a pre-emptive move necessary? And if so was Musoke capable of making it without knocking another piece over? As Price-Allen thought through his options a small thin smile hovered on his lips. He was enjoying himself. This was what made the game intellectually stimulating. The ideal was the mental process combined with the sensual pleasure derived from the infliction of pain – at this far remove, the second might be difficult to achieve, but one couldn't always have everything one wanted in one parcel.

10

Odhiambo's opportunity came sooner than he expected. He had asked Katawi to contact him by means of Cari's office. He was pleasantly surprised on returning with Cari from lunch to find a message awaiting him. Over lunch he and Cari had compared notes. Cari had spoken with Kraxma, but had been rebuffed.

'He's some sort of rude mid-European, James. I explained that I was reviewing Metroarcs' involvement in IBID-financed projects and wanted to know more about the Nigeria fertiliser project. He didn't want to know. Said he was busy with emergency matters and that he understood Glen Hills was his contact point in our office. What's that line from *My Fair Lady*? Kraxma is 'a ruder pest from Budapest' or some such place.'

'What about Hills?' Odhiambo asked. 'What does he say about it?'

'Glen hasn't appeared in the office for a couple of days. The last time I saw him was at the party. Maybe this afternoon I'll try and track him down, 'cos Kraxma's right – Glen is the official contact point and that's unusual; it should be somebody in New York.'

Now their second lead to the inside of IBID had come through. Odhiambo met Katawi as requested in a bar opposite the main IBID building. Katawi was flustered and uncomfortable, but he had achieved the requested double.

'She, Caradonna I mean, is leaving for Nigeria tonight, I think. I spun her a yarn – said you were a visiting official interested in a project similar to the Nigeria one. You needed just a quick briefing. She'll see you at four fifteen. So you've got an hour to look through these.' Katawi produced from a bag two files, one bulging to capacity with papers, the other slimmer. 'These are the general project files – routine correspondence, that sort of thing – no restrictions on circulation. Sensitive stuff is on files that I couldn't access without it being noticed. Technical background stuff is kept in boxes. And very recent memos might not have got on to the central files yet.'

'Thanks, Katawi, you've been a great help. Can I go through them here?'

'Yes. I'll get on, but you should be all right here. I'll come back at four to take them back.'

'And where do I find this Caradonna woman?'

'In the annexe building. Two floors above Chivers' office.'

Odhiambo was not particularly good at assessing documents, although he had some experience at it. Prior to the Eagles Nest case in Kenya he had been involved in two fraud cases involving local firms that had upset the government. He skimmed through the files, starting at the beginning of the time sequence from the back of the fatter one. There was nothing untoward as far as he could see. The project had been approved three years ago. Fertiliser was imported in vast quantities by Metroarcs and was stored, then distributed all over the place by Aginvest in time for farmers to use it. The previous year delivery of the fertiliser to local agricultural offices had gone very much according to plan. The fat file had been closed six months ago. The second file picked up events from that point, at the start of the current planting season. Agricultural extension staff reported farmers complaining of poor yields from the previous crop. Senior officials blamed the poor rainfall in the previous season and urged the extension staff to redouble their efforts.

None of this seemed very unusual to Odhiambo. He had heard of and witnessed several projects in Kenya that aimed to improve the lot of small farmers which had got off to rocky starts or foundered altogether.

Next, as Odhiambo flicked over the pages, came reference to Internal Audit being asked by senior management to look at the project earlier than would normally have been the case. According to a memo from a Mensat Khan to Kraxma this was in response to 'government concern at a high level'. Kraxma had objected. It was too early to judge the project. It needed at least another year. But Khan's hands, it seemed, were tied. In another memo he wrote that 'in view of the fact that this is not only one of our largest projects, but is also intended to be the forerunner of others in Africa, the Managing Director believes it to be imperative that progress is critically and independently evaluated at each stage'. Kraxma gave in, reluctantly instructing the team on its way to Nigeria under the leadership of Romaine Caradonna to co-operate with the evaluator from Internal Audit. There were no communications from Chivers on the file. Odhiambo assumed Internal Audit maintained its own filing system. The only subsequent reference to Chivers was a memo from Caradonna to Kraxma which was dated less than one month in the past. In it Caradonna referred to a phone call from a senior official of the Ministry of Agriculture in Lagos warning her that 'Chivers has secured data direct from someone in the Ibadu Research Station where the original fertiliser trials had been carried out – see analysis in Project Technical Preparation Report No. 6. According to my source the data supplied to Chivers may relate to trials conducted during the last growing season. The Ministry is concerned about data leaving the country without government approval. I reminded him that we have an agreement with the government for the free exchange of data pertaining to projects we finance and that this, presumably, covered Internal Audit as well. I gained the impression that the concern was with the content of the data. Or to put it more properly the Ministry is sensitive to what the data may reveal. I asked Chivers and he admitted he had received some yield data comparing with fertiliser/without fertiliser plots. He said until he had time to look at it he couldn't be sure what the precise specifications were. You may want to reassure the Nigerians formally or informally. Or is there some problem I don't know about?'

There was no acknowledgement of this memo unless a later general circulation to his staff from Kraxma was a slap on Caradonna's wrist. 'Given the sensitivity of relations with Lagos regarding the fertiliser project, references to communications with the government in internal memos should be given a low-level security rating namely 'Restricted'.'

Odhiambo looked at his watch. He had ten minutes in hand. He pushed aside his coffee cup and caught the waiter's eye. He needed a beer even though it was only mid-afternoon. As he waited for Katawi, he drank his beer and thought things through. Caradonna must be bright to be in a professional position with an organisation like IBID. But she wasn't trained in agriculture, it seemed, and was beginning to feel out of her depth with the arguments about the response to the fertiliser by farmers' crops. Chivers, on the other hand, Odhiambo remembered, was a statistician who had worked at the Nakuru Agricultural Research Centre. He would know his way around such data. Had he discovered something? And if so, what? Surely you don't kill a man because he may disagree with the yield estimates used to support a project proposal? He looked up: Katawi was back.

'OK? It's time for you to go to Miss Caradonna. Give me the files and I'll return them to the registry.'

Odhiambo nodded, rose and handed over the files.

'Thanks, Katawi. I owe you one for this.'

Ten minutes later and after a careful clearance check, Odhiambo gained access to his quarry. As he shook hands he found it difficult not to show a reaction to her presence; she had the immediate sexual impact of a film sex siren. Yes, there was the classical Mediterranean face, with the sleek dark hair framing it, and full figure evident even when covered by restrained office clothing of blouse, jumper and skirt, but the whole was more than the sum of the parts: from Caradonna came the overall saturating sensation of sensuality. Place her in an austere office environment in sober clothes and the immediate sexual charge was replaced by the ticking of a sexual time-bomb.

Introductory pleasantries over, Romaine Caradonna got quickly down to business. Her voice was formal, almost clipped in delivery, as if a conscious effort was made to reduce the impact of her physical presence.

'I understand you know that I'm operating on a tight time schedule. You wish to know something about the Nigeria fertiliser project. I'm puzzled that you contacted me through Mr Katawi. Our security officer is not the normal link in a chain of communication on technical matters.'

Odhiambo affected an air of humility and gratitude.

'It's very good of you to see me at such short notice. And you so busy. I'm from the same country as Mr Katawi. I don't know many people in IBID.'

Caradonna shifted impatiently in her chair.

'So what do you want to know?'

'The use of fertilisers by small farmers has always been a problem in Africa. I want to know whether there are big problems with your project. Whether farmers are happy?'

Odhiambo sensed the defensive perimeters being manned inside the lovely head opposite him.

'The fertiliser project is a very large one, Mr Odhiambo. Nothing like it on this scale has been attempted in Africa. It aims to extend access to inputs to farmers across Nigeria. It takes time to deliver such an ambitious service and the project is relatively new – it is too early to discuss its effectiveness.'

'But are farmers buying the stuff?'

'Initial adoption rates are very satisfactory. Over two hundred thousand tons were distributed in the first full year. And the average farmer uses only a few bags. So that's a lot of farmers.'

Odhiambo was reaching the end of his ability to pretend to know anything about fertilisers.

'But I, we in Kenya, even here in Washington, hear that there are difficulties. That an audit was under way.'

'From whom did you hear that, may I ask?'

'My father-in-law works here – at the University. Some of his friends were talking about it.'

'You mustn't listen to outside gossip here in Washington, Mr Odhiambo. Look, if you leave your name and contact address with my secretary, and your affiliation, what company you're with and so on, I will arrange to send you background material including the project design document.'

78

Caradonna started to rise. Odhiambo decided on shock tactics.

'Look, Miss Caradonna, I know next to nothing about fertilisers. I got here by deception. Mr Katawi meant well, he was helping a countryman, but I deceived him. I'm interested in why Mr Chivers was killed. I understand he was working on your project.'

The eyes blazed with anger. Now Caradonna stood erect, very much the outraged executive.

'Whatever has Mr Chivers' death to do with you? I don't appreciate having my time wasted.'

Odhiambo rose too and leaned towards the woman from his superior height.

'My father-in-law is in danger of being charged with his murder and he's innocent – that's why. I'm sorry to have bluffed my way in here, but this is deadly serious. There's a killer in this building. And if it's connected to your work you need to be aware of it.'

'I don't wish to talk with you, whoever you are. Please leave.'

There was ice in the voice, ice and chilli. But there was something else, and Odhiambo could sense it, almost smell it. Caradonna was afraid.

'OK, I'm going.' He turned and went to the door. As he opened it, he turned back towards the woman. 'I was here the night he was killed. Tell me, what were the figures on his computer screen referring to?'

Just for a moment Caradonna started a theatrical gesture with her arm to convey the message 'Go!'. Then, as his words sank in, her arm dropped and she looked at him more intently.

'Figures on his screen? What do you mean?'

'He looked as if he was working when he was interrupted. His computer screen had some sort of analysis on it. There were papers scattered about around the computer.'

'When was this?'

'I was with Katawi when he was called by the police. We were in Chivers' office Monday night with Lieutenant Bolling.'

There was no doubt of Caradonna's attention now. She had moved towards her visitor, curiosity having replaced outrage at Odhiambo's interference.

'And there were figures on the screen? What sort of figures?'

Odhiambo recalled the scene in his mind and searched for an image of the screen. He had got Caradonna interested in Chivers' work at the time he was killed. That gave him something to think over. Now, if he could draw her out a little more . . .

79

'There was a set of figures under a heading, then a sort of conclusion – words, that is. Let me think. Correlation something and a figure and the conclusion – Not Significant, that was it. The figure was a small one, nought point something; one or two, something like that.'

'Correlation coefficient not significant.' The woman paused, thinking intensely. 'Think, man, what was the heading above the figures? It's important.'

Odhiambo seized his chance.

'I'm not sure if I remember. I'll try. Why is it important?'

'Because Chivers had some data from Nigeria on the effect the fertiliser had on the crops – data from a research station. I can't find it on his computer, which had been cleared by Tuesday when I saw it. Nor among his papers. Response data, response of yield to fertiliser.'

'That's it.' Odhiambo was genuinely pleased at his recall. 'Response. That's what it said. Something like Response and then something to do with Variables.'

'How could it be not . . .' Caradonna seemed to suddenly focus on who her companion was. She stopped, then started again. 'Right, well, er, thank you for that information, it helps us to find his data so that we can carry on. I'm afraid I've nothing to say on his tragic death. And I must ask you to leave now.'

Odhiambo could scarcely contain his impatience as he located a taxi rank and directed the driver to Cari's office. The rush-hour exodus from the capital into the Virginia suburbs had started, so Roosevelt Bridge and the road to the Mall were a solid mass of cars, but going the other way to that of Odhiambo's taxi which proceeded without impediment although too slowly for Odhiambo's liking. Cari had done statistics at college level – he remembered her talking about her statistics lecturer and how dull he was. She would know.

Finally, he was in her office. Metroarcs did their Washington staff well in terms of space and furniture. Smart polished redwood desk, leather settee and chairs, large window with expensive-looking curtains looking out on a darkening sky pierced by the needle of the Washington Monument. Impatient though he was, Odhiambo felt an accustomed sense of insecurity. Here he was in his wife's sumptuous office; his wife, known here as Miss Bito; his wife who earned most of their income. How had this come to pass to a Luo boy from a small-holding by Lake Victoria? His relatives would never understand. He fought down the incipient internal panic of being rootless in a world in which he, but not his wife, was inferior.

His wife had risen to greet him, meeting him half-way across her oriental rug and placing a kiss on his lips.

'Hi, James. How did it go? Did you get to see the lady from IBID?'

'Yes, I did. And quite a lady. A real sex-bomb. Difficult to believe she's probably a very bright economist or whatever.'

Cari pouted.

'What a sexist remark, James, you old Luo chauvinist. You mean us office girls are supposed to be plain and dull?'

'No, no. Just painting a picture.' Odhiambo hastened to cover any further implication of his remark. 'And I'm used to beautiful women in offices. I see you all the time.'

'Never mind the flattery, what happened?'

'Tell me, Cari, does Correlation Coefficient mean anything to you?'

She looked puzzled.

'Yes. It's a means of measuring whether one variable is correlated with another – you know, if one goes up the other goes up too. What's that got to do with anything?'

'So if I see 'Correlation Coefficient Not Significant' what does that mean?'

'It means there is no relationship between the variables. Or . . .' Cari remembered her lecturer's cautionary words, 'or, at least, you haven't been able to verify a relationship. But what are you on about?'

'Chivers was working with some data when he was killed. Probably to do with the Nigeria project. Caradonna was throwing me out when I mentioned what was on his computer screen. Then she got all interested.'

'Doesn't help much unless we know what data he was using.'

'From what we know and Caradonna's reaction it was data Chivers had obtained from Nigeria on response to fertiliser.'

Cari crossed to her window and gazed out on the lights of Washington without seeing them. She ran through her mind what she knew, putting the information into some sort of order, then she turned back to face her husband.

'OK. We know the Nigeria project was the delivery and supply of massive amounts of fertiliser. Metroarcs is the supplier. Some company or other in Nigeria handles the distribution. Chivers was conducting an audit. He has some fertiliser response data he's working on when he gets killed. Glen is the contact man for us, a rude guy called Kraxma bosses it for the bank with this bimbo of yours under him, perhaps literally. So where does that get us?'

Odhiambo grimaced at the reference to Romaine Caradonna. She was a lot more than a bimbo. Still, he'd better let it pass.

'Stick with the correlation thing. If it's response to fertiliser – response of what to fertiliser?'

Cari thought, but only for a second.

'Well, the yield of whatever crop they grow on it; what else? Ah, I see where you're coming from. Or going to. There ought to be a good correlation if the stuff's any good.'

'Exactly. How much fertiliser are we talking about?'

'A lot.' Cari's voice had risen with the excitement of the chase. 'Hundreds of thousands of tons. An awful lot of money.'

'Well, we may be closer to a motive, but no closer to a killer.'

'If we're right this could be a huge embarrassment to IBID. No wonder Sally wants to know. Jeez, what they could do with this.' Cari's expression suddenly changed from eager excitement to one of concern with mouth turned down. 'But Glen is the contact man. For Metroarcs, I mean. You don't think . . . no, that's impossible . . .'

'Don't go jumping to any silly conclusions. I still don't see someone committing murder just because one investment is in difficulty. And your boss may have helped to get the contract – but if there's something fishy going on it's more likely to be at the Nigeria end than here.'

Cari was silent, chewing her lower lip. Odhiambo was thinking ahead. Should he tell Bolling what he knew? But what did he know, really? He couldn't see Bolling being very excited about correlation coefficients.

'Come on, James, lover. Let's hit the road. Get home and see what Dad's doing.'

Cari's intention was not fulfilled. When they arrived at the Bito home, Abbie told them Sam had gone to the University and had not yet returned. 'Trying to keep his mind off things,' she surmised. Her own worries were showing on her face.

'What's the matter, Mum?' Cari asked. 'You look as if you've been crying.'

'It's just this thing is getting on top of me.' There was a long pause. 'Oh, Cari. James. The police were here. They had a warrant.

82

They went through Samuel's things. Took some of his clothes away with them.'

Odhiambo swore to himself. While concentrating on the other lead he had neglected the immediate problem of Bolling homing in on his prime suspect.

'Don't worry, Abbie. It's not unusual. They were bound to check for evidence. The fact is, as he didn't do anything, their checks will help to clear him.'

It took a while to calm Abbie down.

The Odhiambos devoted the next two hours to light conversation and preparation of a modest but appetising supper. Both worked. Getting Abbie to talk and then eat did seem to lessen her visible signs of strain. The problem returned after they'd eaten.

'Samuel should've been home by now. He wouldn't stay out as long as this. Not with you and James here.'

Eventually they called. The night caretaker for the wing where Sam Bito's department was situated answered.

'Dr Bito? No. He's not here. Is that Mrs Bito? How are you, ma'am? Yes, he was here earlier, I understand. Before I came on.'

'OK. Thanks. He must have stopped off somewhere.'

'No, hold on.' There was a pause as the caretaker thought through his words. 'You haven't heard, then? From the police, I mean. The day man told me when I came on that they took Dr Bito away. The police, I mean. This afternoon.'

11

Lieutenant Bolling was a frustrated man. Getting information from Kenya was proving to be a slow business. Nothing had been received as yet in response to his request for details of the Omuto murder. Nor had the search of the Bito house produced any promising material. The clothes and shoes he had worn on the Monday evening had been sent for analysis, but the verbal report of his men who had conducted the search was not encouraging. No signs of obvious bloodstains on the clothes or in his car. A few fibre samples from the car had been collected but, again, more in hope than expectation. The one quick response he had received was from the police in England. This served only to confirm that

Odhiambo had been involved in a sensational case whilst there on training and had been seriously injured. He had left for the States to recuperate with his wife. So Odhiambo's story was undented. Could it be that he was on the wrong track? All this Kenya crap was just that. Nothing to do with Chivers' death. No, he didn't believe it. He ran through the links once more. Chivers, Bito, Odhiambo, even the security guy, were all Kenyans. Chivers and Bito had some connection with a Kenyan politician who was bumped off. The Kenyans were launching a new enquiry. Odhiambo was a Kenyan detective. No way all that could be explained as coincidence. He was missing something and he could not make out what it was.

He got up from his desk, leaving a well-chewed pencil on it. Time to go home. As he reached the door his phone rang. He hesitated, then went back and picked up the receiver.

'Bolling.'

'Ah, Lieutenant. We've got some guy on the line, insists on speaking with you. Says it's urgent. To do with some guy called Bito.'

Bolling's concentration snapped back into readiness. He reached for his pencil and rolled it around his finger.

'Put him on.'

'Is that Lieutenant Bolling? Odhiambo.'

Bolling allowed himself a small smile. Sometimes it pays to wait, he thought, to see what happens.

'Yes, this is Bolling. And what have you got to tell me, Mr, or rather Chief Inspector, Odhiambo?'

His smile disappeared with the next words.

'Don't come that with me, Bolling. Where is Sam Bito? Why hasn't he been allowed to call his wife?'

Bolling looked down at the instrument in his hand.

'What are you talking about? We haven't got him. Only some clothes for analysis.'

'You'd better get a grip on your people, Bolling, if you're not lying to me. Sam Bito was arrested at his University late this afternoon.'

Bolling inserted his pencil between his teeth and bit hard. This was a moment to think hard and clearly.

'Look, calm down and shut up a minute. No order for his arrest has come out of this office. If he's been arrested it's for something totally different.'

'You don't expect me to believe that?' But the voice was doubtful. 'That can't be, for Chrissake. Are you sure?'

'Look, Odhiambo, I'm squaring with you. What d'you think we are? We don't make people disappear here, whatever you may be used to. Tell me what you know.' He listened, chewing intently, as Odhiambo recounted the caretaker's story. 'Well, that's simple, the guy's got it wrong. Bito went off with some friends. Maybe he's run away. Scared by our closing in on him.'

'That's bullshit. They told the porter or whatever they were police. Sam wouldn't go anywhere without telling his wife.'

'Look, your information is third or fourth hand. You don't know anything. And I could give you a list of devoted husbands who left without telling their wives. No, no, you listen and calm down. I tell you what, leave it with me. I'll check into it and get back to you. Let's have your number.'

Half an hour later the pencil broke in two, worn away by the chewing. Bolling scarcely noticed. He had checked with the caretaker on campus, obtained the phone number of the day man, spoken to him, and was now digesting the information. Two black men in plain clothes and an unmarked Ford had shown the guard what he believed to be police identification and demanded to know where a Mr Bito was. Somewhat reluctantly he had led them to Dr Bito's study and was then dismissed. He had caught their first words, however – something like 'Mr Bito, Virginia State Police'. Five minutes later they left with Bito between them, their hands on his arms. No, he hadn't seen handcuffs, but he looked like a man who had been arrested. No, he didn't have the chance to speak to Dr Bito. No, he hadn't made a note of the car registration. Newish medium-size Ford. Two big guys. Looked like cops – except, except they seemed foreign somehow. Like Jamaicans. Bolling warned him to keep his mouth shut until he was contacted again and replaced the telephone. This didn't sound good. Bito had been stolen under his nose. But who by? And for what? He spoke to the duty officer to put out an alarm on a white Ford with three black men in it. Hopeless of course. Then reluctantly he dialled the Bito number. This wasn't going to be easy.

Giles Faucon was seated on Sally Eves' balcony, glass in hand, staring at the darkening sky and watching the lights of a jet as it descended past him on its final approach to Washington's National

Airport. Sally had gone back to the living-room to replenish her glass, so Faucon used the moment to review one last time how to proceed: he would miss her, but she was becoming dangerous. He was cross with himself; he prided himself on being cold and emotionless when it came to making difficult decisions and here he was as nervous as a virgin on her first date. The fact was that Sally had burrowed into his nervous system as well as his libido. She was not just a source of sexual release, he found her fascinating on both an intellectual and a physical level. Her very presence affected him, reducing his normal confidence of being in command of his environment. She was mentally his inferior, but that applied to all his acquaintances, professional and social. But in her case, the combination of her tendency to flit conversationally at random intervals from one topic to another and the breadth of her reading meant that she was able to assume the dominant role in their conversation. This novelty he enjoyed, as he enjoyed the novelty of her unusual abilities in bed. Nevertheless, it was over. He heard her approaching through the sliding glass doors and turned in his chair.

'How's your glass, Giles?' She was clutching the eight-year-old Chablis she had retrieved from the ice bucket. 'Here, let me top you up.'

Faucon held up his hand, pushing the bottle gently away. His voice took on a harsher tone that Eves noticed immediately.

'No. Thank you, no. Sit down, my dear, I have made a decision which I must tell you.'

Sally Eves sat with a sense of foreboding. Faucon looked at her in the poor light emanating from the room behind them.

'It is over, Sally. Our relationship. Your activities are no longer compatible with our continued relationship.'

The fighter in Eves was always ready to emerge. She certainly was not going to sit here and be lectured at as if she was some sort of poor relation out of a novel by Jane Austen.

'Don't be pompous, Giles. You're not in an IBID board meeting now. What the hell do you mean, 'activities incompatible' and all that crap? We have a perfectly good understanding that what we do in private and in public are totally separate. If you want to end it, just say so. Don't wrap it up in some sanctimonious moralising.'

Faucon grimaced, but Sally's response was helpful, in a way – it made it easier to be firm.

'Our understanding did not extend to spying. Your tame acolyte Gilbride has stepped over the line of what is acceptable and I'm sure it was done with your knowledge. As SEND is behaving this way, your choice was clear and you have chosen SEND.'

'How the hell do you know what I choose or chose? What makes you think Gilbride is acting for me, whatever it is he may or may not have done?'

'Sally, my dear, don't take me for a fool. I have my sources. SEND has decided to try and embarrass IBID. More than petty pin-pricks. Trying to concoct a major scandal and you're behind it.'

A smile slowly appeared on the woman's face. Faucon, now the decision was made, was able to view her objectively. A smile seemed incongruous on a face that was sculpted for tragedy, particularly when illuminated from behind.

'You've got something to hide, haven't you, Giles you bastard? If I needed proof, this is it. You're running scared.' Faucon started to speak, but Eves overrode him, an experience with which he was unfamiliar. 'No, you listen to me, Mr IBID Director. SEND is going to expose your doings. And I think there's more than environmental issues at stake. I think there's a smell of corruption in the air. And if you can't enjoy being screwed in both senses by the same woman, then you can leave and thanks for the good times.'

Faucon got to his feet and moved back into the living-room. Sally Eves followed him. Once inside he paused.

'No recriminations on my part, Sally. Nor I hope on yours.'

'Bugger off, Giles. Spare me the let's stay good friends bit. It doesn't suit you.'

'Right. But one last thing – and I urge you to pay attention. Think carefully before you proceed on your chosen path. Don't threaten me, Sally. I really do recommend that you do not.'

The woman laughed, but her face was now a vindictive mask.

'You don't scare me, Giles, you little shit. IBID has got it coming and if you're in the way, tough titty.'

'You know, you're really quite a vulgar person. I had not appreciated that fully before. Goodbye, and please take heed of my words.'

Glen Hills sat on the wooden deck of his weekend retreat near the Blackwater National Wildlife Refuge, a huge bird sanctuary in Maryland where ducks and geese stopped in their thousands during one of their regular seasonal migrations. It was dark but he liked to listen to the noises of the night coming from the fields and marshes of this quiet and thinly inhabited area. Outside the park the shooting was excellent and Hills liked to shoot. But now he was alone, and duck shooting was far from his mind. He had a lot to think about. His link with the Nigeria project was a recorded fact. Nothing he could do about that. But his link with the smuggling was known only by one man. Could he trust him? Even if that wretched auditor's death had nothing to do with Nigeria the police investigation could easily get into that area, and once the smell of something malodorous was in the air Hills was sure IBID would put whatever resources were necessary into tracking it down. Yet he had been told not to worry. Chivers dying whilst looking into the Nigeria project was a coincidence, he was told. Keep your head and all will be well. Police will find the killer and that's it. Hills was not so sure. Timing was the key. The early tranches of money were safely laundered into his Cayman accounts and he had the basic documents for his new identity and life far from the outreach capabilities of the fraud squads. Sure, another contribution would be welcome and the scheme should have had at least one more season before suspicion led to investigation. And, after all, the investigation would be in Nigeria with all the possibilities of delay and evidence tampering that were routine in any official enquiry there. No, it had been looking good until this Chivers business. But better get out with the cake than risk prison trying to put the icing on it.

Around the corner of the house came the sound of a car arriving in his yard. Hills frowned – who could this be? His retreat was half a mile down a dirt track – no one arrived here by accident and he sure as hell wasn't expecting a visitor. He rose, reached back inside the room, flicked on the switch that activated the outside floodlight and then crossed to the corner of the deck. He was in time to see a slim man emerge from what looked like a restored old British sports car. As the man looked up, Hills knew the face was familiar, but could not immediately identify it.

'Hello. What can I do for you?'

The man peered into the light, blinking. Hills was hidden behind the light source.

' 'Tis the advantage you have on me, that you do. Would that be Mr Hills?'

The Irish brogue provided the extra piece of information Hills' memory retrieval system required. It was that guy from the Kennedy Center, who directed plays with a heavy social message. Hills had met him on a couple of occasions though his name still eluded him.

'It is. What brings you out into the wilderness? You're a long way from the theatre.'

'That I am. And to be honest with you this is not my scene. Can I come on up?'

'Sure. The door's to your right. It's not locked. I'll meet you on the stairs.'

No immediate answer to his question, Hills noted, as he returned to the interior and crossed towards the door leading to the stairs. The lower floor consisted of a work area, a sort of study, a gun room with small bar to entertain a muddy group of fellow hunters, basic shower and toilet facilities, the boiler room and washing area. On the first floor was a small simple bedroom *en suite*, and a large comfortable living area with log fire. A nice bachelor retreat.

Hills watched as his visitor climbed the stairs with the lithe grace of an actor or dancer and motioned him to pass through into the living-room, where a fire that had been bright was now dying down. Hills crossed the room, gesturing to an armchair, and added logs to restore the flames.

'We've met, haven't we? You're at the Kennedy Center.'

The slim man – clad, Hills observed, in black slacks and black roll-top shirt topped by an open black leather jacket – smiled, although the eyes were wary.

'You're right, that you are. Gilbride, Sean Gilbride. And you're one of the powerful men in town, Glen Hills of Metroarcs.'

Hills stood with his back to the fire, crackling now as the flames bit into the new fuel. Gilbride had seated himself, crossing his legs, looking relaxed and in control. Hills found his irritation rising.

'And how did you know I was here? And why have you come?'

'Fair questions, indeed, and you shall have your answers. But could a passing traveller crave a drink? 'Tis a long drive from DC and I wasn't after stopping.'

Hills' irritation increased. The wretched man had the ability to wrongfoot him, now gently demonstrating his shortcomings as a host.

'I'll get you what you want. But you can talk as I do. I'm not used to night visitors here.'

'A glass of dryish white would be pleasing, kind sir.' Gilbride watched as Hills went over to a cabinet with both refrigerated and non-refrigerated sections. 'I can understand your curiosity, that I can. I'm sorry to disturb you in your solitude, but the matter is urgent.'

Hills pulled a cork out of a Californian white wine bottle. He reached back into the cold section and extracted a light beer for himself. As he crossed back to his visitor he made no effort to hide his growing exasperation.

'What matter? I don't know of anything we're both concerned with.'

Gilbride tasted his wine as if considering its quality.

'Thank you. It's always drinkable this, without perhaps the true balance of dryness with fruit that you get with a genuine Chablis. There's no reason why you should know of my interest in a matter that is of concern to you. But it seems our interests, hitherto on parallel paths, have momentarily crossed.' He sipped his wine as Hills restrained himself from grabbing the leather lapels and shaking him. 'It was the untimely death of an auditor rather than a cosmic event. I and others have an interest in a large project in Nigeria in which Metroarcs is a major player.'

Hills stared at the speaker, genuinely dumbfounded.

'Whatever do you . . .'

He stopped as Gilbride held up an elegant hand.

'Let me reveal myself in all my colours, Mr Hills. The theatre is my inspiration and my living, that it is, but I have other interests. I am on the council of an organisation called SEND. Our aim is to save the planet from despoiling developers. Sally Eves is our most famous colleague. I think you know her?'

'Sally Eves! Sure, I know her and her feminist claptrap. So now she's into the environment – I heard as much. Sally and the arty crowd. You deserve each other.'

'Tut, tut, Mr Hills. I understood Metroarcs was trying to improve its image. Showing concern for our planet. Your beautiful young colleague is thinking of joining us, I'm told.'

Hills was recovering from his surprise, which had kept him on the wrong foot. He spoke with the relaxed air of a man suffering a minor nuisance – nothing more.

'I'm sure we're all in favour of the environment. And my opinion of Miss Eves is personal. Now, Mr . . . er . . . Gilbride, I'm sorry, but I have other demands on my time.'

Gilbride looked around the room as if searching for signs of alternative activity.

'Sure, you're entitled to your privacy if you insist on hiding away in this god-forsaken spot. Do you ever invite friends here with you, or is it your private hideaway?'

'I'm sorry. Get to the point and quickly, or I –'

Gilbride laughed, an unpleasant mocking sound.

'I want your co-operation, Mr Hills. And I fully expect that it will be reluctantly given, it will. I want the inside dope on the Nigeria project. There's something wrong with it and I want to know what it is.'

Hills tried to match his visitor's mocking laugh, but to his own ears it did not sound quite right.

'Look, Gilbride, your curiosity is no concern of mine. The only involvement of Metroarcs with Nigeria is importing and distributing fertiliser – I would have thought that even your gang wouldn't have much quarrel with that, particularly as it's sold cheap to small farmers. Anyway, I'm not prepared to get into a debate with you on it.'

'Helping small farmers is the only defence IBID and its contractors like you offer. If it turns out that even that claim is false, where are you?'

'Right. That's enough. I don't know what you're thinking of, coming down here to talk about fertiliser, but –'

Again he was interrupted. As he spoke, Gilbride rose to his feet and looked Hills in the eye.

'You didn't answer my earlier question, that you didn't. Do you ever bring friends down here? Ernesto Kraxma, for instance.'

Hills erupted with the rage that had been simmering below the surface. He grabbed Gilbride by the collar and pulled him closer.

'What the shit has that got to do with you? I know several IBID people. Kraxma included. We do business together. So don't try to threaten me with non-existent allegations.'

Gilbride smirked in his face.

'I was issuing no threats, I wasn't.' He pulled himself free from Hills' grip and straightened his collar as he continued. 'Kraxma and you were something more than casual acquaintances. I have a source in IBID says Kraxma came here often enough that questions were being asked in IBID.'

Hills turned away.

'Oh, spare me the bullshit. And drink up and get out. Sources in IBID indeed.'

Gilbride flushed. He was being treated with contempt.

91

'Yes, an excellent source. Chief of security, Simon Katawi. It's his job to know these things.'

Hills turned back to face his protagonist. Simon Katawi? Where had he heard that name before? Then it came back to him. He had met him at Cari Bito's party. The night Chivers was killed. Odd, he hadn't known he was IBID. And security.

'Are you saying this man Katawi was following me about? Or Kraxma about? That's ridiculous.'

Gilbride tried a more placatory tone.

'All I'm trying to say is that things are coming out. They're bound to now Chivers is dead. If you co-operate with us, SEND that is, we can be helpful. It's IBID we're after. Particularly Sally.'

Hill scarcely heard the words. His mind was racing and he didn't like the course it was taking. He stared at Gilbride with loathing. Damn the man and that bitch Sally Eves. Sticking their noses in. What he wanted now was to be alone and think out his best course. But then a sounder inner counsel prevailed. He managed to change his expression to one more conciliatory.

'Here, give me your glass. We've got something to talk about.'

12

The small airstrip surrounded by fields of tobacco was still shrouded in the mists of dawn as the pilot turned for his final approach. He was used to landings in unusual locations at unusual times without modern aids and he was very good. The pay was a lot better than he would have received from a commercial airline and he didn't have to be polite to passengers.

As the plane slowed and started to turn at the end of the runway a pick-up truck trundled out from a path on to the grass. Three men were in the back, two of them supporting the third. These two climbed down and then virtually lifted the third from the truck and placed him against its side. The driver joined them as they watched the plane taxi down the dirt strip.

The pilot was surprised at the size of the welcoming party. He was a cautious man and checked through his window with binoculars before he switched off his engines and released his belt. He was met at the plane by the truck driver and voiced his concern.

'OK. Get the stuff off fast. I'm running a bit late. Why the large party?'

The truck driver gestured back towards the truck and one of the three waiting went over to the door at the rear of the plane.

'We'll get it off, but you've got passengers on the return run.'

'The hell I have –'

'Shuddup. Here, read this.' He thrust a paper at the pilot. 'My man has been in touch with your lot. This is a separate deal – contract job. Doing friends a favour. I don't want it any more than you, but we do what we're told, right? You deliver this guy. They'll arrange onward transportation. No sweat, Al goes with him to look after him. He'll make his own way back.'

'I don't fly with hostages or prisoners or what the hell the guy is. Too much can go wrong when you're up there.'

'No sweat. I said. The guy's all relaxed with a nice big jab. And Al will be beside him with the cuffs on. And if you've got an argument you make it with Michael.' The truck driver tapped the paper. 'Now let's get on.'

The pilot continued to grumble as a means of venting his feelings rather than aspirations that his complaints would be met. With the drugs unloaded he prepared for departure, but was able to get a close look at his unwelcome passengers. Both were black, one archetypal bodyguard, squarely built but with the on-the-toes litheness of a former boxer, the other a middle-aged small man; although a cap and scarf obscured most of his face he did not look Caribbean, the pilot thought. He was clearly drugged and allowed himself to be manipulated without protest. The pilot sighed, his not to reason why. A few minutes later he was away from the plantations of Carolina heading for the Keys of Florida, and then on to his base in Jamaica and the attentions of Jasmina, a girl he had met a few weeks ago and who besotted him still. As he climbed he started to hum a tune, the prisoner and escort temporarily forgotten.

James Odhiambo sat in Bolling's office endeavouring to keep his temper in check. Bolling, pencil in corner of mouth, was eyeing him with apparent unconcern – the unease which Odhiambo had detected in his voice the previous night was now gone. Bolling had moved from defence to attack.

'Look, Bolling, if the police didn't pick up Sam Bito he's been kidnapped, as you admitted last night. That should tell you there's something going on and Bito is caught up in it as an innocent victim.'

'There's other scenarios, is what I'm saying. Bito knows we're closing in on him so he does a bunk and makes it look like a kidnap. The sort of thing a son-in-law with police experience would be able to help with.'

'I've just left two hysterical women, Bolling. If this was a put-up job I wouldn't have that to cope with. You've been on the wrong tack since the beginning of this case. Going after my father-in-law instead of getting to the real motive for Chivers' murder.'

Bolling leaned forward and, extracting it from his mouth, pointed his pencil at Odhiambo.

'Now, you listen to me and listen good. Even accepting for the moment that Mr Bito was kidnapped, look at the facts. Your father-in-law was involved in some guy's murder in Kenya years ago.' Bolling held up his hand as Odhiambo started to protest. 'No, I'm not saying he did it or nothing. Just he was caught up in it. Now, that case is back on the front burner in your country and Bito is a witness. His connection with the Kenya case links him with Chivers. He goes to see Chivers who shortly after Bito leaves is found with his brains hanging out. Chivers can't talk about no Mr Omuto and now your father-in-law isn't around to talk either. And you expect me to think these things aren't connected.' Bolling paused and Odhiambo waited; the trouble was, Odhiambo found it difficult to refute Bolling's hypothesis. Bolling threw down his pencil and locked his hands together, elbows on the desk. 'Alternatively your in-law knocks off Chivers to stop him talking and now goes to ground to keep us and the Kenyans off his back. Either way the Kenya connection is where it's at, feller.'

'What about his clothes? You know whoever killed Chivers must have got blood on his clothes. You haven't found any on Sam's, have you?'

'We've got some of his clothes. Maybe not the right ones. The results are not in yet on the ones we got.'

Odhiambo got up and kicked his chair, which skidded across the office until it hit a filing cabinet.

'Never mind all this bullshit. What are you doing to find him? His life is in danger.'

'How do you know that?' Bolling's voice was sharp. 'Do you know or guess who took him?'

Odhiambo closed his eyes, fighting for control of his rage.

'Bolling, for Christ's sake, he's not been kidnapped for nothing. Somebody wants him out of the way.'

'We're doing all we can. We're looking for the car and we've got a description of the men – sketchy, possibly Jamaican, that sort of thing, but it's something. And, of course, we've got a good description of Bito. We'll find them.'

'Oh, you may, you may. But will it be too late, that's the question?'

'There's a full alert out. And the word is being passed around in DC as well as this side of the river. See if anyone knows of a job being contracted to the Jamaicans. You're a policeman. You know we can't do more.'

'Right. OK. I feel so helpless stuck here in a strange place. No contacts. Nothing much to do.'

'Ah, well.' Bolling's pencil was being rolled between his palms. 'I hear you are keeping pretty busy. Thinking of going into the fertiliser import-export business.'

Odhiambo looked at Bolling, trying to make up his mind. 'I was interested in what Chivers was investigating when he died. As my father-in-law didn't kill him, somebody else did, and the likely answer is he was a threat to someone to do with his work.'

'That doesn't give you rights to enter premises under false pretences and attempt to obtain confidential information by deception.'

'So, the Caradonna woman complained. I'll tell you something, Bolling, which you're neglecting. There was some work on Chivers' computer screen when we were with you the night of the murder. I'm told it was gone the next day. Who could have done that? You presumably had someone guarding the office.'

Bolling's interest was aroused, but first he disposed of an Odhiambo assumption.

'It wasn't Caradonna. Perhaps you made an impression on her. There was something on his screen, yes. Some statistical stuff. We had some of his people in checking his papers. They probably switched the machine off. So what?'

'Everybody in IBID, well, everyone connected with Nigeria, seems concerned there's something wrong with a big project there. Chivers was investigating it and Chivers winds up dead. The figures he was working on are wiped out. And all you can say is so what!'

'Chivers' bosses are doing a full check. If there's something missing we'll know today. And I gather if some papers or a computer disc or whatever are missing there's bound to be a copy somewhere.' Bolling got up and moved round his desk closer to Odhiambo, who was standing irresolutely between the desk and the door. 'Look, Odhiambo, I'm having difficulty getting any info from your country; perhaps they don't want me to have it. But London has been helpful. They told me quite a lot about you. In summary they say you're on the side of the angels but you're impulsive and like to act alone. Make the locals look silly. Well, that profile fits a man who will be devious and ingenious when it come to helping a relative who's in trouble. Keep your nose clean, Odhiambo – that's a friendly piece of advice and an official one. Keep your nose clean and don't interfere. Things could go badly for you.'

Glen Hills parked his car in the long strip available for parking off the Washington Parkway on the river side. Coming off Roosevelt Bridge from DC he had missed the exit and found it necessary to do a loop around Rosslyn before getting to the right location. He could have saved trouble by going straight to the IBID building, but the instructions were clear enough and he supposed they made sense. With the police sniffing around and Sally Eves' toyboys interfering it was better they not be seen together. So although the cloak and dagger bit irritated Hills he had gone along with it. It was chilly today, reminding Washington that autumn was ending and winter was not far away. The sky was a pale blue but with high thin cloud starting to obscure it. The wind ruffled the trees, bringing down some of the more tenacious leaves to join the early fallers. Given the lateness of the season and the chill wind there were few walkers on Roosevelt Island and Hills had been able to park close to the footbridge that provided the only access. Hills crossed over and paused as he gained the island. He had never been here in all the years of his time in Washington. Well, he'd had no reason to. It was an interesting oddity, sure. A piece of unspoilt wood on a tiny island in the Potomac left to the nation on condition it was allowed to stay as an unmanaged wood. Trees fell and were left where they fell unless they blocked the footpath when a gap was cut in the fallen trunk. Parasitic weeds were allowed to flourish in competition with more attractive plants. Nature left to its own devices just within hailing distance of the steel and concrete of commercial Rosslyn, and not much further from the Watergate building and the

Kennedy Center. Oddity, but Hills preferred the wide open marshes of the Blackwater River. His instructions had been clear, but there was also assistance by a friendly map at the foot of the bridge which showed the direction to take for the Roosevelt Memorial. Hills walked along the narrow path, fastidiously watching where he put his feet in an attempt to avoid dirtying his polished black shoes. It was only a minute or two's walk through the trees; swishing through the carpet of leaves Hills soon found himself in the only man-made clearing on the island – the site of the memorial consisting of a statue, stone steps and a piazza with two trough-like structures flanking it. Hills thought it would have lacked artistic merit if set in an urban square, but stuck here in a clearing in a primitive wood it seemed to him to be grotesque. He shook his head; he had little respect for Washington architecture, but this was something else from the worst of the mock-heroic period of monument designers. Now, the Vietnam Memorial, that would bring some much-needed quality – though the design was rousing a storm of criticism. Still, he was clearly at his destination and the clearing, sheltered by the trees from the wind, was pleasantly warm. Hills loosened his topcoat and let it flap open. He sat on the stone wall of one of the flanking troughs. It contained water and some pond weed, but Hills saw no movement to reveal the presence of fish.

He looked about him. He was a couple of minutes early, but he hoped he was not to be kept waiting. He had plans to make. His mind was made up. He didn't like the way things were going. One way or another, through the actions of IBID, the police or SEND, the Nigeria deal would be exposed and Hills had a nasty feeling that when that happened the trail would lead to him. The more he thought about it the more he realised that he was the direct link with the Nigeria set-up. In IBID, from Faucon downwards they would claim they were conned – and most of them had been, so it would sound authentic even from the designer of the whole scam. Hills could scupper that claim of innocence, but it would avail him naught. No, it was time to get out. One more year would have been nice, but the successful gambler knew when to ride his luck and when to cash in his chips.

He had sometimes wondered why he had agreed to be a partner. He had a well-paid job with Metroarcs. Not only was he risking that, but more, he was stepping out of the market, out of society. These last days sitting by the Blackwater marshes he had considered the charge that he had risked a lot to achieve little. A million or two in hand – was it worth more than a six-figure salary for another fifteen years? In the end the answer was always the same. It wasn't the money, or not only the money, it was his growing irritation and distaste for his Washington life – sucking up to venal politicians, maintaining a façade of bonhomie when secretly he despised them. Plus the long-cherished, secret desire to let it all hang loose, to stop being respectable, to sail among the tropical islands as a romantic vagabond. Childish, of course, but suddenly he had seen the opportunity to indulge in fantasy – before it was too late. He could never forget his father dying when he was a teenager. And his uncles and their father before them. None had managed to reach sixty. When the doctor confirmed that he too had inherited the weak heart muscle he had abandoned plans for the millennium.

So, time to implement his long-developed plan to disappear. But first there was this loose end to clear up. He was promised a full explanation. Well, we'll see, he said to himself. He had considered the danger but dismissed it, or nearly so. He was still fit and knew his own strength, which was considerable. He had taken one extra precaution; as he thought of it he patted his topcoat pocket – yes, the pistol was there.

His eye scan of his surroundings revealed one young couple in jeans, shell tops and trainers completing their viewing of the memorial and starting to exit the clearing from the far side along the path which Hills presumed would lead around the island. The only other presence was a black man in working overalls brushing leaves into piles. His brush strokes lacked conviction and Hills could see no sign of plastic bags or other means of disposing of the leaves. The man was probably right, thought Hills, it was an aimless activity not meriting energetic endeavour. A typical city employee. Or was this island under Virginia jurisdiction? Or neither, National Parks more probably. Funny, in fact, that he was brushing leaves at all; Hills thought everything was to be left to nature to sort out. Still, that wouldn't apply to the memorial area – it would defeat the purpose if that was allowed to revert to nature.

As these idle thoughts passed through his mind, Hills realised the sweeper was approaching him. Damn it, was he going to ask for money? No, Hills saw the unlit cigarette, it was a light for his smoke he would be after. The sweeper smiled a broad, gleaming-toothed smile. He was young and, Hills thought, Caribbean. One of the recent immigrants glad of a job, even sweeping leaves in this unlikely spot.

'How ya doing, boss?' The sweeper placed his broom carefully against the wall on which Hills was sitting. He held up his cigarette, his other hand slipping into the pocket of his overalls. 'Gotta match I could have?'

Hills allowed himself a small smile to show goodwill before delivering the bad news.

' 'Fraid not. No matches or lighter on me. Sorry.'

To his surprise the sweeper leaned forward with the cigarette now held in his lips as if the answer was in the affirmative and the light was forthcoming. Was he deaf? As he leaned nearer to Hills, he seemed to glance quickly around him. Then Hills felt a pressure on his stomach at the belt line, then a pain unlike any pain he had felt before. He gasped and looked down in time to see the long blade emerge half-way up his chest having completed a savage upward thrust. He spent his last long seconds gazing at the blood spouting through his shirt and vainly clutching with his hands at his stomach as his insides started to spill. The unexpected horror momentarily paralysed his vocal chords and then it was too late.

The sweeper checked his handiwork to be sure he had done enough. He reached inside the dead man's coat and found his wallet. Another glance around to confirm the lack of memorial gazers then he hurried from the piazza into the shelter of the trees.

Cari Odhiambo had at last persuaded her mother to take a sedative and lie down. Since the news of her husband's disappearance the previous evening Abbie Bito had been in a state of near-hysteria. For some time Cari herself had felt likewise – it was as if they were caught in some dreadful programmed sequence in which events worsened as the participants became more deeply involved. She had now got a grip on herself, her mother had fallen into a much-needed sleep and James had returned with at least the "no further news is not bad news" theory. They had discussed endlessly during the night the possible motives behind the kidnapping and there was really nothing left to say, so determinedly she spoke over a late lunch of cold pie and salad of the importance of demonstrating her father's innocence of the Chivers killing.

'I tried to get hold of Glen while you were out, but he seems to have disappeared. He's not at his apartment and his secretary says she couldn't reach him at his weekend place either. We need to know what he knows about that Nigeria project. But I was thinking, James. Those figures you saw – the correlations; even if the data were lost on his computer when somebody switched off without saving the file, the original data must have been there either on a floppy disc or on bits of paper. The people in IBID should have had no problem.'

'But that girl, Caradonna, told me there were no records of the data. She was surprised when I told her what was on the screen.'

'So it couldn't just be an accident of losing the data in the computer's memory. Someone took the source file. And why would someone do that? Because the reason Chivers was killed was to stop him finishing his analysis.'

'But the figures were still on the screen, Cari. When I was there after the killing. The murderer left the computer on.'

'That could have been an oversight. He took the disc or whatever and forgot what was on the screen. It didn't matter 'cos without the disc it was meaningless.'

'In the file I saw, it said he got the figures from some research station in Nigeria. There'll be a copy still there.'

'Yes, and you told me the IBID woman was on her way there. That copy will probably disappear next.'

'Now, Cari. You've got it in for Miss Caradonna. You can't imagine her beating a man's brains out. At least, you wouldn't if you knew her.'

Cari sniffed.

'I haven't had that pleasure. Anyway, I think you should get someone to tell that place to lock the data up.'

Odhiambo thought for a moment, then spoke with a wry shake of his head.

'It's funny. One of the people on that course in Cornwall with me was a Nigerian called Asuma – I think he was in Agriculture. We didn't exactly get on, but I suppose I could call him – he was on his way home. Couldn't wait, he said.'

But Cari's thoughts had moved on.

'Course, James, there's another possibility. A lot of these amateur computer freaks have one at home. Suppose Chivers had the source file at home. Made a floppy disc there to take to the office or the other way round.'

'Jeez, Cari, that's worth a try. I'll ask Bolling if he's looked through Chivers' apartment. I heard someone say he lived alone here, although he had a wife somewhere – still in Kenya perhaps.'

'Well, it's something to do. And I don't trust IBID. I think Sally is right, they're a rum crew. If I could see that data . . .'

Odhiambo shook his head, this time in doubt.

'I dunno, Cari. It's still difficult to see someone being killed because some project wasn't going too well and this might come out. I bet a lot of projects go wrong. A chap called Hargreaves on my course in Cornwall said most of them were disasters.'

'Don't quote the people you met at that bloody course at me, James. A gang of cut-throats and murderers. Anyway, that –'

Cari's further views on her husband's last set of associates were interrupted by the ringing of the telephone. They were still sitting at the table in the kitchen. Cari rose and took the telephone from its wall-hanging behind her. James Odhiambo watched as she listened and got to his feet as he saw her face first furrow then sag in obvious shock.

'What! No. Oh my God! OK. Look, hold the fort. I'll be in to help out as soon as I can. OK? I'm sorry, Cindy. I know what a shock this must be. Hang in there, right?' She replaced the phone and grabbed hold of her husband as he reached her side. 'Oh, James, it's terrible. That was Cindy. Glen's PA. Glen, he's . . . he's dead. He's been murdered!'

13

'This sure is a nice office, ma'am.' Lieutenant Bolling looked around the spacious expanse of Glen Hills' workplace. 'Nice drapes, nice carpet, nice furniture. A man could get on with his work here. Not like what we have to put up with.'

Cari Odhiambo seemed not to hear. She collapsed rather than sat in one of the armchairs as Bolling went over to the desk and started to poke about. There was nothing of interest on the top so he started to pull out drawers. James Odhiambo watched from beside the door. Cari had sent the distraught Cindy home, together with three other staff, leaving one young man to deal with the telephone and deflect enquiries into the death of Metroarcs' man in Washington. Cari spoke, more to herself than to the policeman.

'Roosevelt Island! What was he doing on Roosevelt Island? What a place to get mugged.'

Bolling looked at her and then across at the large man by the door before returning his gaze to the woman.

'You think Mr Hills was taking a lunch-time stroll and ran into a casual mugger? You don't know any reason why Mr Hills would go to the island?'

'Of course not. There's nothing there but trees, is there? What reason could he have?'

'How did he die, Lieutenant?' James Odhiambo was ahead of his wife in his thinking. 'Did it look like a casual mugging?'

'Well, it might be. 'Cept, as your wife says, it's not exactly your downtown mugging area. His pocket-book is missing, if he had one on him. But I'll tell you an odd thing. There was a brush beside him. You know, for sweeping up leaves and such. And leaves had been swept into little piles. And the couple who found Mr Hills say they saw a sweeper working there. Only the Parks people say no one was doing any sweeping for them. Kinda strange, wouldn't you say?'

Odhiambo nodded and blew out his breath slowly. He muttered an obscenity. Cari was alert now.

'What do you mean? Glen was murdered deliberately? I mean, he was set up or something?'

'That's what I'm intending to find out, ma'am.'

'Tell him, Cari.' Cari looked at her husband questioningly. He crossed towards her, speaking with authority. 'Tell him. Metroarcs, IBID and the Nigeria project. And your boss's role.'

Bolling's eyebrows rose and he fished a pencil out of his pocket. As he bit on the pencil with one corner of his mouth he eyed the Odhiambos expectantly.

'Yes, that would be useful, ma'am.'

'IBID, where Mr Chivers worked, and my company Metroarcs are involved in a very big project in Nigeria. Chivers was conducting some sort of audit of the project when he was killed. We, that is James and I, think he was actually working on his audit when he was killed. The Metroarcs link man, liaison officer, whatever, was Glen Hills.'

'Yes, I've heard about the fertiliser project, Mrs Odhiambo, or should I call you Miss Bito – I saw that name on your door? But I didn't know Mr Hills was involved. Is that a routine part of his job?'

102

Cari hesitated, but received an encouraging nod from her husband.

'No. No, we don't get directly involved, normally. We're lobbyists charged with keeping in touch with the US Congress. New York handles contracting matters with IBID. Usually, that is. This one was Glen's baby. He was involved in early discussions, I gather, and wanted to stay with it.'

'But shipping fertiliser around Nigeria – I mean, you can't do that from here. What do you mean, he stayed involved?'

'Metroarcs handles the import of fertiliser and in co-operation with a local company distributes it in Nigeria; Glen liaised with the IBID people in arranging contracts for shipments, legal stuff like that.'

'Which IBID people?'

'I don't know many details. I never discussed it with Glen.' Cari paused as her lower lip showed signs of a tremble. She never would discuss it with him now. She swallowed hard and continued. 'All I know is what I accessed from the company's computer file summary. It gives primary contacts. It's Glen for Metroarcs and a man called Kraxma for IBID.'

Bolling nodded. That was as expected. He looked at the large dark man who seemed anxious to speak.

'So, Bolling. Two men die, both closely identified with the Nigeria project. That's a better link than the Kenya one you were making.'

Bolling grunted and bit savagely on his pencil. The trouble was, he was half convinced Odhiambo was right. He fought a rearguard action.

'I'll tell you another link, Mr Odhiambo. The Kenya connection we've talked about. It's there to be explained. Then up you pop trying always to direct me away from the Omuto case. A Kenyan policeman who should know a lot. Then it turns out your wife is a hot shot in this firm and her boss gets killed. You could argue the common link across these murders is you two. It's you two who span the Kenya connection and Metroarcs.'

'My God, Bolling, try and act your age. We're co-operating with you, which is more than you can say about some of the others. Now, we were talking this morning about the missing figures on Chivers' computer. Cari has a theory, more a possibility, but it's worth exploring. Have you been through Chivers' apartment?'

'Why?'

Cari, her mind pulled away from thoughts of her erstwhile colleague, answered.

'Does he have a computer at home? Did you see one if you went there? If he did he may have copied the Nigeria data there, or put it on his home computer as well.'

'And you think this file or whatever is important?'

'We don't know, but what James saw on his screen was odd. If I could see the data we might learn something.'

'We did go to his place, just to have a look around. There was a study and, yes, he had a computer. Can you recognise the data?'

'I don't know. But he may have named the disc, or given it a recognisable filename, or the original papers from Nigeria or . . . or . . . well, I don't know until I look.'

'Perhaps I should get someone from IBID. That guy Greene or the one with the strange accent, Kraxma.'

'Why don't we look first, Bolling? With Cari to help you identify it. It was her idea. Remember, if something was removed from Chivers' office it was someone in IBID. At least, that's the only logical conclusion.'

Bolling chewed his pencil ruminatively. Then he sighed.

'OK. I'm a sucker for a pretty face. No, not yours, Odhiambo. Now, ma'am, if I can use your phone, I'll get someone to meet us at the apartment. He lived in Alexandria – the old town.'

Bolling used his siren to help them through the rush-hour traffic making its way into Virginia across 14th Street Bridge either on the way home or heading for National Airport. Eventually, they reached the streets of Alexandria. Odhiambo noticed a whole sequence of streets named after royal titles – Prince, Queen, King: it seemed that, although they'd fought to get rid of the British, Americans still hankered after the old ways. Well, there were the same tendencies among some Kenyans, although, he thought, the politicians changed the street names fast enough in Kenya – naming them after themselves in most cases.

Bolling pulled into a side street that rose away from the direction of the river. Half-way up another police car was parked, nose into the pavement, lights flashing. There was very little in the way of parking space as both sides were lined with cars. Bolling drew up, double parking just short of the rear of the other police car. As they got out a uniformed officer appeared from the other.

'I've got the keys, Lieutenant.'

'Right, let's go in.'

Two minutes later, Cari was seated at a computer in a small study. The walls were lined with books on agriculture and economics. There were a few folder-type files and a desk with the computer dominating it. There was no sign of a printer. While Odhiambo flicked through the files, Bolling watched Cari as she checked the drawers of the desk. The second one she opened revealed a box of small discs.

'There are the floppies, Lieutenant. But they're new – unused, by the look of them.' She tried the bottom drawer without result and then turned her attention to the other side. This time the top drawer revealed what they were looking for.

'This is it. Floppies with stuff on them.' She flicked through, stopped and pulled one out. She held it up to Bolling. Written neatly on the tag was "Nigeria: Yield Data". 'Eureka, Lieutenant.'

'Pay-dirt, eh? What now? I don't know anything 'bout these durned things.'

Bolling watched even more intently as Cari pressed a switch that brought the screen to life and pressed some experimental keys on the keyboard. With her husband equally engrossed on the other side, she slotted the thin disc into an aperture in the computer. A few more taps on the keyboard, a pause while the screen flashed 'Loading' and suddenly there on the screen was a heading which read:

Farmers Trials in Northern States.
Paired Plots: With/Without Fertiliser.
Fertiliser Application at Levels 1, 2, 3.
Plot size 20×20.
Crop Code 17.

Cari pressed a key with a downward-pointing arrow. Columns of figures started to roll by.

'So what the hell does all this mean?'

Cari froze the screen.

'It looks like an experiment to test different fertiliser levels on the yield of some crop or other. There may be other crops later in the file.'

'Yeah, I can see that. But so what? Where does it get us?'

'James said that on Chivers' screen it said 'Correlation Insignificant' or something like that. Seems to me he could do more sophisticated analysis with this stuff, but maybe he was just feeling his way round the data. Now, look at those.' Cari pointed at the screen. 'The blanks in the second column mean no fertiliser on that plot. The numbers show how much fertiliser on others. The final figure is the yield. Look here.' Cari's finger traced down several lines. 'The yields are all similar, 105, 98, 108, but the first one had no fertiliser and the other two did. Look at that one, 130, with no fertiliser and that's about the highest on this page.' She turned towards the homicide detective. 'You'll have to get the analysis done properly, but I bet what it was saying on Chivers' screen is that fertiliser does damn all to improve the yield.'

'OK. So the farmers are just as well off without the stuff. So what?'

James Odhiambo rested a hand on his wife's shoulder and answered before Cari could speak.

'Bolling, in Africa we get lousy yields, right? Not like your farmers here. Now, if IBID and Metroarcs are getting these farmers to shell out good money for this stuff, why doesn't it give them more harvest?'

'So they've been sold a bum steer. They want their money back probably. So what has that got to do with Chivers or Hill being bumped off?'

This time Cari got in first. She seemed to be speaking simultaneously with the evolution of her thoughts.

'They've shipped in masses of this stuff. It must have been tried and tested by Metroarcs. It has to have some effect. If they use it right. And these . . .' she tapped the screen again, 'these are proper, supervised experiments. So how can it have no effect? Unless . . . unless . . . The data could be wrong – understating the true relationship – or suppose the farmer is given the wrong stuff? Or the original is adulterated in some way. You know, like diluting medicine or drugs. They pay the full price but they get a load of nothing.'

'I get you now, ma'am.' Bolling was showing genuine enthusiasm for the first time. 'Bunco artists. A scam. IBID shells out for the real thing, but by the time it gets to the lads on the farm someone's cut the stuff so bad it's useless. How much money is involved in this shit?'

'Millions and millions, Lieutenant. I dunno. It can't be as simple as this. But if there is a scam it could be a really big one.'

'Enough to kill for, Bolling.' Odhiambo grabbed the detective by the arm. 'Two men who knew a lot about this thing are dead. It's time you put the IBID people under the microscope.'

'Don't forget Metroarcs, Odhiambo. I think this lady and I have a lot more to talk about. Given Mr Hills can't speak.'

Cari's excitement drained away. The thought of her attractive boss lying knifed in a wood came back to her, followed by her fears of the fate of her father. She felt tears dangerously close to the surface. James retorted for her.

'It wasn't Metroarcs or Cari or Hills that were in that building with Chivers that night. You always have difficulty seeing the obvious, Bolling. First Sam Bito, now my wife. Why don't you go after the IBID people? They too important for you?'

Bolling grinned. He liked to keep Odhiambo on the wrong foot.

'OK. OK. You let me do things in my way. Now, ma'am, what have you done with that bit of plastic – what did you call it? A floppy?'

Bolling used the waiting trooper to deliver the Odhiambos back to the Metroarcs office to pick up their car. He assured them that the search for the missing Sam Bito was not being neglected in the light of the murder of Glen Hills. 'Two murders and a disappearance that don't seem to be linked to a drugs gang is going some for this neck of the woods,' Bolling told them. 'But we can cope. In any case, your father's case now involves the FBI. Kidnapping someone and taking them across a state line is a federal matter. We don't know that for sure, of course, but they've been called in on the basis of suspicion.'

Cari was silent, mulling this over, for much of the return trip into the capital. Her husband busied himself with his own thoughts. Finally, Cari spoke.

'You know, I haven't focused on why Dad was kidnapped. Just the awfulness of the fact it happened. It looks certain now that the fertiliser business is linked to the murders and Dad has no connection at all with that. So why was he kidnapped? And what's going to happen next?'

Her voice, which had started strong and determined, broke at the end.

'It's no good speculating without facts, Cari. I don't like coincidences, but it does seem that your Dad's situation is not linked with these other matters. At least he's no longer a prime suspect.

But still, the coincidence of his link with Chivers and him being kidnapped for some totally different reason bugs me.'

'But why would anyone want to kidnap him? Do you think he's all right? Why don't they contact us if they want something? He hasn't got much money so what use is he to whoever it is?'

Her husband didn't answer, partly because he didn't have any answers to comfort her, but partly because at the very deepest recesses of his mind a hypothesis was beginning to form, the implications of which sent a cold shiver through his large frame.

14

John Musoke was not altogether surprised when into his office came a somewhat heated-looking Amos Kasanga. It was Friday morning and Musoke's day had started early with the telephone call from Nairobi that had roused him from his bed in the middle of the night. Price-Allen in Nairobi seemed satisfied so far, but was worrying about two things, or rather two persons – Odhiambo and Kasanga.

'I want Odhiambo back here quickly, preferably with his wife because she's a woman with an independent mind too. I don't want them causing problems in Washington when the news breaks here.'

Musoke had conveyed the information that Odhiambo was at his in-laws' house, and offered the telephone number, but Price-Allen passed the responsibility right back.

'No. Odhiambo and I have had dealings in the past. He is, shall we say, somewhat sensitive to interference from me. You, Musoke, you will communicate with him on behalf of the government. If necessary I'll get the Minister to speak to the Ambassador. Now, there's another matter. Our mutual friend has got wind that something's up. He's always been sensitive to a scent in the air. He's got a man there in Washington, Kasanga. So take care not to let anything slip. And keep an eye on him.'

Now here was Kasanga, flustered and nervous.

'Musoke, I've heard that Dr Bito has disappeared. Possibly kidnapped.'

Musoke pointed to a chair. Nominally, Kasanga outranked him

but each knew that Musoke's real position in intelligence was senior to the convenience title of Third Secretary he held at the Embassy.

'So I understand. Last seen at his University on Wednesday evening.'

Kasanga waved away unnecessary details.

'Never mind where he was. The question is, where is he now? And who took him?'

Musoke shrugged.

'Good questions, Amos. But no good asking me. Better ask the FBI. One of their men is coming here later.'

'Look, Musoke, don't play the innocent with me. Someone is stealing the cattle from your compound, Musoke. Prominent citizen of Kenya disappears and you shrug your shoulders?'

'He was connected in some way with Chivers. The police were investigating him. Maybe he decided to go into hiding. I can't be responsible for his movements. He's got no official standing. He's virtually an American, he's been here so long.'

'You know as well as I do, Musoke, that Bito still has one long-standing connection with our affairs. He claims to know something about the Omuto business. Then there's his son-in-law. I had him here the other day. He's a senior policeman. And his wife, Bito's daughter, works for some big company and knows half the Congress. This is a big *shauri*, Musoke. The government is concerned. And I think you know more than you're saying.'

'Just stop there. Tell me something, Amos. What business is this of yours?'

'I told you. The government is concerned. And I am here to protect the government's interests. We've got one Kenyan citizen dead, murdered, another disappeared, and three others involved in one way or another. You're supposed to be in charge of intelligence and you don't seem to be saying or doing anything.'

'Three others involved?'

'Yes, the policeman and his woman. And Katawi – he's supposed to be in charge of security over there. Didn't do a very good job of it Monday night. The Ambassador is worried, Musoke.'

'I still don't see why you think all this is my *shauri*. They're not working for me – any of them. The only one Chivers used to see when he came here that I know of was you, Amos. I thought of asking whether you were running your own agents.'

Kasanga looked even more flustered.

'I didn't – I mean, it was the most casual of contacts. Look, Musoke – it's Bito's disappearance I came about. You know his evidence could be damaging – I mean, crucial in the Omuto enquiry. If he's dead he won't be giving evidence, will he? If he turns up in Kenya that's a different matter. I thought he didn't want to go back.'

'Well, then, Amos, I think you've answered your own question. If Bito turns up in Kenya we'll know he was spirited back by Kiwonka's enemies and if he turns up dead we'll know he was taken by Kiwonka's friends.'

'If you had anything to do with it, Musoke, you'd better speak. Some say you dance to the *mzungu*'s tune. And some say our *mzungu* friend may need to be careful. It would not be good for a white man to be seen trying to choose our President.'

'I didn't know the post was vacant.'

Suddenly Kasanga lost his equable demeanour. He rose and shook his fist at Musoke.

'OK. If you want to play stupid, that's your choice. But I warn you, Musoke, neither you nor Price-Allen is fireproof. You may regret turning down my request for co-operation.'

With that he stumped out. Musoke continued sitting at his desk for some time. He didn't particularly like the situation. Kasanga was right up to a point; Musoke believed he had reached a crossroads. If he kept going he was committed and then he relied on his mentor. But if he double-crossed him now the danger was greater. Musoke knew what Price-Allen could do when crossed. He gave a little shudder, then shook his head. No good allowing bad thoughts to break his spine. He reached for his coat; it was time to get an update on events before he got in touch with Odhiambo.

Sally Eves sat in the large plush foyer of the Kennedy Center opposite the entrance to the Eisenhower Theater, one of the auditoriums that led off this central waiting area. She had been told that Sean Gilbride was in the middle of a scene rehearsal, but would be with her as soon as possible. The wait stretched her nerves; she was worried, but also, though she was reluctant to admit it, excited. The IBID affair was now taking on the makings of a genuine front-page story, if only the elusive answer to the prime question could be obtained. Given the crucial stage that had been reached, Sally Eves found it incomprehensible as well as intolerably annoying that her accomplice was concentrating on rehearsing some damn play.

At last Gilbride emerged, trotting lightly down the few steps to foyer level. He could tell, as he crossed the floor towards her, that Sally was uptight. Her demands on him were becoming excessive. It was all right for her – she could choose how to spend her day; what she didn't seem able to appreciate was that most people had commitments involving others that had to be met.

'Sally, darling, what brings you here?' He held out his hands in an exaggerated, theatrical gesture that moved Eves' blood pressure up another notch. 'And is it wise? To meet like this, I mean. Here where we're well known.'

His listener's eyes blazed with an intense, suppressed fury.

'Why the hell shouldn't we meet? We're not doing anything illegal. Well, I'm not. And SEND wants publicity, for Chrissake.'

'OK. Just checking, to be sure. But there must be an urgency. You are more inclined to wait for me to come to you. I'm flattered, that I am.'

'Shut up and listen. Let's go out on to the balcony.' Sally Eves took Gilbride's elbow and steered him towards the doors leading to the great frontage overlooking the river. As they walked, Eves continued. 'This thing is going to be explosive now. We've got to act fast. Without Hills we've got problems.'

'What are you on about? Calm yourself down. I told you already. He's being evasive. Didn't tell me too much. But I've got him worried, that I have. Just a little more time and he's ours. I'm sure of it. I'm seeing him tonight.'

His companion stopped, grabbing his arm once more to bring him to a halt also.

'What are you talking about? God, don't say you don't know.'

Gilbride felt the stirring of concern.

'Know what?'

'Hills, you dummy. He's dead. He was knifed yesterday. On Roosevelt bloody Island of all places.'

She had her companion's full attention now. Gilbride stared at her, mouth open, astonishment writ large on his face.

'Dead? What, murdered, you mean? Hills?'

Sally Eves almost pulled Gilbride on to the stone balcony and did not speak until they reached the outer edge, protected by a waist-high wall. She leaned towards him and Gilbride found that with his bottom pressed against the wall, retreat was impossible.

'Yes, he's been murdered. I take it you know nothing about it?' Gilbride spluttered his indignant denial. 'Right. But you saw him the night before and, in your words, "leaned on him" to tell you what he knew. You told me that he admitted there was something going on in Nigeria, but needed time to consider taking us into his confidence. Don't you see the implication? Before you can follow up, somebody makes sure he doesn't tell us anything. Who did you talk to other than me?'

Gilbride had recovered his wits.

'Nobody. Nobody. You think I'm a fool? This'll be IBID's doing. He probably went to see his contact there. Where did you say it happened? Roosevelt Island, wasn't it? Well, there you are – right next to IBID.'

Sally Eves looked doubtful.

'Now you listen, Sean. We have to be careful. If the police find out about you and Hills it could be tricky. If Giles Faucon's people are involved in getting rid of Hills, we could be at risk too. He warned me when he ended our relationship.'

'The answer, my dear woman, is to go on the offensive. Charge IBID with causing a disaster in Nigeria and trying to silence its critics. Now you're not bedding Faucon what's stopping you?'

Eves' face tightened.

'Now, you listen. I'll decide when to move on IBID. You may remember that you have failed to come up with what is wrong with the Nigeria business. Now I'm going to pursue the Bito woman. She must know something about what Hills was up to. And you are going to check your theory why Hills was over the river. Use your IBID contacts to find out who in IBID Hills might have been working with if your theory is right. And do it fast. Leave your little friends prancing about the stage without you for a bit.'

Gilbride watched the woman striding away a few minutes later. What a bitch she was. He was concerned about Hills. He thought back to their conversation: had he inadvertently brought about Hills' death? He shivered. If so, he was at risk. It was time to think about looking after himself. He had not told Sally about Hills' connection with Kraxma. He needed to keep some information to himself – one never knew when such information could be used as a bargaining chip.

Cari and James Odhiambo were at the Bito home, partly to act as companions for the distraught Abbie Bito and partly waiting for news from Bolling. Metroarcs management had told Cari not to worry about the office, a team was flying in from New York to handle office caretaking and arrangements regarding the deceased lobbyist. Cari had spoken to a New York Vice-President and had mentioned the Nigeria project, Hills' connection with it, and the possible complications for Metroarcs. She was irritated to be told once more not to worry, 'New York will take care of it!' Although grateful to be relieved of the onus of looking after the Washington office, given her personal worries, Cari had the certain feeling that New York was sidelining her because she was not trusted to run the show. Well, she had no confidence in New York. She had liked Glen Hills and she felt in some way responsible. After all, she had helped put Bolling on to a line of investigation that could embarrass Metroarcs and Hills. She could not just sit back and do nothing. So when the call came from Sally Eves, Cari was in a more receptive mood than her caller might have expected. James had passed her the telephone and he was watching her anxiously. He had been very quiet since last night: Cari recognised the symptoms – James was uneasy in his mind, something was troubling him. It reminded her of his mood when they arrived from London. She had known then there was something on his mind. Recent events had driven his preoccupations into the background, but now he was withdrawn again, although Cari was sure that this was to do with their current problems. She listened as Sally pleaded her case.

'I know what you asked me to do, Sally, but events have overtaken me. My father has been kidnapped and now Mr Hills has been murdered. It's terrible.' She listened again. 'Well, I did find out some basic facts, yes.' Another impassioned interjection hit her ear. 'I'm looking after my mother. It's difficult.' She paused, thinking rather than listening to the continued pleas, and then came to a decision. 'OK. But look, Sally – this is a two-way thing. We share knowledge. Pool our information. OK? Right. I'll try to make arrangements to get away for an hour. Right. 'Bye.'

She looked at her husband, who looked at her as if she'd gone mad.

'Cari, what are you doing? This is no time to keep up with your pressure group friends. We've got enough on our plate now.'

'Look, James – Sally and her friends were digging into that Nigeria project. She wanted me to find out what Metroarcs was doing. She was looking into IBID. She might know something. You can hold the fort here for an hour.'

113

'It's Bolling's job, Cari. You're meddling in something that isn't your business.'

'It is. It is. Metroarcs is my business. I work for them, remember. It keeps us in our comfortable lifestyle.' She saw that she had struck a nerve and that it hurt. 'Oh, James, I'm sorry. I didn't mean that. I'm on edge. But I do owe them loyalty and I haven't been very loyal, leading Bolling to matters that could embarrass the company. At least I owe them to find out what I can. And . . . and . . . Glen is my business. He's . . . was . . . my boss. And I liked him.'

James Odhiambo turned away. He was hurt. Nothing touched him on the raw more quickly than the reminder that Cari earned the bulk of their income. Kenya police officers were not well paid, particularly when you converted Kenya shillings to dollars. He should order her to stay home. But that was the point of her barb – whether she intended to launch it or not. He had no right to order her. She had a job, responsibilities, and supported him. Although the spirits of his ancestors mocked him, he recognised another emotion. He was proud of her.

Abbie was trying to busy herself in the kitchen, preparing a meal much more elaborate than was required. At least she was functioning again, although her emotions were still such that one felt she was walking a tightrope as she moved about concentrating determinedly on something, anything, other than her dread and fear. Cari explained that she had to go out. Abbie nodded absentmindedly. It did not matter to her. In a strange sort of way Cari's presence kept bringing back the thoughts she was trying to keep suppressed lest they break her.

'James will be here and I'll be back before you've cooked that pie. OK, Mum?' Cari gave her mother a brief hug and turned to her husband, brooding in the background. 'Thanks, big guy.'

'Thanks for what?'

'For not stopping me going. You're something special, you know that. I got a feeling, James. Sally may have something that will help.'

James nodded but without conviction. He saw her off and hoped he had not been a fool as well as a weakling. Well, no harm could come from having a heart-to-heart with that Eves woman. Meanwhile, he had his own thoughts to pursue. He returned to the kitchen and helped himself to a can of beer. A little small-talk with his mother-in-law that neither focused on and then he retreated to the lounge with his can. He sat and thought. Whoever killed Chi-

vers had blood on him. A lot of blood, probably. How could someone in that state walk out without the danger of being noticed by
Katawi's people? And no clothes had been found in the building. A
change of clothes available and a bag. Someone who normally
carried a bag with sports clothes in, perhaps. Chivers, Caradonna,
Bito, Hills, SEND and the long arm of Omuto. There could not be
one uniting link. Were there two chains of actions and reactions
which ran in parallel except for one link in common – Chivers? He
took another drink from his can as the telephone rang once more.

15

Romaine Caradonna had survived the incredible chaos of the
Lagos Airport arrivals area. Doing a stint with West Africa Projects
might be a necessary rung in building a career ladder, but no one,
no one, she thought, should have to put up with Nigerian public
services. The airport was organised so as to maximise the discomfort felt by paying passengers – the unpaying (politicians and their
business cronies) were whisked through a totally separate system –
with staff trained, it seemed, to masters degree level in arrogance,
bullying, indolence and sheer incompetence. The final touch was
the overlay of military and administrative corruption so that only
by bribery could one traverse the slimy obstacle course dotted with
mantraps. The only airport, as far as Caradonna knew, where a
boarding pass did not guarantee a seat: hiring a 'toto' to go ahead
and occupy a seat on the plane was the only way to do that. The
only airport where you needed to seek out the bag-handlers before
proceeding through immigration – an experience in itself – to buy
their goodwill to ensure that your bags got on to the luggage belts,
and got on to them intact.

The trouble was, she thought, that one's troubles did not end with
the retreat from the public areas. She had now spent a night in the
most expensive hotel in the city, in a room costing IBID as much as
one in the Grosvenor House in London or the Waldorf in New
York, but where the bedside tables had no light bulbs, there was
only a torn and worn single towel in the bathroom, tepid water
flowed, or rather trickled, from both hot and cold taps, and, most
annoyingly, the air-conditioning system emitted stale, warm air.

Caradonna felt the sweat trickling down her back between her shoulder blades and fanned herself futilely with a document on which she was attempting to concentrate. She was relieved when the telephone rang. Relief that it worked and relief that it probably signalled some action. Anything was better than sitting in this dump.

She had not availed herself of a rest-stop in London because she was anxious to get on with the task in hand. She knew there was something going on in this benighted country that could put her reputation at risk and she was determined this time to find out what it was. Besides, she found it easy to sleep on long flights as long as she had a comfortable, reclining seat in the first-class section, which IBID duly provided. So she was ready to get going and the call lifted her spirits for her wish was bearing fruit.

An hour later she was on her way on the congested roads out of Lagos heading for the agricultural research establishment situated some one hundred miles inland. Her companion, who had provided the car and driver, was a United Nations technical expert working in Nigeria. Caradonna had met him socially on a previous visit. He was a young, good-looking Colombian, who was potentially eminently beddable – Caradonna had mentally filed him away in her mind under the index 'Future One Night Stand' – but his value to her now was very different. His expertise was in agriculture and he was in Nigeria as an expert in farmer co-operatives. On Monday she was due to start the official part of her visit seeing Ministry of Agriculture officials and representatives of Aginvest. Then she would fly north to visit some of the distribution centres. But she had come to the conclusion in Washington that on technical matters she was too easy to con. It was then she had remembered Roberto and she knew that he was what she needed when she made a visit to the Ibadu Research Station. She had called him; he had offered her his assistance as long as she was there by Friday. So, here she was. Better still, they were on their way now without the Aginvest people knowing. She did not want their people or Ministry officials inviting themselves along.

They were out of the built-up area now, the road, a major highway, good if dangerous, being heavily populated with some of the world's worst drivers. Roberto's driver, however, seemed competent and watchful. The palm trees gave way to scrub and smallholdings with cassava and bananas much in evidence, but Caradonna was intent now on her companion.

116

'So the farmers are unhappy? On a general scale?'

Roberto nodded.

'Your project is going down the tubes, Romaine. Two seasons now the farmers have used your seed and fertiliser and it has been a washout for them. Extra costs but no increase in production. Or not enough to be worthwhile.'

'Across the country? This is so everywhere?'

Another nod.

'I get about to most parts. Everywhere the story is the same. This is setting back the efforts of those of us trying to modernise farming systems. We encourage the farmers slowly. You come in with multi-millions, a conglomerate, political clout, the farmers have their arms twisted to take what you're peddling and find out they've been let down.' He looked at his companion more in sorrow than in anger. His voice was light, not aggressive. He did not wish to alienate her. Quite the reverse, she was damnably attractive. 'I don't mean you personally, of course. But some of your people should have known better.'

'But why didn't they benefit? That's the question, don't you see? Their yields should have doubled, trebled. Trials show that. We had experts here when the project was being designed. Couldn't miss, they said. As long as it rained. What about the rainfall?'

'Not bad. No droughts, if that's what you mean. We've had a good couple of years, in fact. Anyway, some of the farmers have irrigated land – they're no happier than the rest.'

'So what else can explain it? Perhaps the farmers don't put the stuff on in the right quantities, or plant the seed at the wrong time, or they're cursed by witch-doctors.'

The driver looked over his shoulder with a large grin.

'Ah, madam. Perhaps it is your fertiliser that is cursed. They say it comes from far away in the North. Heathen people.'

'North Africa. Highly developed fertiliser industry. And towns you can drive about in. You just watch where you're going.'

'The man you're going to see at Ibadu.' Roberto was anxious to keep the woman from becoming angry. 'Is it Dr Atendu?'

'Yes. The cereal breeder. He did the early trials. The ones the experts said were conclusive. And he may have done some recent trials on farmers' fields.'

'And the results . . . ?'

'I'm not sure about the latest ones. Someone said they're not impressive.'

'So maybe the company that's importing the stuff is bringing in rubbish and selling it as prime grade.'

Caradonna had been looking out of the window again as they went through a village. Now she turned her head towards her companion. God, thought Roberto, what a profile.

'Not possible. The source delivers fertiliser all over – no complaints. On arrival here the government claims to inspect it before its dispersal to the regional centres.'

Roberto laughed.

'Government inspections here are not exactly foolproof. Documents can be forged here quite easily. It's an industry in its own right.'

Eventually the conversation drifted on to other matters. Only when the car turned off the road under an arch proclaiming the home of the Ibadu Centre did Romaine Caradonna return to the subject of her mission.

'Now, Roberto. I want your assistance. I'm an economist not an agriculturalist. You make sure that this guy Atendu levels with me, OK?'

'He has a good reputation. He's a good scientist.'

'He may be good, but will I be able to understand him?'

In fact, Dr Atendu, a slightly built, middle-aged man, was extremely articulate and intelligible. His tale was soon told. Yes, the original data collected from properly organised trials on experimental plots on the research station were still on file. Shown the annexe to the project document, he nodded; yes, those were the results. Very satisfactory. Yes, he had arranged trials this last season on farmers' own fields but with supervised fertiliser application and harvesting. A copy of the data had been sent to a Mr Chivers in IBID. He had received some criticism about this from the Ministry. They had taken his file with the data. As he wasn't prepared for this he had no copy. No, he hadn't had time to have the data analysed.

'Shit,' said Romaine Caradonna, to herself, but audibly. 'So you say the data are back where I just came from, in Lagos?'

Atendu smiled. It transformed an otherwise glum face.

'I'm afraid so.' He paused. 'Although it may not be so easy to discover. Er . . . sometimes things taken to Lagos are not meant to be seen, if you understand me.'

Roberto shifted uneasily in his chair, but Caradonna nodded.

'Sure, I understand. You don't have to deal with those guys long to understand.'

Roberto tried to be helpful.

'No exploratory analysis was done before sending it to IBID?'

'No. We have no time for sophistications like that. I did look at the print-out when the data were put on to a diskette.'

Caradonna leapt in.

'And what impression did you get? An experienced man like you. You must have a feel for such data.'

Atendu inclined his head, acknowledging the compliment.

'Not promising. Yields were poor whether fertiliser was applied or not.'

The standard possible explanations were bounced about among the three of them, but with no discernible advance. As he wound up the meeting Atendu offered his visitors the use of the guest house on the station as darkness was upon them and night-time journeys on the road back to Lagos were even more dangerous than daylight ones. The woman exchanged glances briefly with her companion. He caught her eye and although their expressions did not alter, nor were words exchanged, both knew that, as Romaine Caradonna accepted the offer, a compact had been made. Their hospitable researcher walked them over to the guest house in the cooler air of twilight, promising that the driver would be looked after and that a cook was available for guest-house residents.

'Your appetites will be satisfied,' he said. Caradonna shot him a quick look, but Atendu's face had blended into the approaching night. Was there a twinkle of mischief in the voice? Her ears tuned in more carefully as Atendu resumed in a voice that now had returned to its normal dry, earnest delivery. 'I do not like to talk of these speculations in formal session. But, Miss Caradonna, one cannot but hear the rumours as one travels.' As if by prearrangement the three walkers stopped, their destination, a good-sized bungalow with colonial-style verandah, still visible across the well-kept lawn rising from the path on which they stood. 'You may care to consider this in your further enquiries. The fertiliser comes in – all is well. Somewhere between the import and the distribution it gets adulterated or switched. What the farmer gets is not what he paid for.'

Roberto whistled.

'I've heard similar tales, but put them down to the Nigerian gossip industry. It doesn't seem possible.'

Caradonna was thinking hard. She voiced the problem that Roberto was presumably alluding to.

'We're talking huge quantities here, Dr Atendu. Thousands of

119

tons. We're not talking of swapping a couple of lorries. It would be a big operation. Huge stores. And where would the real stuff go?'

Atendu laughed softly.

'You don't know Nigeria well enough, young lady. Particularly Lagos. Anything is possible if the reward is big enough. The local subsidiary of the company supplying fertiliser has a huge quarry and stone-crushing complex. The fertiliser is stored there after importation. A lot could happen.'

'Do you have any evidence of this?'

'It is not wise to dig too deep. That is if, like me, you are a Nigerian with a family to support. Perhaps someone like yourself, from outside, protected by a powerful institution . . .'

Atendu left the sentence hanging. Caradonna could scarcely see him now.

'Let's get to the house where we can see to talk.'

But Atendu had said all he seemed prepared to say. Once inside the guest house he returned to his former taciturnity and soon took his leave. It was later when they lay exhausted on the bed that Roberto returned to the subject.

'You know, I think Atendu was only willing to talk freely in the open. I wonder if he thinks his office is bugged. I didn't think people were that suspicious.'

'What, and this place as well. Oh dear!'

They laughed. Roberto turned back on his side towards the woman – the most sensual partner he had encountered.

'Let's give them something worthwhile to listen to.'

Back in Washington Giles Faucon was closeted in his office with his Directors of Audit and Africa Projects and his Chief of Internal Systems.

'So, Mensat. What more can you tell us about the Nigeria project? And you, Greene – have you confirmed what Chivers was working on when he was killed?'

Mensat Khan coughed delicately, wiped his mouth with an immaculately folded handkerchief, and then spoke, choosing his words with some care.

'We're not very much further forward, I'm afraid. Miss Caradonna is in Nigeria now with instructions to focus on the distribution system. If there is something untoward, the difficulty will be to penetrate the local Nigerian company working with Metroarcs.'

120

Faucon revealed an expression of distaste as if he had bitten into something sour. His eyes moved to focus on Greene. He nodded peremptorily. Greene glanced again at his notes and started hesitantly.

'We have confirmed Chivers was preparing his report on the Nigeria project. From his notes it seems he had grounds for concern. We have not been able to retrieve the er . . . er . . . data that apparently should have been on his computer. Nor has the er . . . er . . . hard copy been found. If the data have been deliberately removed it would confirm that preventing him completing his analysis was a motive for the murder.'

Faucon closed his eyes briefly as if despairing of the folly of his subordinates.

'Your logic is faulty, Greene. Not for the first time. Even if deliberately removed there are other explanations. Removed subsequent to the killing is but one. You did, I assume, look for the data in Chivers' apartment?'

Greene shifted uneasily in his chair.

'Not until yesterday and then we were informed the police had barred entry.'

'Exactly. Because the police, I am told, did what you should have done earlier. Looked in Chivers' home computer. My information is they were successful.'

'So where is it now?' Mensat Khan leaned forward across the large desk. 'Can we get a copy?'

'I understand Lieutenant Bolling is making private arrangements. You may make such representations as you think worthwhile, but in my estimation we shall hear when Bolling wishes us to hear. And as much or as little as he wishes.'

The two men fell silent. The third in the row facing Faucon decided his turn was about to come – he was correct. Faucon's eyes met his.

'So, Steen, there is work for you to do. I want all the files relating to the Nigeria fertiliser project impounded and sealed. Central registry and departmental. And individual unofficial files. Make a thorough search. Without delay. It may already be a case of shutting the stable door after the animals have departed. I include as files computer discs. Use administrative staff, not the security personnel. The latter will be posted at all exits from the Annexe building. Any member of Africa Projects leaving the building for whatever reason prior to the completion of your task is not to be allowed to take documents or discs with them. In case of doubt, stop everyone if necessary. You will also issue a memo to all staff. No one is to speak of these events to anyone other than the police. Specifically, no one is to speak to any contractor or non-governmental organisation: particularly not to SEND.'

Khan showed visible signs of injured pride.

'Giles, we must consider morale. Staff will regard themselves as under susp –'

'Your protest does you no credit, Mensat. Can you not see? Chivers is murdered. We know what he was working on. A man called Hills has been murdered in very strange circumstances not far from here. He is, or was, Metroarcs' Washington agent. Metroarcs is the contractor for the project and Hills was our contact.'

Greene's mouth fell open; he had not heard of the death on Roosevelt Island. Khan was made of sterner stuff.

'Nevertheless, there is no evidence against my staff. We must observe the proprieties.'

'Proprieties.' The word was repeated with sarcasm hanging on every mini-syllable. 'I am concerned with the reputation of this institution, not the *amour propre* of your staff.' Faucon paused and waved at the waiting Steen. 'Go. Put these matters in hand.' He turned back to Khan who was flushed with indignation. 'I have specific instructions for you. Recall the Caradonna woman. I will arrange an independent team to conduct an investigation. Meanwhile all disbursements to be suspended. And while we talk of suspensions, Kraxma to be placed on leave with pay.'

'I must protest, Giles. All this –'

'Mensat, I am not interested in your wounded pride. You have let me down. IBID down. We must limit the damage.'

Faucon rose: the audience was over.

Out in the corridor Greene, feeling himself lucky to have escaped lightly, thought it appropriate to mutter a word or two of sympathy. Khan looked at him.

'Either the man has lost his wits, or he wishes to prevent further enquiries he does not control. One may speculate on the reason, whichever it may be.'

The young lovers were deeply asleep when the guest-house attendant knocked on the door with the early morning tea, which he left on a table outside the door. Romaine Caradonna regarded early morning tea as some quaint relic of colonialism, but her companion had become accustomed to the practice. He padded over to the door and retrieved the tray. In addition to the expected crockery there was a folded piece of paper. Curious, he opened it and read.

There is man I meet who is relative of my wife. He knows about business you and lady talk plenty about. I bring him to you here so many ears do not listen.

Agmeya.

Agmeya was the driver. Roberto turned to the woman lying with her face buried in the pillow.

'Romaine, wake up. My driver has someone who wants to see you.'

When they emerged into the living area they discovered that Roberto's driver was waiting in the kitchen with his new acquaintance.

'This is Adama. He was a driver with Aginvest. He knows what happens to the fertiliser.'

After a confused exchange Caradonna began to get the picture as Adama settled into a coherent delivery. He had left Aginvest's employ for unexplained reasons three months earlier. Whilst with the firm he had driven one of their large articulated lorries.

'The fertiliser it come into the main area OK. Then we take it to regional stores like Kaduna. But what goes there has been re-bagged. Only little of real fertiliser. This mixed with stuff they make in that place where they dig stone too. Look OK, but not good.'

'And what happens to the real stuff?'

'Only one bag in three opened to make mixture. Others go on my lorry and I take to Cameroon. I and others. It fetch plenty big price in Cameroon. Aginvest has big business there only call it by different name.'

Caradonna turned to her handsome young Colombian.

'It's unbelievable. They're making a profit on the distribution in Nigeria only they're distributing rubbish. Then they sell the stuff they've already covered the costs on in Cameroon at double the prices, there's no subsidy there.'

Roberto Elandor shook his head in bewilderment.

'Jeez, it must be worth millions.'

After some further probing of an increasingly nervous Adama, the IBID and UN professionals fell silent. Both realised their predicament almost simultaneously.

Their own driver, Agmeya, spoke. He too was thinking on similar lines.

'This man, he not willing to be used. I promise him reward later on. But it is too dangerous to say these things in Lagos.'

Elandor looked at the woman beside him. She had dressed hurriedly and was unwashed with hair uncombed. Yet still she had a presence, both overt in terms of the sexual charge that seemed to emanate from her person and less obviously but distinctly in the sense of personality that would command.

'What do you think?' Elandor was hesitant. 'What should we do?'

Romaine Caradonna had had in succession a night with a Senator, a night on a jumbo jet and a night with the young man she was looking at, yet, somewhat to her surprise, her brain was running like a Porsche.

'Mr Adama, it is good you have spoken to me. When we put things right for farmers here you will be remembered. Believe me. But now you must stay quiet for some days, maybe some weeks.' Adama nodded. He was quite willing to be told to be careful. 'And you.' She turned to her, or rather Roberto's, driver. 'You too have done well, but you too must keep a silent tongue. Roberto, I must go back to Washington. We need a full and high-powered team here. So that an investigation cannot be suppressed.'

They hurriedly prepared to take their leave, but as they got in the car Agmeya had news that made Caradonna's mind race once more.

'The houseman here he disappear into town. He should wait for you to go, I think. He would expect good tip from foreigners. I think maybe he hear too much.'

Caradonna had left some money with a note and for one moment felt inclined to retrieve it. She was silent as the car headed back towards the capital. Finally she made her mind up.

'Roberto, I don't want to be making false worries. But if Aginvest know you and I have uncovered their scam, then funny things could happen.'

The young Colombian's mouth turned down.

'I too am worried. This is too big a thing for me.'

'Here's what we do. I stay away from the hotel and you stay away from wherever you live. We go straight to the UN office. Get someone senior to get me on the plane today to London. Once there, I can speak to my bosses. You keep your head down. Stay with a friend. Hang around the UN office. Once the story's out you'll be OK. And our friend here.' She pointed at the driver. 'Can you send him back to warn his relative to move away somewhere safe so long as we know where he is?'

The driver grinned through the windscreen. This was some woman. His boss should take this woman for himself. He would do no better.

When the first part of Caradonna's plan was executed she was surprised to discover at the UN office in Lagos a telex requesting her return to Washington immediately. One of the senior UN personnel was a Brazilian woman with whom Caradonna had become friendly during her previous visit. She listened to Caradonna's tale, or such of it as the IBID woman revealed, and offered her both hospitality and the services of a local UN employee to retrieve her belongings from the hotel. Relaxing by her new friend's swimming pool, Caradonna breathed a sigh of relief. All should now be well.

Later still the same day a senior manager of Aginvest found his colleague from the Ministry at his Ikoye home.

'She's not at the hotel. I'm worried she may leave on the flight to London. What can you do?'

'We can verify whether she does or not. Is that what you mean, my friend?'

'No! She knows too much. Can you not stop her?'

'Ah, my friend, you have simple mind. Me, I think as so. If she goes to airport without going to hotel then it is sure official will pick up her things and official will take her to airport. You think we want diplomatic incident? No. Accident on road back from Ibadu, that you could have arranged. After all, many accidents on such roads. But now is too late, my friend.'

'So what do we do?'

His host opened his hands from where they had been folded across his large belly.

'It will be in the hands of bigger men. But I would say, probably start a row with the World Bank and IMF and so IBID too. Government say delegations not welcome until row is resolved. Gives you time to cover your tracks, my friend. It is time our farmers got some good fertiliser, no?'

He laughed, a deep, genuine rumbling laugh. There was no matching jollity to come from his guest.

16

Sally Eves had come to a decision after a night in which her temper had cooled. Cari Bito had proved to be a major disappointment. Just a week ago Sally had been confident that Cari was succumbing to the force of Sally's personality and that soon she would be receptive to suggestions of becoming a friend of the environment within Metroarcs. But at their meeting yesterday Cari had become quite hostile. She had claimed that there was no evidence against Glen Hills or Metroarcs and if there was something wrong with the set-up in Nigeria it was probably the government's doing. She had gone so far as to imply that Sally and SEND were conducting a vendetta. The worst thing of all was that, too late, Sally had realised Cari was drawing out information from her. She had responded to Cari's defence of Hills by telling her that Hills had given every sign of guilt when Gilbride had visited him.

'Visited him?' Cari had said. 'What do you mean, visited him?'

'At his place in Maryland – the night before he was killed. We wanted him to tell us the details of what was going on in Nigeria and who in IBID was in on it.'

'And did you get anything?'

'Nothing concrete. Gilbride felt he was cracking. But then he was killed. To stop him talking, most likely.'

'But for Gilbride to go then he must have had something to threaten him with. Or Glen would have tossed him out on his ear.'

'Someone in IBID told Sean that Hills and a man called Kraxma were involved together.'

Cari had tried to continue the questioning, but Sally realised the role reversal that was taking place and attempted to reassert herself although with little success.

Now that bloody Gilbride had gone missing. Everyone was letting her down. Starting the other night with that bastard Giles. Well, it was time to strike back. Even if she still lacked proof, with her skill she could come up with a press release that would involve some mud sticking. She sat at her typewriter and started to compose.

*

Lieutenant Bolling chewed ferociously on a new pencil as he summarised his position in his mind. He had returned from talking to
the professor who had analysed the Nigeria data and with whom
he had discussed the implications. Put simply, Nigerian farmers
were being sold fertiliser that did not fertilise – they were being
conned, and to the tune of tens of millions. The Nigerian company
distributing the stuff and Metroarcs, the importers, must somehow
be involved. An IBID auditor about to report on this scam gets
killed and the evidence stolen. The IBID staff most closely involved
were a young woman, Caradonna, a mid-European, Kraxma and a
suave Pakistani called Khan. Kraxma was the link man with Metroarcs through their Washington representative, a guy called Hills.
Hills is found ripped open on Roosevelt Island.

The other Kenya angle with Bito as the suspect had come to
naught. Bito might have had the motive and opportunity to kill
Chivers, but no physical evidence was available, and now he had
disappeared. Bolling's contact in the FBI had told him the word on
the street was that the Bito kidnapping was a contract job with a
Jamaican drug gang which was prepared to freelance as long as the
money was right: client, however, unknown. So that ruled Bito out
of the Hills murder – and anyway, Hills had no Kenya connection.

So Caradonna, Kraxma, Khan or some less obvious IBID official.
The trouble was the lack of substantive evidence. Bolling, personally, discounted Caradonna although she was an important witness who unfortunately was currently in Nigeria. Kraxma was
Bolling's favourite, and Bolling believed that the man had had the
gall to wipe out the data on Chivers' computer in Bolling's
presence. But why hadn't he done this at the time of the murder?
Nor did he have any tangible evidence to place Kraxma in Chivers'
office at the time. Mensat Khan was a long shot not least because he
had an alibi which appeared to be holding up. No, Kraxma was the
man and it was time to pull him in for a formal interrogation. There
were diplomatic overtones, but Kraxma did not have diplomatic
immunity. Bolling used the chewed end of his pencil to stab the
numbers of his captain's extension. Better get the proper authorisation. He sighed. He didn't like to get into an interrogation phase
without a couple of forensic aces up his sleeve. Bloodstained
clothes or the hired punk responsible for the Roosevelt Island
job. One or both of these he needed to be on safer ground, but

procrastination was not an option either – given the high profile of the victims, the rumblings of impatience from above were already shaking the ground under his feet.

On her return to her parents' home, Cari Odhiambo had briefed her husband about her conversation with Sally Eves, but he had seemed uninterested, as if IBID and SEND had returned in his mind to the status of incomprehensible acronyms. One reason for his lack of attention became evident only the next morning as they took an early lunch together near the Metroarcs office. He told her of the telephone summons the previous evening and his visit that morning to the Kenyan Embassy.

'They want us back in Kenya, Cari; me particularly, but you as well. I got the orders over the phone after you left to see that woman, but I wasn't having that. They said the Ambassador or First Secretary or some such would confirm it, if I doubted that it was a government directive, but I wanted to see the man who probably knows the background. A call or two and I got his name – Musoke. I went to see him this morning. He played it cool, but I got something out of him. I'll bet you my last shilling that he's a Price-Allen man. And I'll bet Price-Allen is behind this in some way. And I'll go further and say it's connected with your father's kidnapping and the Omuto business.'

Cari felt her head spinning and after that a frisson of fear at the mention of Price-Allen's name. She remembered that terrible day in Nairobi when James was in a cell and she was a puppet in Price-Allen's scheme that culminated in dead men and a narrow escape for James. A multitude of questions jumbled in her mind.

'I thought you were somewhere else last night. Not talking. I could tell something was wrong. Why didn't you tell me you'd had a message? And you didn't say you were going to the Embassy.'

'You had your own problems what with that bloody woman Eves and your head office people here. I didn't want to worry you. How are things at the office?'

She knew he was not being frank. She knew the symptoms. He was worrying away at something in his head. He liked to confide in her when he had the facts assembled, but he didn't like it when he couldn't see a pattern.

'Oh, the New York people have taken over as if I didn't exist. I warned them about the Nigeria problem. They said they'd get some sort of investigation under way. Oh, James, I liked Glen. I feel like I'm being disloyal somehow.' She paused; momentarily she had returned to her local difficulties, but now James' news swept these concerns away. 'But what do you mean, James? Darling, what's going on? What's Price-Allen got to do with anything? Are you sure?'

Odhiambo felt a familiar pang of guilt. All he seemed to be bringing Cari was grief and worry. They were sitting in a French-style café restaurant, Cari with a low-calorie salad in front of her that served to emphasise the self-indulgence of his hamburger and fries.

'Musoke, the Embassy man, I put him under some pressure. Said I needed to ring my boss to find out what was going on. Also, we couldn't leave until we'd found out what happened to your father. He tried the heavy hand. Only here on sufferance and so forth. I told him you've got resident status and I'm your dependent.' Odhiambo grimaced. 'Well, it's the truth, it wasn't difficult to be convincing. Anyway, he let something slip. Said if we went back he understood there might be news of your father there. I grabbed him, asked what the hell he was talking about. But he shut up. Eventually, he said he would speak to Nairobi and see what he could find out. "See what they want you to tell me, you mean," I said. Then I made what might have been a mistake, but his reaction was interesting. "I know people too," I said. "Important people. One a *mzungu* you must have heard of." He smiled, started to say something then went into his shell. But for a moment it was written clear on his face; I could see it. Price-Allen is who he's going to call. I'm sure of it. He's one of Price-Allen's men.'

Cari was alternately amazed and ashamed that she had managed for periods in the last two days to put her father's kidnapping to the back of her mind. How much could she be expected to focus her concern on? Her father missing, her boss dead, and James in the middle of another crisis when he was in America to recuperate. Now he had brought her father back to centre stage.

'My God, James. This is terrible. It only needed Price-Allen to make it a nightmare. But what can he have to do with Dad?'

She watched the handsome head shake slowly.

'I don't know. It's a hunch. No, more than a hunch, I think. Sam had nothing to do with Chivers' death, but Sam and Chivers both knew something about the Omuto killing. Chivers is dead so Sam is the vital witness. Sam can put the finger on Kiwonka, so

129

Kiwonka might want to keep him out of Kenya. On the other hand, those who want to stop Kiwonka's rise up the political ladder would need Sam available.'

Cari's hand was at her mouth.

'Oh, James. You don't think they've killed –'

'No. Stop thinking like that. He's been kidnapped. If someone wanted him silenced they could have shot him or whatever. But he was taken alive. Someone wants to keep him safe, ready to give evidence.'

Cari's voice rose with the underlying hysteria beginning to surface. One or two diners at adjacent tables looked around with mild curiosity.

'I can't take any more, James. I can't take it all in. You still haven't said where that bastard Price-Allen fits in.'

'Hush, Cari. Keep on top of yourself. You underestimate your strength. You've been magnificent.' James reached across the table and enveloped her slim hand in his large fist. 'Price-Allen is the Big Man's agent. Kiwonka is in the same group as Aramgu. You remember him? Price-Allen did everything to do him down. So Price-Allen is most likely to be organising the enquiry to incriminate Kiwonka. So he needs Sam. So, knowing Price-Allen as we do, he's had him spirited away.' He paused, seeing the strain in his wife's eyes. 'If my theory is right, Cari, it's good news. Sam will be safe somewhere and Price-Allen or his slaves can tell us where he is.'

Cari could feel the bile in her throat. She felt nauseous. She pushed her plate away and cradled her head in her arms on the table. The tears stained her forearms. Her husband watched her anxiously and with some embarrassment. She straightened again, keeping her face lowered, and fumbled in her handbag for a handkerchief.

'Wait here, James. I'll be back in a moment. I'm OK. Really.'

Odhiambo waited, chewing moodily on his french fries. Somewhere at the back of his mind there was the nagging feeling he had missed something. It was frustrating – the more he tried to pin it down the deeper into the recesses of his mind it went. He looked up: Cari was back, a wan smile, make-up repaired, and looking incredibly lovely. He felt a great sense of longing. Why, oh why, couldn't their lives settle down in normalcy; time to love and time to seek forgiveness, time to build their fenced compound in which their relationship would grow even stronger, safe from predators.

'James, darling. I'm OK. And ready to move on. What do we do next? I won't pretend I'm not scared – scared for me and you and scared for Dad. But not broken.'

Again he took her hand. 'One day soon, we'll be alone, without problems, and I'll make it up to you. I promise.'

'OK, big guy. Don't get sentimental. What do we do next?'

'Musoke is the key, I'm sure. The Embassy man. He promised to see me again this evening, but not in the Embassy, he said. The next time you come here, he said, you're likely to find yourself bundled on a plane. He said he'd meet me at a bar on 17th Street. Five o'clock, I've got the address.'

'So what can I do?'

'Go home as soon as you can. Get Abbie to let you go through Sam's desk, files, whatever. Those he kept at home. There may be something.'

'What do you mean, something? Something about what?'

'He told me the story of himself, Chivers, Kiwonka and Omuto. In more detail than he told you. But I have a feeling he kept something back. Something that might be relevant. Anything that relates to his Kenya days.'

'You're getting rid of me. A makework job.'

'No, Cari. It's important. You know my instincts are often right. We may not have too much time. Anything we can get may help.'

'And where are you going now?'

'I'm going to find my friend Katawi. The security man at IBID. Tell him I think he fed me some *ugali* made with unmilled maize.'

And that was as much as he would tell her. Outside the restaurant, Cari watched him stride away, leaning forward in that purposeful way. She had offered him a lift but he said he had mastered the Washington Metro underground system and it was pretty efficient. Just a couple of stops to Rosslyn and he even had his farecard. She turned towards the garage where she had left her car. She wasn't going home. James had wanted her out of the way at home rather than needing a search of her Dad's papers. They could do that together tonight. No, she was going to see one of her acquaintances who claimed to be a minor functionary in the US Treasury. She had met him at a couple of parties and he claimed to have fallen madly in love with her. She had heard he was an agent engaged in surveillance on foreign diplomats. She wanted to know more about the mysterious Mr Musoke and his colleagues in the Kenyan Embassy.

Musoke was finding the conversation difficult. The telephone cradled in his shoulder, he cast his eyes around his office as if looking for an escape. All the while listening; it did not pay to fail to listen to Price-Allen.

'. . . Our package is well on its way, undamaged. You did well, Musoke, on that bit of posting. But now an ordinary mailing and you fumble. Odhiambo must return now. As he is still recuperating, his wife must accompany him. Leave of absence will be given by her bosses for that. I want Odhiambo here when the package arrives. Have I made myself clear?'

'Yes, bwana. But Odhiambo is like the buffalo, slow, cautious but determined. He is sniffing the wind.'

'Don't give me your game-hunting analogies. You have the tickets?'

'Yes, I have them. Bwana, I think he suspects you're behind this. Can I –'

'You fool. How could he suspect unless your tongue wagged? Musoke, I may have to make other arrangements.'

'No, wait. He told me he wanted to call you. To get you to get me off his back. He sees you as his *rifiki*. But I thought perhaps he guessed too that I am in touch with you.'

To Musoke's surprise he heard what sounded like a chuckle. He had never heard Price-Allen's mirth before.

'Oh dear. Odhiambo, he will blunder about so. So. If you can't handle a simple task without further inducement tell him this.' There was a pause and Musoke waited, afraid for a second that the line had gone dead. 'Tell him his mentor endorses the urgency of his return. Tell him I am investigating the Bito matter and back here I can bring him into the action. But tell him also that if he delays the Bito problem may become insoluble. You have that, Musoke? Get it right.'

Musoke felt in urgent need of a beer. Talking to Price-Allen was like walking towards the barrel of a gun: you found yourself imagining the black hole suddenly erupting, followed by the impact. He had heard too many stories of what happened to those who crossed or failed the small man with the eyes you didn't wish to probe. Well, at least he had been given some leeway. Just his luck that a job that could be handled with no loose ends gets screwed up by the chance presence of a policeman who happens to be Bito's son-in-law. Now he had another awkward interview. He glanced at his watch and hurriedly reached for his jacket on the back of his chair. He was late; Michael would be waiting and he too would not make a good enemy.

Twenty minutes later he was seated at a corner table in the dingy bar that was becoming almost familiar to him. Strange that until so recently he had not been there more than once in the last year. He nursed his beer and waited. He was a few minutes late so Michael could well be here, but out of sight while his minders ensured that Musoke had come without followers. After a few minutes three men emerged from a side door. The middle one, broad-shouldered, nondescript shirt and trousers, both black, Caribbean hair cut short, no flashing jewellery or Rolexes, sat opposite Musoke and fixed him with an unblinking stare.

Musoke broke off eye contact by looking at his glass.

'You wanted to see me. That's unusual. I hope there's no problem. The money was transferred as agreed.'

The slightest of nods.

'You Africans – I thought you were simpler than the locals, man. Say nothing of the Caribs, including mine. But now I'm not so sure. You playing games with me, man?'

The voice was low, flat, unthreatening, but Musoke for the second time in an hour felt a frisson of fear in his gut.

'You've got me lost, Michael. No games. You did the job. Did it well. Handed over on schedule, I'm told. And you've been paid. *Shauri kwisha*. In my tongue meaning that's it, all over. No sweat.'

'You sent word you were interested in the other dead guy, Hills. Seems to me you should have known everything necessary about him, Mr Kenyan. Another of your citizens works the Hill with Hills, you get my meaning?' The white teeth flashed briefly and there was the sound of a polite giggle from the supporting chorus. 'And that citizen is married to another of your citizens, Mr Kenyan, who just happens to be a pig, man. Coincidence don't stop there neither. Both of them live with our man, the one we transported for you.' Suddenly the head thrust forward across the small, beer-stained table. 'You got some explaining to do, man.'

Musoke swallowed hard. He felt the tension and sensed rather than saw the looming figures behind the Jamaican drug lord.

'I know all that. Coincidence, as you say. Didn't affect your job. I wasn't interested in Hills as such. I wanted to know who killed him.'

'Well, that's where it gets really crazy, man. I got the word around and we got us a little blade man. Too friggin' fancy for me. What some of my customers would call too theatrical. Don't use no one who likes to play around when doing a job. Do the job. No frills. Anyways this fancy nigger he told us about him and Hills in those woods.' Another flash of teeth. 'Leastways after we tested his own blade a little. Time he finished talking seemed to me you have some explaining to do. Why you got me chasing about when it's an all-African scene, man?'

Musoke felt a hand on the back of his chair. Somehow his bemusement gave his voice more courage than he felt.

'What the hell you talking about? I didn't have Hills killed. Why would I be willing to pay to have you tell me I fixed it? Come on, Michael, get with it.'

The tension around him was palpable and Musoke swore a silent oath that if he got out of the bar in one piece he would never use these crazy Jamaicans again. The man opposite him was silent, eyes fixed on Musoke's as if trying to penetrate his mind. Suddenly he laughed out loud.

'OK. So you ain't in the picture. Perhaps we should be dealing at the top of the pack.' Michael half turned and gestured. A cigarette flared into life behind him and was placed between his fingers. He drew on the cigarette and inhaled deeply. 'Simeon behind you there said these things were more dangerous than the stuff we deal in. I tell you they watch too much friggin' television. Now you listen, Mr Kenyan. Then you tell me you don't know what's going on among your own kind?'

Musoke listened and as he listened his mind started to function again and raced ahead. What did this mean? He needed to make a call before seeing Odhiambo. Things were getting out of control. Call Price-Allen? No. He'd better sort this one out himself. He pulled his mind back. First he had to flatter this monomaniac in front of him. Raise the fee in thanks and convince him he wasn't being led around by his nose.

If Cari Odhiambo had been less than honest as to her short-term intentions, her husband was in no position to moralise for he too had concealed his immediate destination. He did, indeed, cross under the Potomac River by Metro train and emerged in Rosslyn. But IBID was not his first destination. Instead, after a brisk walk, the recording of his request and a lengthy delay, he obtained access to Lieutenant Bolling in a designated interview room.

'So, Mr Odhiambo, you wanted to see me informally.'

'Yes. Look, I've got a favour to ask. I want to get into Hills' home here in Washington. And maybe into his weekend place in Maryland. My wife says he was there the day before he died. He came back to Washington sometime during the night.'

Bolling looked at the man across the table. There was something about him he couldn't quite fathom. Perhaps it was that his size and demeanour somehow conveyed the impression of a stolid, plodding, unimaginative policeman; Bolling was beginning to believe that, to the contrary, he was dealing with a mind of some astuteness.

'You wouldn't care to tell me why? Or even if the reason is good, why you should be involved? If you've got information about Mr Hills I'll be glad to hear it.'

'Look, Bolling. We've got this man Hills, he's shaken by the murder of the IBID auditor, he goes to his country place to get some privacy and think things through, suddenly he rushes back to Washington in the middle of the night, then in the morning sets off for a remote wooded island and meets his killer. Doesn't that tell you something?'

Bolling smiled, a thin widening of the lips rather than a sign of humour.

'I don't know what standards you're used to in Africa, but here we do know how to conduct an investigation. In fact, we're interviewing one man now and we're looking for another. Let me put the question back to you, Mr Odhiambo: what do Mr Hills' movements tell you?'

'That he had a visitor that evening. Which from another source I can confirm. And something was said that required him to rush back and make an appointment in a remote spot. Something that is the key to this whole business.'

Again the thin-lipped smile.

'Your intuition is not bad. He did have a visitor and we think we know who. That's who we're trying to pick up. We've gone through Hills' place in Maryland, or the Maryland boys did on our behalf. Yes, there was evidence of a visitor, enough to probably pin down the person even if he denies it, but so what?'

'What about his place here? You see, I'm looking for something specific. Not fingerprints or mud on the carpet. I want to see if he made a note.'

Bolling looked a little unsure for the first time. He plucked a pencil from his shirt pocket and bit on it.

'What sort of note? We'd have seen it if it was lying around.'

'Not that sort of note, no. You see, I have a crazy theory beginning to form in my head. I don't want to waste your time with it. But if I'm right he would have had to make a call and he might have noted it in some way.'

Bolling was intrigued despite himself.

'And you think you're the only one who would recognise its significance?'

'Well, yes, in the sense that I'll know if it fits my theory and then I could explain it to you.'

'Look, Mr Odhiambo. You and your wife put me on to that disc thing. It looks as if there is some scam going on in Nigeria. And we're bearing down on that angle. It looks promising. I appreciate your assistance. Are you telling me now that you've got some other cockaninny theory?'

'Not necessarily. But there's something nagging at me. Just send someone with me to his place. What harm can it do? Humour me. I have a strong instinctive feeling. We Africans are known for it.' Odhiambo smiled in what he hoped was an ingratiating way. 'If I find what I'm looking for I'll be straight back here without interfering with anything.'

Bolling sighed resignedly.

'He lived in DC. That's another jurisdiction. OK. I'll make a call. Get someone to meet you at his place. You know where it is?'

'Yes, my wife gave me the address. Tell the DC police I'll be there at four.'

Bolling nodded and got up.

'I must need my medical. I'm going soft in the head.'

Odhiambo joined him at the door.

'Thanks, Bolling. Thanks for the confidence. If there is anything, I won't let you down.'

The grunt he got back could have meant anything.

Odhiambo's next stop was at IBID. It was gone three but he wanted to see Katawi before heading back across the river, even if it meant he had to take a cab instead of his new-found means of rapid transport. He had phoned Katawi before his lunch with Cari and he had confirmed his likely presence in his lair at the main IBID building. On enquiry now, however, Odhiambo was disappointed. The security guard at the reception desk phoned through,

136

only to receive the news that Katawi had been called away on business.

His walk back to the Metro station took Odhiambo past the building where he and Katawi had come to view Chivers' body. On a hunch, Odhiambo crossed the road and entered the narrow passageway between the IBID building and the one next to it. Emerging at the back, Odhiambo found himself at the closed end of a cul-de-sac with a road leading back in the direction of the river. It was clearly the access for service vehicles and there adjacent to a set of double doors were two rubbish skips. Odhiambo wandered up to them and peered over the top. The usual plastic bags of rubbish, boxes, and office detritus met his gaze.

'Hey, man. What you doing there?'

Odhiambo looked around. A security guard was approaching with a hand on a baton in his belt. Odhiambo stepped back.

'Just nosing about. I had an appointment with Mr Katawi, but he's been called away. I'm with the police.'

The guard accepted the explanation without demanding further proof. Odhiambo started to retrace his steps then stopped and turned back.

'Tell me – how often are these things emptied?'

The guard hesitated, but Odhiambo's air of authority overcame any lingering suspicions.

'Three times a week.'

'Which days?'

'Nights. Or evening. Mondays, Wednesdays, Fridays. What's the problem?'

'No problem. Just filling in the picture. Thanks.'

'No sweat. Have a good one.'

Odhiambo headed back to the Metro and the taxi-rank in front. Time to get to his next appointment. He needed a lucky break and he needed it fast.

17

Odhiambo paid off his taxi. He was running a little late, not helped by the driver's ignorance of Washington geography. Odhiambo, who had acquired the usual visitor's respect for the encyclopaedic knowledge of cabbies in London, was surprised that here in America's capital many of the taxis were driven by recent immigrants speaking Spanish. He turned to face the townhouse and as he did so a casually dressed man closed up towards him. The appearance was casual, but the quick scan of Odhiambo's person by the concentrated eyes gave the game away.

'You the guy the Virginia boys sent over?'

Odhiambo smiled and held out his hand.

'Yes. I certainly am. And you must be from this side of the river.'

He felt the appraisal continuing.

'You're not from around here. Nor the Caribbean. Where you from?'

'Africa. Kenya. I'm a detective. I happen to be involved with Lieutenant Bolling on the Rosslyn murders – including a Mr Hills who lived here, I'm told.'

'Yessir, he sure did. We've been through the place, of course. What are you looking for?'

As they spoke, Odhiambo fell into step with the detective as he mounted the steps to the townhouse. It was a substantial property in an expensive area. Glen Hills' lobbying duties clearly incorporated a high lifestyle.

'I'm not sure. A note. An indication of why he was where he was when he was killed.'

'You don't see it as a mugging?'

'More important I don't think Bolling sees it that way. I'm just playing a hunch. Sorry to be a nuisance.'

'No sweat.'

They were inside a hall. The Washington detective led the way, opening doors, allowing the two men to glance around.

'Is there a study, somewhere he worked?'

'Let's look on the other floors. There's two above this.'

Off the second floor landing they found what Odhiambo was looking for. A study, furnished with a desk facing the window looking out over a green wooded area. Shelves of books including law books and many political memoirs, biographies and modern political histories. No computer, Odhiambo noted, but three telephones including a fax and an ancient-looking teleprinter.

Odhiambo went in and cast an eye over the desk. He remembered a similar experience in Nairobi where the key of the case lay before him on a murdered man's desk although he only recognised it much later. His Luo instincts were working full bore. There was something here if only he could find it and realise its significance. His guide watched him with an air of resigned boredom.

'No suicide note, right? So he didn't commit harakiri?'

'Harakiri?'

'That's what they do in Japan, right? Slit their guts open. I hear that's what happened to your man.'

'No, he didn't do that.' Odhiambo focused on a daily flip-over diary. It was open at Monday's date. There were several entries. 'Breakfast, Smolling, Hemmings.' Then 'll. Sen. Morgan' and an indecipherable name against the word 'Lunch'. The bottom entry said 'Cari party'. He flicked over the pages. There were several appointments noted but nothing to indicate his departure to Maryland or his return. The morning of his death was blank. He shook his head. 'No. Nothing.' There were very few papers on the desk; Hills either didn't use his desk for writing or he was a tidy man. Such papers as there were related to some piece of legislation and looked somehow as if they had been untouched for some time. He sighed and repeated, 'Nothing.'

The telephone on the desk was not accompanied by a notepad. Odhiambo turned to the table under one set of bookshelves. Two more telephones and, yes, a notepad. The top page contained the message "Cindy – cancel Wed." and a telephone number. Under this page the pad was blank. The waste-paper plastic bin was empty. A man in Hills' position probably had somebody in to clean at least once a week.

Odhiambo was disappointed. He was missing something, he was sure of it. His eyes scanned the shelves. The bottom one was devoted to storing large volumes, reference books and telephone directories. There was a gap in the middle of the several directories. He looked down again – yes, there in the far corner of the table, to the right of the telephones, was the missing directory. Odhiambo felt the familiar tingle of expectation. He rummaged through the directory, no page of personal numbers; he picked it up by the spine and shook it – nothing fell out. He glanced at his companion who shrugged and grimaced.

'Probably kept most records in his office. Got a fancy one close to Congress.'

'Yeah, I guess so. I was hoping he might have noted something here when he made an appointment to see someone.'

'So. Want to see anything else?'

'Better look in his bedroom.'

Odhiambo turned to follow the policeman through the door. He stopped. A long shot, but what the hell. He turned back, picked up the directory on the table and flicked through the pages until he found the page he was looking for. A shiver ran through his body. There it was – the name and number were underlined. He closed his eyes. When he opened them his companion was looking at him quizzically.

'Found something after all?'

'Could be. I don't need to see any more. Bolling may need this directory.'

'I guess it'll still be here. I guess they've cancelled his cleaner. Tell Bolling to buzz if he wants it bagged for delivery.'

The two men left the house and Odhiambo watched as the policeman set the locks.

'Thanks. Sorry to trouble you. But it just may prove to have been worthwhile.'

'And you're not saying, right?' The detective laughed. 'That's OK, buddy. Where you heading?'

Taking advantage of his companion's friendliness, Odhiambo found himself with a lift to his next destination.

Cari Odhiambo had returned to her office, which gave every sign of business despite the fact of it being a Saturday afternoon. She rang the home number of her quarry but there was no reply. She tried his personal office number and was pleasantly surprised when the voice of the man she was seeking answered. He had excused himself on the grounds of having someone in his office, and promised to call back, exhorting her to stay put. Keeping her head low to avoid the New York praetorian guard, Cari tried to concentrate on a paper on GATT negotiations. This she quickly abandoned – you needed to be in a quiet and rested state to grapple with tariffs and trade – and then she fiddled with her computer. She almost welcomed the interruption when her secretary, returning from a late lunch, discovered her presence.

'You're supposed to be staying away. You've got enough on your plate without worrying about us. Although we need sympathy, with the men from New York all over us.'

'I'm just killing time before an appointment. Don't worry, I'll be out of your hair again in a minute. Why are you here on a Saturday afternoon?'

'Oh, the New York men want everything done like yesterday, and Cindy is too broken up to come in. Any news of your father? It must be terrible not knowing.'

'No, no news. And yes, it is terrible. That's why I'm trying to keep busy. Keep from brooding.'

'And your Mum. How's she taking it?'

Cari felt a stab of guilt – an increasingly frequent assault on her conscience. They were leaving her alone too much. The trouble was, her mother had retreated into a private inner world and didn't seem to want company, even the company of her own daughter.

'Oh, OK in the circumstances. Yes, I know, I should be home with her.'

Cari's secretary realised she had touched a raw nerve and sought a change of subject.

'I heard Miss Eves has issued an attack on IBID. A journalist friend told me at lunch. She's alleging corruption and what have you somewhere in Africa. The trouble is, I gather she's getting at us too. Blaming poor Glen – Mr Hills. It's not fair when he's dead.' The secretary's voice broke. 'Do you think I should tell those guys?' She gestured at the wall but in the general direction of the office housing the New York men. 'I guess it'll be in the *Washington Post* tomorrow.'

'If she's issued a press release see if you can get hold of a copy. But, yes, you'd better tell them so that they're prepared. Damn the woman.'

As she spoke there came the insistent low tone of the telephone. Cari lifted the receiver.

'Cari Bito. Metroarcs.'

'Cari, it's Chuck. Sorry for keeping you waiting, but if at long last you're chasing me I needed to be alone to respond appropriately. Must be my lucky day.'

'Chuck. Thanks for calling back. Yes, it's been too long, but I need to see you urgently. Want to ask for your help.'

'Not something you want to do on the phone, right?'

'Exactly. I'll come by, if that's all right? If you can fit me in.'

'Any time for you, honey. But somehow I get the impression it's not my body you want but my brain. Any clue you can give me as to the type of pitch – fastball or curve?'

'I'll explain when I get there. It's kind of difficult, embarrassing even. I'm sorry.'

There was the slightest of pauses, then a chuckle.

141

'OK, mystery lady. Any reason's good enough for me if it brings you to me. You on your way?'

'On my way, Chuck. And, Chuck, thanks.'

Another chuckle, but a wry one.

'I'd be one happy camper if I hadn't heard that your husband's here too. He's a big one, I understand.'

Cari replaced the receiver and, ignoring the curious look she was getting from her secretary, hurried from the office. As it was a Saturday, the homeward-bound traffic did not cause a major delay. And for the same reason she found a parking spot near the Treasury building. She fed the meter and glanced at her watch – yes, it was past five; James would be seeing Musoke now. She found her way into the annexe building where Chuck Bayer had told her he worked and, after the usual checking and issue of a visitor's clip-on badge, was directed to his office on the ninth floor.

'Cari! I'd forgotten just how beautiful you are.' He was out in the corridor as she left the elevator. You're not bad yourself, thought Cari, looking appreciatively at the slim, handsome black agent. Dammit, she thought, he might even be younger than me. I'm getting old. Bayer leaned forward and they touched cheeks briefly and chastely. 'Come on into my little cell.'

It was small compared to Cari's spacious office, but she knew enough about government to know that power and office size were not perfectly correlated. Small and tidy. Maybe he was just too good to be true.

'It's lovely to see you, Chuck.' She allowed herself to be guided to a standard issue straight chair. Her host parked himself on the corner of his desk and looked down on her with a smile. 'And I feel guilty about this after neglecting you so. I know I promised lunch, but what with having to go to England and see if my husband was in one piece it's been dreadful. But I need your help, Chuck, and I can't explain why – not fully anyhow.'

Bayer's mouth turned down as he listened to her fast, almost gabbled delivery.

'And you sound as if you've no time either. I was going to suggest going out for a beer while we talk.'

'Oh I'd love to, Chuck, but you're right, I haven't the time.'

'OK.' Bayer moved back to his own desk chair. 'Fire away.'

'We've – that's James, my husband, and me – we've got ourselves in the middle of a big problem. My Dad's been kidnapped, but before that a friend of his who worked in IBID was murdered and now my boss, Glen Hills, has been murdered also.' As she spoke it sounded fantastic to her own ears. Summarised in a sentence, the events of the last week were unbelievable. Cari watched Bayer's face anxiously. Would he be totally incredulous? She didn't have time to go into full explanations. 'I don't know how much of this you had heard, but it's all true.'

Bayer's face showed no emotion.

'I didn't know about your father. That's awful. You must give me more fill-in. The two murders, yes, I've heard of them.'

Cari allowed her desperation to show through in her voice.

'Chuck, just imagine how I feel. My father, my boss and a friend of my father's. You see, the IBID man, Chivers was his name, was a Kenyan in fact. He and Dad worked together once. The two murders – well, they look as if the connection there is some big-scale corruption in an IBID project in Nigeria. But Dad's kidnapping can't have anything to do with that. James thinks there's a Kenyan political angle to it. Now he's under pressure to get on a plane back to Nairobi, preferably with me with him.'

Bayer smiled.

'Well, we gotta see what we can do to stop that, right?' He leaned forward, serious now. 'Tell me, Cari, why have you come to me? I'm anxious to help but what are you expecting of me?'

The crucial moment had come and Cari suddenly found herself losing her nerve. She might be about to cause considerable embarrassment, and any hope of information was a very long shot indeed.

'I don't know how to put this exactly. Forgive me, but, well . . . oh hell, out with it, woman. Chuck, one hears things, you know, from mutual friends. About your real job, I mean.' Cari watched Bayer's face carefully, but his expression remained one of benign puzzlement. 'The pressure on James is coming from a man called Musoke. In the Embassy. I just wondered if you knew anything about him? I mean, is he a sort of intelligence man or just a functionary? There, I know I'm stupid, but I'm worried what may be happening to James.' Her voice cracked. 'After all, when your father disappears your mind starts imagining things. James has had his problems in Kenya before.'

Bayer stared at the woman a moment or two longer as she lapsed into silence. God, she was beautiful, but there it was, you win some, but not all. He got up and came round his desk to his original perch on the corner beside her. He leaned forward and spoke softly.

143

'Cari, you mustn't listen to all you hear. It's a great coincidence that I do know who you mean.' Having got the mandatory lie out of the way he didn't bother to try and rationalise the coincidence if indeed her supposition was wrong. 'Musoke has been seen associating with some local characters, or rather non-locals but active locally, that meant he interested certain people. I was asked to find out something about him. Whether he was stepping outside his terms of reference, shall we say. Yes, he's the intelligence man in the Embassy. We have no problems with Kenya, of course. Friendly country. Glad to see it doing well. So, as long as he's discreet – no problem.' He paused, choosing his next words carefully. 'So if Musoke is the guy handing your man a one-way ticket home, it's likely the strings are being pulled by his security people at home. That's just an inspired guess, of course.'

Cari heard what she had come to find out, but it was his first comment that she hung on to.

'What do you mean, non-locals? Not Kenyans presumably? People he sees, I mean.'

'No, not Kenyans. Well, they may have come from Africa originally, who knows. Men who are trading in goods on which no tax has been paid and who declare no income.'

'You mean drugs. Stop being so damn obscure, Chuck.'

'OK, Cari. Yeah, we've got Jamaicans here trying to get a hold on the market. Your Mr Musoke has been seen around. No indication he's into drugs, mind.'

Cari's mind was racing.

'The men who took Dad. The porter said they were West Indian. You think . . .' She was interrupted by the buzz of the telephone on the desk. Bayer muttered an apology and picked up the receiver. Cari could hear the voice of the caller and to her amazement found it familiar.

'I'm sorry to trouble you, but I'm trying to trace a Miss Bito. Miss Cari Bito.'

Bayer frowned and looked questioningly at his visitor.

'Yes, Miss Bito is with me. Who is this?'

'It's her secretary. I have an urgent message for her.'

'Hold on.' He handed the receiver to Cari. 'It's your office.'

Cari took the phone.

'Yes, it's Cari. How did you know where I was? In my log. Chuck under C. Oh, well, that's good detective wo –' Bayer, watching, saw her face suddenly tense and freeze. 'What? . . . Oh, no . . . It can't be.

Oh, my God ... Where? ... OK ... Right, I've got it ... Yes, and thanks.'

Bayer took the receiver from her unresisting hand as it fell into her lap. As he replaced it he placed his other hand on her shoulder.

'What's wrong, Cari? What is it?'

'Oh, Chuck. This is a nightmare. I can't take any more. That was my secretary. The police called. There's been another killing and they've arrested James!'

18

Odhiambo had been deposited by his new police friend on the corner of the block containing the bar where he had agreed to meet Musoke. He was now a few minutes early, so he walked past it at a leisurely pace in a practice he had heard described here in the States as 'casing the joint'. It was a typical Washington downtown bar, capturing at this time of day the thirsty businessman leaving his office, consisting of a long bar at which a line of men were sitting and a row of small tables along the wall where couples or small groups could drink and talk and be tempted to eat from a surprisingly extensive menu. Odhiambo walked on to the corner of the next block for no particular reason, or rather, when he rationalised it, because he needed to establish some order in the maelstrom of his mind. He had the solution of at least part of the puzzle, he was sure of it, but he needed to understand the logistics involved and who was pulling whose strings. He had begun to see the picture emerging, but there were still pieces that were out of place. Perhaps he should have gone straight to Bolling and stood Musoke up, but he believed that Musoke was the man who could adjust the pieces and perhaps bring together what appeared to be two independent pictures.

Odhiambo retraced his steps and pushed open the door to the bar. It was growing dark and the inside presented a contrast of a brightly lit bar and shadowy tables lit by small individual lamps in the wall. If one wanted a drink with a lady one need not be conspicuous about it. This discretion on the part of management did however present Odhiambo with a problem; the row of tables was long and it was impossible to pick out the faces at the more distant ones. It hardly seemed practical to walk the length examining the occupants, so Odhiambo compromised, walked half-way down the bar and eased himself on to a spare stool. He at least was conspicuous, so Musoke could make himself known if present. No one exhibited any interest, however, except a young barman. Odhiambo ordered a draught Miller Lite and kept an eye on the door.

Ten minutes later he knew something was wrong. It was not just that Musoke was late – ten minutes was trivial, especially for a Kenyan, he knew that. No, his Luo instincts told him that he was going to wait in vain and he had learned to trust such intimations when they expressed themselves as forcefully in his mind as now, reinforced by a shivery feeling that seemed to course up and down his spine.

'Another one, sir?'

Odhiambo looked at his glass, which was two-thirds empty. He shook his head.

'No. Not at the moment. I'm waiting for someone. A shortish, heavily built African. You haven't seen someone like that?'

The barman looked at Odhiambo with a clear message in the downward twist of the mouth and the sceptical raise of his eyebrows. How do you expect me to notice one black guy? The single word merely underlined it.

'Sorry.'

He started to move away, but Odhiambo leaned forward.

'Wait just a second. I've seen people appear from up that end.' Odhiambo gesticulated to the darker recesses of the room. 'Is there a door there? From the street?'

'Not the street, no. From the elevators for this building. It's the way up from the garage if you park there.'

The barman moved away and Odhiambo picked up his glass and took another swallow of beer. Would Musoke come by car? Probably. It was too far from the Embassy to be a light walk. Why had he nominated this bar, anyway? Why not one closer to the Embassy?

He caught the barman's attention once more.

'I'll have that other beer please.'

Quickly and deftly the order was filled and placed in front of him.

'You want to pay now or keep the tab running?'

Odhiambo had a ten dollar note ready and held it out.

'Now. Thanks.'

Change was expertly produced from a wallet in the barman's

apron. Odhiambo pushed two one dollar bills back to the barman's side.

'For you. Tell me – are there any Embassy offices above here? In this building, I mean.' The barman pocketed the notes.

'Your friend a dip, is he? Yeah, two or three of them have offices in this building. Just for visas, I think. You know, it's where you go if you want a visa. There's a list in the hall by the elevators. List of the offices, I mean.'

Odhiambo nodded his gratitude.

'And they'd have reserved spaces in the garage, right?'

'Sure. You see it painted on the wall, so and so associates or embassy or whatever. There's two levels; reserved places are on the first.'

Odhiambo pushed the saucer with the remaining change across the bar.

'Thanks again. I'm just going to see if his car's there. If a black guy asks for a large black guy, tell him I'll be back.'

'Sure. Thanks. Hope you find him.'

Odhiambo walked to the door he had enquired about. He scanned the faces at the tables as he passed, but no Musoke. Nor did he expect him. He obviously was not in the bar. What was less clear to Odhiambo was why he was heading for the garage. No good reason. Except maybe Musoke chose this bar because the Embassy had car spaces here. So free parking for Musoke. But he wouldn't be sitting in his car, would he?

Once through the door Odhiambo could see the elevators. He crossed towards them. Sure enough, next to them was a board with a list of tenants. Odhiambo scanned the metal lettering. Yes, there it was, 'Embassy of Republic of Kenya: Visa Office. Hours 9.30 a.m. – 12.00.' Inside a list of destinations included Garage Level A and Garage Level B. Odhiambo descended to Level A and found himself in a typical concrete underground car-park – bare walls, painted lines emanating from them and substantial pillars giving evidence of the size of building they were supporting. To his left he could see the commencement of what was presumably the entry and exit ramp. Cars occupied some of the allocated slots but a number of them were empty. Again, Odhiambo wondered why he was here but the answer, irrational though it might be, was that every cell of his subconscious had joined in series to create a charge in his brain that said, yes, this was the course of action to take. The garage was lit well enough to read the painted reservation signs.

Odhiambo turned right but reached the side wall without seeing what he was looking for. He retraced his path and continued on past the door by which he had entered: seven or eight slots later he saw an empty bay with the words 'Kenyan Embassy' painted on the floor. Next to it was a Japanese saloon looking small compared to the Cadillac parked beyond it. As he approached the rear Odhiambo saw the number plate had a diplomatic tag. He felt the hair prickle against the nape of his neck. He peered in and for just a mini-second saw nothing, then he did see it – a body slumped from the driver's seat with the head face down on the passenger seat. He yanked at the door handle with unneeded strength; bending his head in, he touched the hand that lay across the gear lever – the hand was still warm, but there was no pulse. He leaned further in, resting his hand on the hip of the dead man. Looking down, he did not need to turn the body – even face down he could see who it was. He could have waited in the bar for ever. Musoke would never have arrived.

Pulling his head out of the car, Odhiambo stood for some time in thought. His mind was full once more of racing, jumbled thoughts. With an effort he cleared his mind of everything but the options for the present moment. These quickly narrowed, for with the distinctive screech of tyres on the concrete floor of an enclosed space a car entered the garage and passed him before pulling into an empty bay a few places further along from where he stood. A woman got out and started to walk towards the door leading to the elevators. She glanced nervously at the large black man standing irresolutely beside a car with the door open. It was Odhiambo's move and he could see only one play.

'Excuse me, er . . . miss. There's been an accident here. Would you stop at the ground floor and ask one of the bar staff to call an ambulance and . . . er . . . the police?'

The woman stood still as if shocked into stone.

'What . . . what sort of accident?'

Odhiambo concentrated hard to keep his voice reassuring. The last thing he wanted was a hysterical woman.

'I'm not sure. The driver of this car is unconscious. Please hurry. I'll wait here.'

For a moment he thought she was not going to obey. Finally her arm moved to raise her hand to her mouth and as if this unlocked a mechanism her legs started to function. She half ran to the door and vanished from Odhiambo's sight.

Odhiambo turned back to the car and the body of Musoke. He bent inside the car once more to look more closely at the body. He could see now the growing stain on the passenger seat and, as he pulled Musoke's shoulder to turn the body slightly, he could see the signs of an entry wound in the side of the neck. He removed his head from the car for the second time and turned to examine the concrete of the empty parking bay on which he was standing. There was a tiny pool of water and further forward a spot or two of oil. Difficult, of course, to tell but Odhiambo thought it likely they were fresh deposits from the air-conditioner and oil filter of a car that had occupied one of the two Kenyan Embassy slots and waited for Musoke to drive in and occupy the other.

Once more he turned his attention to the car, this time opening the rear door on his side. Musoke's body was coatless but Odhiambo had caught sight of a jacket that had slipped from the back seat on to the floor. He hesitated but only for a second. Retrieving the jacket he removed a wallet and a notebook from the inside pocket before dropping the jacket on to the seat. A quick look at the inside of the wallet revealed nothing but dollar notes and credit cards. The notebook was in fact a pocket diary which seemed to contain only the usual abbreviated notes of times of meetings and appointments. Odhiambo found the page for the current week. There were two entries that gave a time and the letter M. Odhiambo's appointment that he was not destined to make was shown as '5–0'. Two other entries caught Odhiambo's eye. 'Ring P-A' was one and 'Update P-A' the other. From behind him he heard the noise of a door shutting – damn, no more time. He quickly bent inside and replaced the wallet and diary in the jacket as a voice said, 'What's up?'

Odhiambo found he was being approached warily by two men, one, by his attire, a member of the bar staff, the other a large burly man who was presumably a customer who had offered his physical presence as insurance.

'There's a dead man in this car. Have you called the police?'

There was no need for the new arrivals to answer Odhiambo's question for the noise of a siren intervened, growing in volume and accompanied, shortly before the car swung into sight, by the tortured squeal of the tyres.

Two minutes later and Odhiambo found himself facing the police car, legs apart while hands patted and probed his body. He felt his anger rising: this was ridiculous – up to now he had gained a positive perception of the police in the capital and across the river, but this time he seemed to have struck a couple of morons who seemed to engage in a cross-talk act.

'You run down the body, Art,' said the big-framed, black member of the duo. 'I'll shake down my brother here.'

The slimmer, shorter and white policeman waited for his cue.

'This stiff look like one o' yours too, Mo.'

'Don't make no difference once you're worm-bait, Art. Ain't no racists 'mong those worms.'

'Reckon you're right there. Get right down to it, meat's meat.'

Odhiambo tried to break up the routine.

'Look, I told you. I just found the body.'

'But he knows the stiff, ain't that what he said, Art?'

'That's how I heard it. Came right out with it.'

'I had an appointment, for Chrissake. I was looking for him.'

'Sure found him, brother, seems to me. Found him good.'

'And he weren't going no place, no sirree.'

Odhiambo gritted his teeth and stayed leaning against the car. He didn't want to make any sudden moves – this pair might be trigger-happy as well as irritating.

'My brother here's clean.'

'So's his friend here. Leastways no hardware. Ain't too clean. Lotta blood here, Mo.'

Odhiambo was relieved to hear other vehicles making their tyre-protesting arrival. Any newcomers would be an improvement. Indeed, relief of sorts was at hand: an ambulance was followed by an unmarked car containing a detective who seemed as irritated by Mo and Art as Odhiambo was. After ensuring that activity around the car was organised and authorised, and splitting the duo by detailing Mo to get names off the bystanders who had grown to four, the detective pulled Odhiambo to one side.

'You wanna tell me the story, mister? Like what's going on here?'

Odhiambo commenced with reference to being dropped off by a policeman, said he was due to meet a fellow Kenyan and explained what had happened after he entered the bar.

'So why did you come down here?'

Odhiambo realised this was the tricky question. Luo instinct would not be a persuasive answer.

'He didn't turn up at the bar. So I went searching.'

'You thought he might be just sitting in his car here?'

'Well, not exactly.'

'So what is exactly your answer?'

The detective was interrupted by the policeman, Art, who was waving a folder.

'Hey. This guy told Mo and me his name was Odambo or something like that. This here's some airline tickets. Looks like they got the same name. They were in the stiff's jacket.'

Another car heralded further reinforcements, but Odhiambo had a sinking feeling he was destined for the station. He needed to think carefully. He had no intention of revealing all he knew, at least on this side of the river. He needed to speak to Bolling. Also Cari.

The detective was looking at the open wallet that Art had also handed over. He pulled out Musoke's identity card and then looked at Odhiambo.

'This Musoke, he's a diplomat.'

'I guess so. He was with the Embassy.'

There was a hurried consultation with the last arrivals which quickly led to a sense of greater care and purpose in the organisation and urgent messages being sent from the car radio. Then Odhiambo's prediction came true; he was ushered into one of the police cars and driven off.

Bayer had insisted on driving Cari to the precinct where her husband was being detained. He had some difficulty in keeping her calm; she seemed to think that events had got out of control. Well, if her father had disappeared and her husband had been arrested, he supposed she had good reason to think so. He ushered the woman into the scruffy entrance and insisted on her sitting while he made enquiries at the desk. He returned with what he hoped was good news.

'He's not under arrest, Cari. He's just been pulled in for questioning, that's all.'

'But who's been killed? And where does James come into it?'

'I don't know. An Embassy man, apparently.' He looked at the woman, who was chewing the corner of her lip. 'It could be the man we were talking about. Anyway, he'll be able to tell you. You'll be allowed to see him soon.'

Bayer's confidence was misplaced. Odhiambo had asked for a call to be made to Lieutenant Bolling. The detective complied, only to be told that Bolling was unavailable as he was interviewing a

151

suspect in the Roosevelt Island killing; he then decided to put Odhiambo on ice, as he expressed it, until an increasingly confusing situation was clarified.

19

Bolling had hopes of Gilbride. He recognised the type, full of bluster and confidence, but when you applied the right pressure at the right point he would spill everything he knew. He was, in short, the complete opposite of Ernesto Kraxma. Bolling allowed the interview he had just concluded to run through his mind as he waited while Gilbride gave various standard personal details to the detective conducting the interview. Kraxma had sat and smoked, impassive, rumpled with tie loosened, but his hands were steady and his eyes met Bolling's without shifting away.

'You admit that you and Glen Hills worked closely on the fertiliser project?'

'Of course. It is my responsibility. Hills represents the importer. It is proper we talk, no?'

'We've evidence there's a scam going on, Mr Kraxma. A big con-job.'

'Pardon? In what context you speak?'

'Your fertiliser, Mr Kraxma. When it gets to the farmer it's no bloody good. Someone is selling bum goods and you're financing them and Hills is shipping them.'

'You make big mistake. Fertiliser, many thousand tons go from North Africa to Lagos. Inspected on departure and arrival.'

'Come on, Mr Kraxma. Mr Chivers discovered something was wrong, didn't he? He was going to blow the whistle. Then someone smashed his head in.'

'If Chivers discovered fraud, someone after him will discover also. Chivers not only man capable of evaluation. So killing Chivers does nothing to hide anything. You right, possibly. Something wrong in distribution system in Nigeria. Would be not new. But doesn't mean I organise it. Or Hills.'

Kraxma turned his head to look at the detective accompanying Bolling as if looking for confirmation.

'It's not "if", Mr Kraxma, not "if" Chivers discovered fraud, he *did* discover it. We've got the figures he was working on.' At this point Kraxma's head had swung back and his eyes focused again on Bolling. 'Putting your fertiliser on the plots didn't make a damn bit of difference. The corn or whatever was just as well without it.'

Kraxma's glowering look was one of anger rather than fear. He was going to be a tough nut to crack.

'I tell you, already. Yes. Looks like Nigerians up to something.' A heavy shrug. 'This is, what you say, par for course out there. But we will find out and fix it. Hills . . .' Another shrug distanced Kraxma from the dead man. 'Hills, I don't know. Not possible to ask him now. But me, I have no, what you say, insider contact.'

Bolling had pulled his trump card.

'Your officer, Caradonna, is on her way back here. She was summoned back by your bosses, but IBID received a telex this afternoon from the UN. She was already planning to return double quick. Wishes to report on significant findings, it said. Concerned about security. You know what that means, Kraxma. She's found the local end of the operation and fears for her safety. She's ready to blow the whistle. Also, I got some friendly agencies here to do a bit of checking for me. The local distribution is handled by a firm called Aginvest. Dubious lot, is what I'm hearing. But more interesting still, my friends tell me Metroarcs owns controlling interest in Aginvest. You and Hills got this whole deal sewn up, right?'

'Then you go talk to Metroarcs. Maybe if this correct we've been slow. Caradonna not too experienced. She not see the problem soon enough. But IBID will make full enquiry.'

'Come off it, Kraxma. Hills couldn't run this past an old hand like you. Especially as you and Hills were close buddies.' At last Bolling caught some reaction in the other man's eyes. 'Oh yes, Mr Kraxma. We know you were a regular visitor to Mr Hills' home in Blackwater. And there's another thing – Hills couldn't have killed Chivers. And he sure as hell didn't slit himself open. But I believe you were there, in the building, when Chivers was working late. You must have thought he was getting too close. When were you last on Roosevelt Island, Mr Kraxma?'

Kraxma retreated into himself. Bolling could see the thought processes at work. The stubby fingers reached for and extracted another cigarette from a pack that was nearly as crumpled as its owner, but the eyes stayed focused on the wall behind the two detectives. At last, he seemed to shake himself.

'Look, Mr Homicide Detective. I am responsible person in

responsible institution.' He raised the hand holding the cigarette as Bolling opened his mouth. 'No, you hear me this time to finish. Because we are not, what you say, cowboys and we want to be open, I tell you all I know. Even what I not know. Only guess. OK?'

Bolling nodded.

'That's what I'm here for, Mr Kraxma. A little co-operation.'

'So. For some time I worry about Nigeria project. Some things not smell right. You will find memos on file. From me. Saying this. I warn Caradonna but she is not agriculture expert. Nor she knows Nigerians. So my responsibility but I am busy man. Lots of problems in all projects. Nothing simple in Africa, I tell you. Now no need for me. Independent evaluator. Best of all worlds, no? Let him do necessary checks. So I stay and go spend time with Hills. Hills take close interest. Too close, my nose says. So I hope to find out what Hills doing. Hills plays cards close to heart, no? Chivers returns like man on to something. Caradonna worried. I say to her, "Go back only this time never mind farmers. Find out what Aginvest doing. If Chivers knows what is smelling, important we have plan." '

Bolling listened in growing frustration. It sounded like Kraxma had his trail covered, but Bolling had listened long enough to other plausible liars. He was probably telling the truth on details, but his innocence was another thing.

'So, what is your hunch as to what's going on?'

'I think perhaps fertiliser gets in OK. But somewhere in Nigeria it takes wrong road. Ends up in other country. Maybe, Cameroon. Price is high there and supplies good now. Farmers in Nigeria get something else in original bags, no? Metroarcs get paid twice. Farmers get the shit.' Kraxma recognised his pun. 'Or maybe not even that, no? Maybe they be happy with that to make crops grow. They get something not so good.'

'So you put it all on to Metroarcs? You and IBID are the guys in the white hats?'

Kraxma shrugged.

'Maybe we slow on, what you say, uptake. But IBID will make full enquiry now. But you must understand. This is Africa. Nigeria. Not the USA. Not Virginia. Maybe Hills not know either.'

Bolling snorted.

'You make it sound like any old problem. You forget, Kraxma, two men are dead. Two men who could have told us what is going on. You haven't come fully clean, have you, Mr Kraxma? And the people who could have called you on it are dead.'

154

But all to no avail. Kraxma had grunted and expostulated and shaken his heavy head, but nothing more of any relevance had he said. Now Bolling had Gilbride. If he couldn't get this guy to wet himself, Bolling reckoned he would need to think of early retirement.

He had received a tip-off that Gilbride had visited Hills the night before Hills was killed. Then when he sent a detective to elicit details it seemed that Gilbride had dropped out of sight. It was fortuitous that one of Bolling's men was talking to the IBID security chief when Gilbride came into the IBID building. Gilbride claimed to have been staying with a friend.

Bolling waited while the other detective extracted from Gilbride an account of his visit to Hills' Maryland home. At last, he tapped his junior on the thigh, extracted the chewed pencil from his mouth and leaned forward.

'Mr Gilbride. I'm anxious you know where you stand. You're helping us with a serious murder investigation, so I'm sure you want to tell us all you know, like a responsible, eminent citizen, am I right?'

Sean Gilbride looked at the new speaker with a mixture of defiance and nervousness.

'Sure and that's what you keep telling me. I'm "helping". That wouldn't be to stop me asking for a lawyer now, would it?'

'Lawyer? Why would you need a lawyer, Mr Gilbride? Just some information is what I'm looking for. From a lawful citizen.'

Gilbride took his time replying. Then he seemed to come to a decision.

'Right y'are then. I'll take you at your word. I have nothing to hide, d'you hear? Apart from knowing Hills and going to ask him about the dirt on Nigeria. And that was for SEND, not myself, mind.'

'If you thought Hills and his company were pulling something, why did you think Hills would talk to you about it?'

'You never can tell. Look at the *Washington Post* fellows. They keep asking questions is what they do and occasionally someone spills the beans. So it was worth a try, it was.'

'Come on, Mr Gilbride. You're a busy theatre director. You take the time to drive all the way into the sticks just to play at being an investigative journalist? Get real!'

Gilbride shrugged.

'Sally Eves was getting impatient. If you know of Sally you'd know that when she's in a hurry she expects you to be up and doing.'

'And Hills denied all knowledge of anything wrong. That's what you told the officer, here. Right?'

'Sure, that's what I said. Didn't necessarily believe him, mind. But he wasn't about to give much away.'

'And so untroubled was he by your visit, he rushes back to DC, makes an appointment to see someone on Roosevelt Island and gets himself sliced apart.'

Gilbride gave a little theatrical shudder.

'Can't stand blood myself. Terrible business, no doubt of that. Yes, maybe I rocked him a little. He decides to share his worries. I don't know what his thought processes were.'

'Let's stop dancing around, Gilbride. We're not on stage in one of your productions. I'll tell you what I think happened. One of two options. One, you knew something about Hills and went there to put the arm on him. See if you could get him to give you what you wanted. You named someone else. He blustered, but was worried. He rushes back to report you're on to something. Only instead of something nasty happening to you it happens to him. Or . . .' Bolling pointed his pencil at the man opposite. 'Or, you know more than he or anyone believed. But he hung tough. He threatened you. Went back to see a man about doing you over. But you followed. You were scared maybe. So you thought better not let him organise any grief for you. Better get your blow in first. Maybe you do need a lawyer, Mr Gilbride.'

Gilbride's already pale face was now an unhealthy grey colour.

'You're mad. I'm not involved, I tell you. You're building a house of straw. You've no evidence of any of this.'

Bolling rolled on, ignoring the protestations.

'And you dropped out of sight, either because you didn't want to be interviewed about Hills' murder or because you're afraid that whoever eliminated Hills might come after you next because of what you told Hills. Which is it?'

'It's rubbish you're talking. It's nonsense, I tell you.'

The words were emphatic, but the voice was faltering.

Bolling leaned forward and tapped the table with the pencil tip. It was time to gamble.

'We're interviewing someone else in here right now. And you know who he is. You knew Hills' collaborator. You had a source, didn't you, Gilbride? That's why you were useful to SEND. You're well connected in, shall we say, certain circles. You hear things from your friends. They're the gossipy kind, aren't they? You have such a friend in IBID, don't you? If you want to be clean you gotta come clean with me now. I've no time to keep horsing about.'

'You mean you've arrested . . .' Gilbride stopped himself. Bolling could almost see the mind working overtime behind the staring eyes. 'Has he confessed? I mean, whoever you've arrested.' Bolling smiled, hoping it had the enigmatic quality of the Sphinx. 'Look. Right y'are. I'll tell you all I know. 'Tisn't much, mind. But what there is you shall know. Then you let me get on with my life. There's a bunch of expensive talent sitting around across the river at the Center waiting to be rehearsed.'

'Tell on, Mr Gilbride, and then we'll see. Co-operation, that's what is needed here.'

'Look. Hills was in cahoots with a guy in IBID, sure. They were getting rich on some fertiliser rip-off. I don't know whether the first fellow to get murdered knew something. That's what I was trying to confirm, d'you see? I told Hills I could document their relationship. But he didn't crack. Stayed pretty cool. But I thought I had pushed him nearer the edge, that's all. I told Sally, Sally Eves, I told her it was worth sticking to Hills; keep after him. She told me he was dead.'

'And who's the collaborator Hills was working with? The one in IBID.'

The final hesitation and then Gilbride took the plunge.

'A middle-ranking official. Responsibility for steering the Nigeria project through the IBID board. Kraxma. Ernesto Kraxma. Mid-European, still has a thick accent. He and Hills were in each other's pockets for some time when the project was being set up. Lately they've been getting their heads together. Or so I'm told.'

It was Bolling's turn to hesitate. Now for the biggy.

'Who's your source, Gilbride? You've got to go all the way now.'

'A man called Fulton, Guy Fulton. Nasty bit of work, if you want to know. But I'd met him . . . er . . . socially, shall we say. He likes young theatrical talent.' Gilbride laughed with apparent amusement. 'Younger the better. He's in IBID. He's got it in for Kraxma and Hills. Wanted them exposed. Their deeds exposed, I mean.' Again, the laugh.

At last, thought Bolling. I'm nearly there.

'So you went to Hills claiming you could tie him to Kraxma and the fertiliser scam. You revealed your source.'

'No, not exactly. I kept Guy Fulton up my sleeve, as it were. There's another IBID man I knew of, involved with security, a Kenyan. I met him once when I was with Sally Eves at some IBID do – she was involved with the head of IBID. This man, Katawi, was like Faucon's security man. Anyway, I sought him out. He knew Kraxma, of course. I asked him if he knew Hills. He said yes. The daughter of a Kenyan friend of his worked for him. I asked him if he knew Kraxma and Hills worked together. I was looking to confirm Fulton's story, you see. He didn't know, or he wasn't prepared to say. All he said was he'd seen Hills at some party the night the IBID murder happened. So I bluffed Hills a bit, I used Katawi as my source when Hills asked me, rather than Fulton.'

'So Hills would have had no reason to contact Fulton when he got back to DC?'

'Fulton? No. Well, not as far as I know. Why should he? You're never thinking . . .'

'Fulton was trying to nail Hills. You said it, Gilbride. Hills and Kraxma.'

'For sure, but in a professional sense. Do Kraxma down, really. In a career sense. Jealousy or whatever. In any case, I never mentioned Fulton to Hills.'

'But did you mention Kraxma?'

'Of course! I told you. Hills' association with Kraxma was why I was there.'

'Did Hills admit . . .' Bolling stopped. The door had opened and a female police officer stood uncertainly in the opening. 'Yes? What is it? I'm interviewing.'

'I'm sorry, sir. The DC police are on the line. They called earlier. They say it's urgent.'

Bolling sighed.

'OK. OK.' He turned back to Gilbride. 'Right, Gilbride. You're wise to be now co-operating. Go through the details with this officer here. More fully, so he can write up a statement. I'll be back.'

With a nod to the detective who had commenced the interview, Bolling followed the messenger from the room. She held the door for him and spoke after closing it behind them.

'It's a Captain Williamson. Some diplomat's been killed and he's holding someone who knows you.' She looked at a scribbled note. 'A James Odhiambo. Kenyan. Same nationality as the victim.'

Bolling almost clutched the woman for support. This was getting too much.

158

'Holy Mother of Mary! What's that bastard gone and done now? Where's the damn phone?'

20

Cari Odhiambo had finally succeeded in seeing her husband. Her friend Chuck had got in to see the local Captain of Police and things started to happen, including, Cari gathered, contact with Lieutenant Bolling. She was ushered into a small room already seemingly full with the large frames of James and an even larger policeman. Cari restrained herself from rushing to embrace her husband. He was looking solemn and intense and she instinctively knew he would not want displays of sentiment in front of his guard or watch-dog.

'James, darling. Are you OK?' She took his hands in hers and managed a smile. 'Whatever happened?'

'I'm sorry, Cari. It must have been a shock. Are you holding together?' He saw the small nod, but was not deceived. 'Listen, sit down, we haven't much time. There's no need to worry. At least, on my behalf. I'll be out of here soon, but soon may not be in time. There's things to do. OK? Are you able to take things in?'

'James Odhiambo! I'm not some weak little girl from the bush. If you're holding up then so can I. What's going on?' She sat down on one of the two plain plastic chairs as James gingerly lowered himself into the other. The policeman shifted a wad of gum from one corner of his mouth to another and leaned his shoulder against the wall. He hadn't been given any particular instructions. Presumably the mike was on, so whatever they talked about wasn't his specific concern. 'Who's dead, James? And how did it happen?'

'Ssh, Cari. There'll be time for explanations later. The man from the Embassy was shot. Musoke. Look, I think I'm beginning to –'

'Musoke. I guessed as much. Look, James – I went to see a guy I knew vaguely. He's Secret Service or something like that. He confirmed it. Musoke, I mean. He's the state security man here.'

James Odhiambo waved a hand in an impatient gesture.

'Yeah. We don't need the American Secret Service to know that. The question is –'

'It's not just that. Musoke has connections with one of the

Jamaican gangs here. You see what that means. Dad was taken by Jamaicans.'

She had her husband's attention now.

'Is that right? Well done, Cari. Who is this agent of yours, anyway? OK, never mind, now. So that's another piece of the puzzle. It's beginning to –'

'But who killed him, James?'

'Hold on. Time's running out. Bolling's on his way over. I need you to do a couple of things. Get home and check out that your mother's OK. And stay with her. But most important, ring Nairobi. Get hold of Price-Allen.' He saw the grimace of distaste appear on his wife's face. 'Yes, I know. The fact is, I'm pretty sure Musoke was one of Price-Allen's men. Get him at all costs. Then you're going to have to bluff a little. I need confirmation of what I think's going on that involves Sam.'

'James, the important thing is to get you out of here.'

'Leave that to me. Or rather Bolling. You go now and do what I say. It's important for your Dad, for me, for both of us. Now, listen while I tell you what I want you to say to Price-Allen. What's the time? Eight, Saturday night, right? I've almost forgotten what day it is. It's the middle of the night in Kenya. No, early morning. There was a number Musoke had in his diary. It seemed familiar. I've written it down while I've been sitting here. I think it's Price-Allen's home number. Here, you remember it?'

Cari forced herself to pay attention. In the back of her mind she could see the hated figure of the man who had been responsible for her only act of betrayal of her husband during those dreadful last Nairobi days: the sardonic voice, the saturnine smile camouflaged by the ordinary appearance of a white Kenyan businessman, medium height, build, unobtrusive – a typical Nairobi clubman, except for those pale eyes behind which lay the mind of a psychopath.

James Odhiambo watched the play of emotions on that beautiful face that seemed to have aged in recent days. He knew that, of all the reasons why Cari was reluctant to return to Kenya, the fear that Price-Allen would once more envelop them in his scheming was most to the fore. The dawning realisation that his baleful influence extended even here was a considerable shock to her. He waited and saw the internal battle won; she was still his wife, the woman whose inner strengths he was still only learning to comprehend. She nodded.

'When you get hold of Price-Allen, tell him that Musoke is dead – murdered carrying out his orders. Tell him I know who did it. But I don't know who's on which side. As far as he's concerned he can prove where he stands in only one way – proof that your father is safe and free.'

'You know who killed Musoke, James? Then tell the police.'

'Wait, Cari, wait a bit. We're approaching the endgame now – got to be careful about each move. A mistake now could screw it all up. That's why you've got to do your bit with Price-Allen. For the moment we've got him on the defensive. We've got to use that leverage to get guarantees about your father. It's our best chance. Meanwhile, I'll talk to Bolling. I think he's a reasonable guy. Now, when you've spoken to Nairobi, phone me here or phone Bolling if I've left here. I'll leave a message. Then you stay home and look after Abbie.'

'Oh, James. I know you. You're playing with fire again. What are you going to do?'

'Cari, go please. Time is not on our side. I'll be all right. I promise.'

Cari got up. She felt feverish but knew it was a combination of adrenalin and dismay.

'OK. But James, what happens if I can't get Price-Allen? Or he says he doesn't know what I'm talking about. What then?'

'He'll be expecting Musoke to call. I'd bet on it. And when he realises you're serious he'll react. This is a nasty problem he's got here.'

'What problem? What hold have we got on him? Why should he react as you put it?'

'Because he knows, or you can tell him, that I could tell Bolling a story that would have the Americans spitting mad. They don't like diplomats pursuing their national vendettas in their capital. The Kenya government could be embarrassed – after all, we rely on American aid, and it wouldn't thank the man who got it into trouble. On the other hand, if I scratch Bolling's back maybe he'll scratch mine and we can avoid a diplomatic mess. But first, Sam Bito must be freed.'

'Oh God, James. I hope you're right.' Cari turned to go and saw the second large man in the room. She had forgotten they had a silent observer. She turned back. 'What about this officer? I mean, we've been talking . . .'

Odhiambo laughed.

'We've said nothing illegal. Now go, Cari. Get out of here before you run into Bolling.'

Cari left the police station. She had insisted that her friend Chuck return to his duties when he had satisfied himself that James was being held only as a witness. He had given her back her car keys and left in search of a cab. Standing in the dusk of a chilly Washington night she couldn't for some moments remember where Chuck had parked the car. 'Come on,' she said to herself, 'concentrate, woman. Don't become unravelled now.'

She found the car and drove home, struggling to keep her mind on the task of negotiating Roosevelt Bridge and the George Washington Parkway with the Saturday night traffic. An image of the tanned white face with the small, sneering smile kept imposing itself outside the windscreen. Bugger Price-Allen. Why did he haunt her life so? Finally, she gained the drive of the Bito home and, leaving the car unlocked, hurried into the house. Her mother, hearing her arrival, met her at the door.

'Cari, thank God you're back. What's going on?'

Cari's guilt complex came flooding back. In all of this, they – yes, it was James' fault as well – they had left Sam's wife without comfort, news or even notice of what they were up to.

'Mum! Are you OK? What's happened?'

Abbie Bito had gained a sort of ledge on her mounting concern about her husband. A level place where a strange sense of placidity temporarily eased her tortured mind: a respite that helps those at risk of losing all reason through worry to hang on to their sanity. But now tonight's news had removed the level ground and she was frightened as well as worried for her husband.

'On the news. There was an item on the news. A Kenyan diplomat found shot in a garage somewhere. Oh, Cari – I didn't know what to think and I didn't know where you or James were.'

Cari took her mother in her arms. She could feel the trembling in what had always been a sturdy frame.

'It's OK, Mum. I'm sorry. There's been so much going on: Dad, Glen and the guy in IBID. I haven't been able to get my feet on the ground. I shouldn't have left you the way I have. But it's OK. At least I hope it's going to be OK. James thinks he knows what's going on.'

The two women entered the house and Cari poured them both a stiff drink. She talked, but without giving her mother the facts of Musoke's murder and James' detention. That's the trouble, she thought, I still don't trust her to handle it. Yet all my life she's been the rock I could rely on.

'Oh to hell with it. Listen, Mum. I'm insulting you. The fact is I don't know what's going on, but James was on his way to meet the Kenyan who was killed, so the police are questioning him. No, it's OK. He's on good terms with the Rosslyn cop. James thinks he's on to something that may help to get Dad back to us. Don't raise your hopes, but just maybe we're getting somewhere. I'm going to make a call or two. One to Nairobi. Then I'll explain more, OK?'

Abbie Bito looked stunned for a long moment, then she raised a smile.

'Oh Cari, I've been so wanting to feel I'm part of it. I had the feeling you were keeping me away from things. I don't mind so much if I know. What can I do?'

'Nothing, except sit tight. No, wait a minute.' Cari remembered the earlier instruction James had given her over lunch. God, that seemed like an age ago already. It would give her something to do, however useless. 'Look, Mum – James thinks Dad might have something that relates to the old days in Nairobi. Particularly the Omuto affair. He might have forgotten he had it, even. Has Dad got any old boxes, files, bottom drawers?'

Her mother looked doubtful.

'He never talked about those days. He didn't keep anything as far as I know.' The opportunity of a task sank in. 'But he's got a couple of drawers he keeps locked in his study. I know where the key is. I guess it'll be all right if I open them.'

'Sure it will. It's in case there's something that will help.' Although I can't think what, thought Cari. 'OK. Mum, you go to it while I try the phone.'

Bolling stared at Odhiambo across the bare table, his frustration evident in every pore of his pock-marked face.

'And that's all you're prepared to say? That we've ... I've ... been chasing my own shadow and missing the real story? What use is that? I need some facts.'

Odhiambo sighed.

'I'll give you what you want. I just need two pieces of the jigsaw, but they're important pieces. And I can't get them sitting here.'

'If you're not careful you'll be sitting in less comfortable places than this, and for a long time. You admit having an appointment with this guy, Musoke, you meet him in the garage and, boom, he's dead, clutching tickets with your name on.'

'Don't insult my intelligence, Bolling. You don't believe I killed Musoke. The police here don't believe it. I just want to get out from here and bring things to a head.'

'With another body or two, I suppose.' Bolling sat back in his chair with an exclamation of discontent. 'I did you one favour already and you promised to level with me. What did you find in Hills' apartment?'

Odhiambo considered for a moment. He could understand Bolling's impatience. He leaned forward, beckoning his visitor to do likewise, and lowered his voice.

'OK. Although I'm not quite ready with a case, I'll tell you all I know and my theories and hope you decide to play it sensibly. But we can't talk here, you know that. You and I may agree, but could you order these people here to keep their hands off?'

'DC police are an independent jurisdiction from mine, you know that.'

'Exactly. Get me out of here, Bolling, and we'll sit down in a bar and talk. Things are coming to a head. We can't waste more time.'

Bolling's face twisted as if he was in pain although the cause was indecision.

'OK. But you listen here, Odhiambo – you'd better play fair with me. No more stalling, no more grandstanding. I want everything you've got and quickly. Do you read me?'

Odhiambo nodded.

'It's a deal. Now let's get on with it.'

Price-Allen roused himself from sleep at the insistent ringing. The curtains of his bedroom window were not drawn but the view out towards the Athi Plains was still shrouded in darkness. The sky, however, was starting to take on vivid colour. Dawn was at hand. He groaned but reached a hand for the instrument on the bedside table.

'Hello.'

'Is that Price-Allen?'

It took only a second or so for his mind to clear and for the memory trace to be retrieved.

'It is. Am I correct in supposing –'

'Odhiambo. Cari Odhiambo. Speaking from Washington.'

He chuckled.

'Yes, my dear lady, I recognised the voice. And I'm aware of your present location. Although we hope to see you here in –'

'Look, this isn't a social call. God knows you're the last person I'd call unless I had to. I have a message for you from my husband.'

Price-Allen's mind was now in top gear. He was trying to get ahead of his caller. Like a chess player he wanted to see the coming moves. He stalled for a little more time.

'I had hoped my efforts on your behalf when you were last in Nairobi would have softened your attitude to me, dear lady. Not to speak of promotion for –'

'Cut the crap. If my belief that you're a scheming bastard had changed, which it hasn't, it would have been confirmed by your latest effort.'

'I cannot believe you have woken me to insult me. What is your message?'

'James told me to tell you that Musoke is dead. He was killed in a garage here somewhere. Murdered.'

Price-Allen's grip on the receiver tightened. There was a slight pause, then the woman's voice continued.

'Are you still there? I –'

'I hear you. I know of a Musoke in the Embassy there. It is him you mean?'

'Of course. Your man in Washington, James says. No, don't interrupt. Your work means nothing to me. Musoke was due to meet James, but the killer got there first. James says he's getting to the bottom of things, but he needs to know who's playing on whose side.' Price-Allen remained silent. Let the fool woman talk away while he thought. Musoke dead! Why hadn't the Embassy phoned? He listened on. 'Specifically, I'm talking about my father – Samuel Bito. Before James lifts a finger to help you out of the mess here I need proof that he's safe and well. . . . Do you hear me? I need an answer.'

Price-Allen sighed almost theatrically down the phone.

'This talk of sides and messes that I'm in. You're fantasising again, Mrs Odhiambo. You and your husband are always looking for conspiracies.'

'I said cut the crap, Price-Allen. We know each other too well. Where is my father?'

'As it so happens, my dear, I had hoped to get a message to the worthy Inspector about your father. Mr Musoke was the messenger. His unfortunate accident must have prevented him from delivering it.'

'Accident! You call murder an –'

'Never mind semantics. I was sending good news. I can assure you that Dr Bito is alive and well and I have reason to believe he will arrive in Kenya shortly. My message included air-travel authorisation for you both to hurry here.'

'You kidnapped him, you bastard. Why? What are you trying to achieve?'

Price-Allen sighed again, the sigh of a patient martyr to unjustified abuse.

'Please. Don't alienate the only person who can do you some good. Politics are involved in this business as I'm sure your husband has deduced. The Chivers affair precipitated matters, although, in truth, Dr Bito had behaved stupidly. My motive is to ensure Dr Bito's safety and return him to the bosom of his family. No, hear me out. This is very important. To ensure Dr Bito's safety delicate negotiations are involved. I need you here to assist.'

'What about my mother? His wife.'

'What about . . . oh, I see what you mean. Yes, her return can also be expedited. You see, I am willing to do everything in my power.'

There was a long pause. Price-Allen waited patiently. He knew when the bait was being nibbled on.

'I . . . we, we'll need guarantees. Proof. Proof that Dad is there and free.'

'I have known you to be a determined and intelligent young woman. Do not disabuse me of my belief. I'm not asking you to do anything dangerous or illegal. Just come home. Your husband is due back anyway. If you wait there you are wasting precious time.'

'You're holding him as a hostage for us. Why, in God's name? Why?'

'You're being stupid. Now pull yourself together. I've no interest in you. Dr Bito is in danger, but not from me. And your husband could make matters worse by getting in the way there. The course of action I propose is both an order, his duty, and the most sensible for all concerned. That is all I have to say on the matter.'

He could feel the woman fighting for self-control. He smiled. He might yet retrieve a situation that was getting out of his grasp. It was always vexing trying to manipulate pieces by remote control. Like playing chess by post with an erratic mail service. The response was cool but receptive. He quickly gave instructions on how

166

new tickets were to be obtained from the Embassy if the originals remained with the police. He told her the number where Odhiambo could contact him later in the day. Then he terminated the call. He needed to make more calls urgently. What the devil happened to Musoke?

Cari replaced the receiver, feeling frightened and tense – the usual reaction to finding the tentacles of that sinister monster closing around you. But also there was hope. She must tell her mother. She turned to find Abbie hovering in the doorway, looking anxious and holding an envelope.

'Mum, what's the matter? What have you got there?'

'Cari, I found something. It was stuck with tape on to the bottom of his drawer.' The hand holding the envelope moved forward as if cranked by an invisible lever. 'This is it.'

'What is it? What have you found?'

Her mother's hand was fully extended now and Cari rose from her chair beside the telephone and moved towards her.

'Read it. You'll understand it better than me.'

'OK. But Mum, there's some good news. Well, I hope it's good. I think Dad may be safe and on his way back to Kenya. God knows what's going on. But somebody senior in Nairobi wants us back there. Says he thinks he can get Dad out of whoever's hands he's in.'

It was Abbie Bito's turn to sink into a chair. Hope, confusion, fear chased across her face, but were displaced by a look of stoic endurance that settled her mouth into a determined line. She gestured towards the envelope in her daughter's hand.

'I need to get my thoughts together, Cari. You read.'

Cari looked at the envelope; it was addressed 'Abbie'. She inserted her fingers in the flap at the narrow end and removed the contents, which were two lined sheets of folded quarto-sized notepaper. She read quickly.

My Dear Wife

If you come to read this it may be because I have miscalculated and am no longer able to be with you. We have made a good life here in America and raised a daughter we are so proud of. I wanted to let the past stay buried. For the last few years even Omuto's face has faded from my nightmares, but he will not rest it seems and he returns to haunt us again. I am so sorry, my dear, that I have made a mess of things – I think that must be the truth if events are such that you are reading this.

I have been pressed by Chivers to volunteer my evidence to the Omuto enquiry. You know my role and the guilt that has stayed with me. And how Chivers prevented me being set up as the sacrificial goat. What you don't know and what I didn't know until yesterday is that Chivers knows more than I thought. He sent me a note, very cryptic and instructions to burn it! The gist was that when he interrupted the men trying to plant the gun on me – the gun that killed Omuto – he caught sight of one of them. Not much light and only a fleeting glance. But something happened to jog his memory. Now he knows who it was and most likely he is the gunman who killed Omuto. He says we must talk.

I intend to go and see him this evening before our party for Cari and James. If he knows who did it and that person is tied to Kiwonka then Chivers is the vital witness, not me. But if he steps forward and needs me to back him up I may have to reconsider my position. I can't see how I'm in any more difficulty than I was already, but Chivers' note ends with a warning that I am in danger. He's been reading too many political thrillers from Crown Books. But if you read this he may have been right.

As I don't know what Chivers is afraid of I can't advise you what to do after reading this. I must leave it to your good sense. You've always been the sensible one. The important thing is to keep yourself and Cari out of anything to do with this affair. Particularly Cari. It's not good to be in Kenya with knowledge of past crimes.

Your loving husband.

It was signed with a giant curly S.

Cari looked up. Her mother was watching her intently and spoke as soon as her daughter's eyes left the page.

'It's too late, isn't it, to keep it from you? Too much has happened.'

'Of course, Mum.' Cari crossed over and, kneeling, took her mother's head to her breast in an action of love and penitence. 'I've been too busy with my own affairs, haven't I? We haven't talked enough.'

'Oh, Cari. I thought I was strong but these last few days . . .'

'You have been strong. And alone, and that's my fault.'

'What do you make of Samuel's message? And what do you know about what's going on?'

'There's a *mzungu* in Nairobi. Bad news. We, James and I, had problems with him before I came back. But he's important and influential. He just told me Dad is in Kenya or will be. And he's trying to free him. Don't ask me what's going on. But it must be because of all this.' Cari tapped the pages she was still holding. 'Chivers was right, Dad was in danger, but so was he. He got killed and Dad kidnapped. Once Chivers was dead Dad must have needed time to work things out, but he didn't have enough time. And he must have forgotten the message. It had been overtaken by events – he'd have removed it if he remembered.'

'Cari, if Mr Chivers was killed because of Kenyan politics, what about your Mr Hills?'

'Look, don't worry now, Mum. I think, incredibly, we've got two separate murders – well, three as a matter of fact, but at least two different motives. James thinks he knows what's going on so we'll let him worry that one out.'

'So what do we do?'

'We track down Lieutenant Bolling and show him this. And where Bolling is we may find James.'

The two women rose to their feet, Cari's hand locked in her mother's larger one. Cari felt a bond of love and understanding that she had not experienced with her mother for a long time. She smiled and the older woman smiled back, but the moment was severed by the intrusion of the telephone announcing a caller.

'Hello, this is Cari Bito.'

'Cari, it's Sally.' The voice was strained and higher-pitched than normal, but was still unmistakably that of Sally Eves. 'We need to get together. Or I need to see your man, what's his name – Odhiambo.'

'Sally, what's up? I'm kind of full up with my own crises at the moment.'

'This is all one with your problems. You see, I remembered something. I think it's relevant to the murder. Something that happened the night of your party. Something someone said. The security man. Then tonight I was talking to a *Washington Post* man. Turned out he'd been in Kenya. Knew about the incident. What he said got me thinking.'

'What on earth are you talking about, Sally?'

'Look, I wouldn't put it past Giles to tap this phone. So can't say more. I'm busy too right now. Come here in the morning, early. Do you hear? It's urgent. You or your husband may be able to explain. If not, I must tell the police.'

'OK. But what are you talking about? Sally? Sally?'

But Sally Eves had hung up. Cari turned back to her mother and this time it was the daughter who sought reassurance.

21

Giles Faucon sat very still in his chair; the two men flanking him at the top of the table waited. They had gone over and over the likely implications of the Nigeria fertiliser affair if, as seemed increasingly likely, it involved a massive fraud. A lot depended on the details Caradonna provided when she arrived back in Washington. She had spoken to Khan from London and given him a broad outline. In a few hours she would be on the Pan-Am flight to Dulles. They had discussed Kraxma's position. Mensat Khan had tried once more to make the point that Kraxma's involvement was by no means certain.

'I've seen him, Giles. The man is in a nasty spot. Suspected of murder, fraud and God knows what. He's upset rather than worried, I'd say. He seems to have confidence that nothing can be proved against him.'

Faucon had gestured with the back of his hand as if dismissing Kraxma's posturings as unworthy.

'If there's been fraud on a big scale involving the Metroarcs contract, Kraxma is responsible in any case. Furthermore we know of a social relationship with the Metroarcs man who's been killed.'

'If he's involved and he's made money out of it why would he sit here and bluff it out? When Chivers and Hills were killed he could have fled. He'd know of places he could go where if you've got sufficient resources you're safe.'

'Over-confidence does not equate with innocence. Besides, Kraxma does not concern me. With or without Kraxma we have a media problem.'

It was at this point that the third man present, an American in charge of public relations for IBID, received a bleep of his pager. When he returned it was with news that had sent Faucon into his silent concentration.

'It was my contact at the *Post*. Miss Eves has suggested an exclusive on a scandal within IBID. The *Post* is seeing her tomorrow. Her press release was bad enough but if she's got the basis of a fuller story the *Post* will make a meal of it.'

Faucon's period of mental retreat was completed; his eyes returned to rest briefly on his two companions in turn. Then he reached for the telephone beside him and pressed a button.

'Is Katawi there? He's gone.' A frown marred the smooth forehead – a rare facial manifestation of irritation. 'Yes, it is Faucon. You have a list. Yes, I know what it refers to. Bring it in to my office. Immediately.'

He replaced the receiver and looked again at his companions, his pale eyes seeming to reflect an inner intensity.

'I thought it prudent to use a consultant security agent to monitor Miss Eves' calls.' The PR man shifted uneasily in his chair and looked down at the table. A hint of a smile widened Faucon's lips, millimetres only and briefly. 'He keeps Katawi's people notified of calls. Tapes follow.'

'You don't need me to say be careful.'

'No, Mensat, I don't need telling. Cover is included in the contract. I am concerned if too many of Katawi's people are involved.'

A tap at the door heralded Faucon's secretary who in turn ushered in a pale, thin man, no more than thirty, Khan surmised, who had the look of a frightened rabbit. He fixed his darting eyes on Faucon and almost trotted to the head of the table. The secretary hovered, not sure if she should have allowed this nondescript individual into the presence or whether she should have delivered the sheet herself. As always her instincts proved faultless.

'Thank you, Jane.' The communication between them was of long standing and Jane withdrew. Late though the hour was, she was there whilst he needed her. Her loyalty was to him rather than to the institution. Faucon turned his attention to the messenger who had already turned to leave. 'Wait. You are?' The man turned back and seemed to hesitate.

'Moore. I work for Mr Katawi.'

'Quite so. How many of you know of this list and its origins?'

'Just him and me, sir – er . . . I think. And I don't know the source number. Mr Katawi had to go out. Just after these details came through. I'm . . . er . . . I have to stay to type summaries of the tapes when they come.'

'I see.' Faucon scanned the list. There were only four entries. 'Right, thank you.'

As the messenger withdrew Faucon read the entries more

carefully. It claimed to be a log of calls covering the period from four o'clock that afternoon until eight. The telephone numbers were listed followed by the name of the person Sally spoke to and a remark by the recorder. The first was to someone called Gilbride, reference his police interview and information on IBID. The second and third were to the same individual with the remark, 'Washington Post re story on scandal of misused funds in IBID.' The last entry was to a Washington number on domestic detail. It was the next and additional entry that Faucon concentrated on. It said, 'Agent called although next report not due. Subject made call at 9.17 to Virginia number. Person called identified herself as Cari Bito. Conversation referred to subject's knowledge of evidence of a murder. Said she suspected phone was tapped by someone referred to as Giles. Talked of going to police but after meeting in morning. Subject sounded under strain.'

Faucon leaned forward to speak to his intercom.

'Jane, speak to that man who was just here. Tell him to arrange for delivery of the tape covering the late evening without delay. And to bring it here.' He turned at last to his silent companions. 'So, gentlemen. You have at best twenty-four hours to counteract whatever this woman is intending to say. It may be worse than we think. She is claiming to know something about the murders. She is losing control of herself. When we get the tape we will be better informed, but go and start your counter-offensive now. Everything we know about SEND, and everything on our processes to prevent fraud and our depth of investigation when, rarely, these processes fail.'

Sean Gilbride looked at the man who had reluctantly allowed him into his apartment with barely concealed distaste. He had never liked the sardonic, arrogant demeanour of Guy Fulton, but now that he found himself reliant on Fulton's goodwill his dislike intensified.

'Now see here, Fulton. 'Tis past time for game playing, that it is. I couldn't help but tell the police you were my source.'

Fulton had not offered his unexpected guest a chair. He stood stiffly in his lounge facing this dishevelled late-night caller.

'God you're a little shit, Gilbride. You dig yourself into a hole doing that Eves woman's dirty work and then you try and drag me into it.'

Gilbride's spirit was far from broken.

'You gave me half a bun, Fulton. Typically, I may add. Put me on to Kraxma and Hills, but nothing Sally could use. I had to put the arm on Hills. Now the police are harassing me.'

'I hear they're interrogating Kraxma.'

'So I believe. But I don't know if they've got enough to charge him.'

Fulton let out a crude oath, then turned away as if he could bear Gilbride's presence no longer. Gilbride watched. He knew Fulton well enough to know that at bottom he was a weak if vindictive man. Sure enough, he saw Fulton turn back to face him.

'You're a clown, Gilbride. You're like something out of one of your French plays. Kraxma and Hills have been running a scam in Nigeria. That doesn't mean Kraxma killed Chivers. Kraxma is smarter than he looks. If he's sitting it out it's because he thinks he's fireproof – on the murders and the fertiliser money. You were supposed to go after them on the Nigeria business, not get tangled up in Chivers' murder.'

'But if Kraxma didn't kill Chivers – or closer to home if he didn't kill Hills – then who did? That's what I was after telling you. I don't want the police coming after me. If you deny you got me involved it could be awkward, that it could.'

Fulton opened his arms, in a mock insincere gesture of concern.

'Your problems are no concern of mine, Gilbride.'

But the voice tailed off a little uncertainly as his visitor advanced towards him. Gilbride extended a finger and held it close to Fulton's face.

'You keep forgetting, Mr Guy bloody Fulton, that you rely on my discretion with regard to that young lad in my company. It could have been a bit awkward for you, that. Still could if I had a mind.'

There was a strained pause. When Fulton spoke the arrogance was missing.

'Damn you, Gilbride. I should never have got involved with you and your sodding SEND. I'll do what I can, but we need to have a cover story. I can't have it put about I was blabbing IBID's secrets to outsiders. Where would that leave me with Faucon?'

'Better that than if other stories reached his ears, I should say. OK. If you would make a fellow a mite welcome and give him a drink we might be able to put our heads together and that's a fact.'

22

Bolling sat behind his desk chewing furiously on a new pencil. James Odhiambo sat facing him across the desk sipping from a styrofoam cup of coffee. Finally, the phone rang and Bolling snatched at the receiver. He listened and shook his head slightly at Odhiambo.

'OK. Put out an all-station on him. Pull him in when seen. And keep a snooper on the house. Right.' Bolling replaced this phone. 'The guy's gone to ground. No trace since early this evening.'

Odhiambo drained his cup and tossed it into the trash can beside the desk.

'I don't like it, Bolling. I got a feeling about this. He's panicking. Thrashing about.'

'You mean he ain't gone to no movie tonight.'

'He was seen after Musoke's death, right?'

'Yessir, he was back in dear ol' Virginia, going about his business.'

'Yeah. That's what worries me. What made him rush off again?'

Bolling rolled the pencil across his mouth until it was comfortably lodged in the other corner.

'You're sure you've got the right man?'

'For Chrissake, Bolling, we've been over and over this.'

Bolling nodded.

'Just doubting aloud, you might say. Trying to convince myself we haven't got ourselves heading down a false trail.'

'You know as well as I do that either we've got two separate murderers and causes for murder involving many of the same people or there's one unifying reason and the rest is irrelevant. The Nigeria business may be big with IBID and Metroarcs involved but it has nothing to do with Sam Bito who's disappeared or Musoke who's dead.'

'Except Sam Bito's daughter works for Metroarcs and the first victim knew Musoke as well as having the means to blow the whistle on the Nigeria scam.'

'Oh, come off it. That's too tenuous.'

'Chivers, Musoke, Bito, OK. But it's you that's on tenuous ground with Hills. There's no connection.'

'Except he rushes back from his country home after seeing the SEND fellow, gets out this telephone directory, circles a name, makes a call and goes off to Roosevelt Island. The only thing I didn't understand is what Gilbride told him that triggered his actions.'

'Well, I've told you what Gilbride told me, but we can pick him up and have another go.'

'I think he's given us the clue. Gilbride's claimed source in IBID. OK, so he mentions the name and that starts the alarm bells ringing in Hills' head. I think he saw something. Suppose Hills had been to see Kraxma at the IBID offices before coming to the party. He must have seen our friend in the building. You need to get this out of Kraxma. Hills' visit, I mean. Hills doesn't make the connection until Gilbride reminds him of the name. Then something strikes him as odd. He goes back to town, rings, makes an appointment and sets himself up. So that's one of the missing jigsaw pieces.'

'And the other? You said there were two.'

'The other is what caused the hurried interception of Musoke. Was he going to tell me something? Or was it something he'd found out that would be relayed to Nairobi? Did Musoke ring him up too? Same as Hills did. Asking for an explanation and so signing his death warrant? What's the matter with everyone? They got a death wish or what?'

'It's all a castle in the air, Odhiambo, you know that.'

'No. There's the car, the missing clothes, the data file stolen but the screen left on, the Caradonna interview, and most of all the name and number circled in Hills' directory. With all of that you'll break him once you get hold of him.'

The door opened and a close-cropped head appeared around the edge.

' 'Scuse me, Lieutenant, a Mrs Odhiambo is here.'

'Thanks. OK, Odhiambo, you get on home with your better half and I'll let you know as soon as we get somewhere.'

Odhiambo looked at his watch. Cari had made good time since he called to say he was back at Bolling's station. He rose from the chair.

'Yeah. Meanwhile I'll get hold of the big white chief at home. See if he can confirm some link at the Kenya end. And thanks for listening.'

'So long, feller.'

As Odhiambo emerged to the general reception area, Cari rushed to him as if she hadn't seen him for weeks rather than three hours.

'Oh, James. Thank God it's working out. You said on the phone you and Bolling were agreed?'

Odhiambo looked around. There was the usual flotsam and jetsam from the streets to be found in a police station at night. He eased Cari back to arm's length, holding her gently by the elbows. He looked into her eyes and winked.

'We're on our way. I'll tell you about it when we get to the car. Come on – let's get out of here.'

They eased past an incoming group of two drunks escorted by a tough-looking uniformed policeman and made their way to the street. Cari gestured towards the parking lot beside the station.

'It's in here.'

They walked towards the car. Odhiambo sought confirmation of the message his wife had delivered on the telephone.

'So Price-Allen reckons Sam is safe – and all will be well as long as we get back there.'

'Yes. I don't understand it. He surely wouldn't kidnap Dad just to hurry your return?'

'No. He needs Sam as a witness. But I don't understand why he was taken right after Chivers' death.'

'Oh, James. Mum found a letter Dad wrote the day of the party. Apparently, Chivers knew more than Dad thought. About Omuto, I mean. He knew who the gunman was.'

Odhiambo grabbed his wife by the arms again.

'That's it. That's it. Chivers was a main witness. When he was eliminated Price-Allen knew Sam might be next. So he got Musoke to organise the snatch. God, I'll break the bastard's neck when I get back.'

Cari pulled away and rubbed her upper arms – her husband's grip had been fierce.

'Only after he gets Dad free. Yes, Dad wrote that he was going to see Chivers to discuss what Chivers had just remembered. So whoever killed Chivers might have thought Dad knew too. So if Price-Allen had him kidnapped, perhaps it isn't so bad, given what happened to others like Musoke.'

They were in the car with Cari reversing from the parking slot. As she drove away Odhiambo gave her a quick summary of his conclusions. Cari immediately posed the same question as Lieutenant Bolling.

'But why Glen? Where's the connection? I wonder if Sally knows? She said it was something that was said at our party.'

'What are you talking about, Cari? What's Sally got to do with it?'

Odhiambo listened as Cari told him about the call from Sally Eves. He urged her to remember Sally's words as precisely as she could.

'That's it, James. Oh, and she said she was afraid her phone was tapped.'

'Her phone's tapped? Why would her phone be tapped? Is the FBI investigating SEND or something?'

'No. She's going after IBID so she thinks her ex-boyfriend, what's-his-name Faucon, she's afraid he may be bugging her.'

'And she told you Katawi had said something at your party to do with Chivers' death?'

'Relating to our problems, is what she said. I tried to put her off by saying we were up to here with our own problems and she said that's what she wanted to see me about.'

'And she thinks IBID is listening.' Odhiambo lapsed into silence as he digested this latest information. Cari drove on, heading now up the Washington Parkway with the lights of Georgetown across the river and receding behind them. 'Oh my God!' Cari looked across at the muttered blasphemy. 'Cari! Turn off this damn road and turn round. We've got to go back.'

'Back! Back where? To Bolling?'

'No. To Sally Eves' place. And quickly. I'll explain later. I may be wrong, but I need to be sure.'

Odhiambo sank back into a troubled silence, unheeding of his wife's demands for information. The trail of blood, he thought, was becoming a river. He had seen this before: a killer who kills for some pressing reason, believing the murder will be an end in itself, who finds he has to kill again until like a deranged scorpion he strikes again and again heedless that the next lash may be self-inflicted. He knew with a terrible certainty that he must this night bring this sequence to an end. But would it be too late?

Cari, now gripped, by a process of osmosis, with her husband's sense of urgency, drove across Roosevelt Bridge at a speed well in excess of the limit, passing some late-night cars heading into the city. She turned left and left again and soon was approaching Sally

Eves' apartment building overlooking the river. Next to the famous Watergate building, linked for ever with the fall of Richard Nixon, it was more anonymous but equally sumptuous. Cari parked in a spare parking bay.

'OK, James, we're here. You want to see Sally, follow me.'

The Odhiambos' entrance into the building was observed from inside a brown Chevrolet parked across the street.

'Shit, man,' said the passenger to the driver as he tapped his cigarette pack to release another cylinder. 'Two more, only these drive right up to the front door. This here rap is a turn-off, man. What the f –'

'Shut up.' The driver was curt. 'Michael don't care what you think. You ain't asked for no opinions. Never mind who else is going in, it's the dude coming out you gotta see, if you don't wanna lose them eyes of yours.'

James Odhiambo followed his wife to the porter's room that guarded the door to the internal foyer and, presumably, the elevators. The porter, an elderly black Washingtonian, too old to change his old-fashioned chauvinist ways, looked past Cari's shoulder at Odhiambo.

'We've come to see Miss Eves. Odhiambo and . . . er . . . Cari Bito.' It was always difficult to refer to his wife by her maiden name, but that is how the Eves woman would know her. 'She wants to see us.'

The porter's mouth hung open in an expression of bemusement that changed rapidly to one of suspicion. His hand crept towards the bell inside the doorway in which he was now framed.

'Od-iam-bo, you say. Why, there's a Mr Odhiambo gone up to see Miss Eves a few minutes ago.'

Odhiambo pushed Cari aside and went to grab the porter's lapels but contented himself with holding the arm that prevented the hand reaching the alarm bell.

'Look, I'm Odhiambo. I'm a policeman. Take us to Miss Eves now. She's in danger. Quick, man. The other visitor is dangerous. Come on!'

The porter hesitated but Cari's intervention won the day.

'My husband's who he says he is. I'm a friend of Sally's. You've seen me before.'

'OK, ma'am. Yes, I know you. It's just this gen –'

'Never mind.' Odhiambo felt the blood pounding in his ears. 'Come on and bring the pass key.'

'Maybe I'll just ring through –'

'There's no time. And we need surprise. Now move.'

Finally the porter pressed the release button on the trellised door and they hurried through the carpeted foyer.

'308,' Cari said. 'Oh good, there's an elevator open.'

'All muffled up he was,' said the porter meditatively. 'Anyone'd think it was a cold night.'

The porter turned left on the third-floor corridor and with Odhiambo almost dragging him into a run they reached a heavy door with the numbers 308 engraved alongside it. Odhiambo grabbed the key from the porter's hand and with one motion turned the lock and hurled himself against the door.

Simon Katawi was in the process of wrecking the lounge to simulate a violent burglary. He was about to drop a sideboard drawer as Odhiambo burst in. For a split second only he froze as his heart jumped, then instinctively he hurled the heavy drawer at Odhiambo's head, catching him a glancing blow before he had time to gain his balance after the undisciplined entry. Without hesitation Katawi ran to the balcony doors, released the catch, pulled them open and dashed out. Vaulting on to the protective wall, he took a quick glance, then lowered himself at full stretch holding on by his fingers. With a quick swing of his body he let go and landed on the balcony below. Struggling for his balance, he waved his arms then repeated the manoeuvre.

Odhiambo reached the balcony of Eves' apartment as Katawi gained the street. He shouted.

'Stop. The game's up, Katawi.'

Behind him he heard Cari scream, watched for a second more as Katawi ran off to the left, then went back into the lounge. Cari was looking at something behind a large settee, her hand now to her mouth. Odhiambo hurried over. As he feared, there lay the body of Sally Eves, blood still oozing from a wound at the side of her throat. Odhiambo bent and felt for a pulse, knowing it was too late. He straightened.

'Call the police, Cari, and wait for them here with him. OK?'

A nod confirmed the instruction. The porter also nodded as Odhiambo looked towards him. As he reached the door, the question came.

'Where are you going?'

'He ran off on foot. I'm going to try and cut him off.'

'Here's the car key. Be careful, James.'

Odhiambo caught the tossed key and ran for the elevators. Seeing stairs on his right he opted for the direct route and bounded down. Reaching the car he quickly pulled away from the building and navigated on to the road where Katawi had landed. As far as Odhiambo could tell, the route Katawi had taken would lead to either Roosevelt Bridge or the Kennedy Center, framed in light on his left. Had he left his car this way? Answers to both questions came more easily and certainly than Odhiambo expected. As he peered through the windscreen he saw a figure pass under a light on Roosevelt Bridge: a running figure! Odhiambo almost missed the access lane to the bridge. He accelerated, moved to the middle lane to pass a dull-coloured Chevrolet moving very slowly in the inside lane, and then regained the inside lane scanning anxiously the pedestrian sidewalk. Yes, there he was, well on his way to the exits off the bridge. I've got you, thought Odhiambo, as he came up behind the running figure. Katawi glanced back, staring momentarily at the lights about to draw alongside, then, to Odhiambo's amazement, he jumped on to the wide guard rail of the bridge, swung his feet over to the river side and disappeared from view. Odhiambo braked his car to a halt. Damn! Katawi had jumped into the river. Odhiambo had no intention of following. He had recently survived one immersion in water without being able to swim, but that had been involuntary. He hurried back to the spot where Katawi had jumped and looked over. To his surprise he found himself looking at the branches of a bush, still containing a fair proportion of its autumnal leaves. The bridge stretched on and curved to the right with the glint of water below it. For a long second Odhiambo was confused, then realisation dawned – this was Roosevelt Island, the untamed island where Hills had been disembowelled.

Odhiambo hesitated, but his excuse of being a non-swimmer was invalidated and no other came to mind. Following Katawi's example he hopped his bottom up on to the rail, swung his legs over, hesitated for one moment more and pushed himself towards the bush. He fell only a few feet, stumbled, fell forward, scratched his forehead on the base of the bush, but otherwise found himself on the island without serious damage. He picked his way forward carefully and within feet of his landing area found himself on a muddy path. He had heard talk about the island: its unspoiled, untended woods with just one main path around its perimeter and a path across the interior where the Roosevelt Memoiral was situated. He had seen it from the car – the whole thing was probably only a mile or so in circumference. Which way to go? The only access to the Island, he remembered, was on the Virginia side – a pedestrian bridge from the Washington Parkway. That would be what Katawi was making for. Odhiambo turned left and moved as swiftly as he dared along the dark narrow trail lit only by the reflected light from the moon, where it managed to penetrate the tangled foliage of the trees.

His senses had failed to record the arrival of a second car behind his as he made his jump off the bridge.

Cari heard the strident sound of the siren of the first police car arriving below her. She had contacted the police emergency number, but was now attempting to reach Lieutenant Bolling in Rosslyn. At last she heard the thin voice of her quarry.

'Look, this is Cari Bito, Mrs Odhiambo. I haven't got time to explain now, the DC police are arriving. Sally Eves is dead – murdered. James is chasing the killer. I think they may have headed your way over Roosevelt Bridge. He'll need help, please.'

Bolling's pencil snapped in two. He heard his caller talking to someone entering the room.

'Hello, Mrs Odhiambo, you still there?'

'Yes, but the policeman wants my hands in the air or something. Help James.'

The line went dead. Bolling swore. Well, what he knew of Mrs Odhiambo she'd cope for a while. He'd better see what was happening on his side of the river.

Around a bend in the path, Odhiambo saw ahead the moving lights of cars on the Parkway. The footbridge could not be far away. The glance ahead to the mainland proved his undoing, however. His foot snagged a trailing root and with a muffled curse he fell forward, protecting himself by taking his weight on his hands. In his role of night hunter with all senses at full alert he felt the sting as a sharp stone in the path dug into the flesh below his thumb. His inner senses screamed a different sort of warning, but lying prone he was unable to respond with sufficient speed. He felt the chill of the metal pressing against his neck and in what he expected to be his last second he irrationally wondered what Sally Eves' last

181

thought had been in the same situation a little earlier. But no oblivion came. Instead Katawi's voice.

'Get up, Odhiambo. Slowly.'

Odhiambo obeyed. The moon shone brightly on this spot, but he could not see his quarry turned hunter, who stayed behind him.

'What now, Katawi?'

'You walk slowly, bwana. To the bridge. You come with me to my office.'

Odhiambo stayed where he was.

'It's no good, Katawi. My wife will have called the police. Bolling is looking for you already. You'll get nowhere near IBID.'

'You're my passport, Odhiambo.'

Odhiambo took a deep breath and with his arms held well away from his body turned ever so slowly to face his adversary.

'I'm telling you, Katawi. A police car sees the two of us they'll be shooting first and asking questions later.'

The moonlight highlighted the eyes, the whites showing wide in the dark face. Odhiambo could not see the pupils, but he could sense the dilation. He was looking at the eyes of a madman.

'You say Bolling is looking for me. I say you're bluffing.'

'No, Katawi.' Odhiambo was playing for time. Here in the woods, in the dark, surely an opportunity would come. 'He and I know what's been going on. You started with Chivers and carried on from there.'

'Start walking, Odhiambo, or you'll walk no more. *Sasa*, *sasa*. I warn you.'

Reluctantly Odhiambo turned and started walking, but slowly, contrary to the Swahili instruction.

'Give yourself up, Katawi. You've no other option.'

'How did you guess it was me?'

'No guessing. Just too slow. The Nigeria business was a clever false trail. You stole the disc in the computer, but left the screen on to draw attention to the theft. It was smart, that. Then you were quick on your feet when given the chance to help me down the wrong road by giving me those files and steering me to Caradonna. Bolling was right from the beginning. Kenyan politics held the key. Chivers recognised you, didn't he? He recognised you as the man he saw with the gun that killed Omuto. He was potentially a deadly witness if you could be shown to be a Kiwonka man. So he had to go. Was Bito going to be next?'

'You're bluffing. There's no proof of any of that crap.'

'I'm not bluffing. Did he recognise you when he first saw you or did it slowly come to him – something familiar, then memory suddenly triggered? After all, it was a long time ago.'

'Just walk and keep your damn fantasies to yourself.'

'I knew you were at the office at the right time. Your car was still in your slot in the garage. The blood puzzled me. The killer must have got it on him. Did he change? Then I remembered – one of your guards said his wet weather suit was missing. You had access to the guards' room. You were due at Bito's party. You waited for him to go, put on the rainwear, killed Chivers, stuffed the bloody clothes and the weapon in the skip, knowing it was about to be emptied, and went to the party. The trouble was, Glen Hills saw something, didn't he?'

'All right, Odhiambo if you're so bloody curious, I'll tell you. It isn't going to do you any good, bwana. I was doing OK here and then the *mzungu* arrives. I knew the name and I remembered that night at the Centre. But there was no reason why he should recognise me. A couple of times we spoke, when we kinda met in the lobby whatever; I could see something in his eyes, he was puzzled. Then just a couple of weeks ago we were both at a cocktail do, someone from the Embassy also who said something about we were both from the Nakuru area, and I saw the memory come back. I knew he knew. Then, that night I saw Bito arrive. I checked the log – he'd gone to see Chivers. I was panic-stricken. Would he tell Bito? I didn't have a gun, but I'd seen his office. I knew the clubs were there. I put on the plastic pants and top and went to his office. Bito had left. "I don't want to talk to you," he said. "There's laws against libel in this country," I said. He laughed and turned back to his computer. "Don't worry. I'll talk only when I'm back at the enquiry." That was it.'

'But Hills, what did he see?'

'It was a bad medicine, Odhiambo. I came down in the elevator to get the car. As I entered the garage I saw a car parked next to mine. Door partly open so interior light was on. Hills was sitting there. I was in a hurry. It was important not to be too late at Bito's party so as not to be noticed. So I went back up and took a taxi. Then later I see him at the goddam party. Gave me a turn, that did.'

'But he didn't put things together until Gilbride told him he knew you. Katawi is the security chief at IBID, he says, or something like. And Hills links the man he met at the party with the man he caught a glimpse of in the garage. He hadn't told the police about being at

IBID for obvious reasons. Then he makes his mistake. Rings you up. I found your name circled in his telephone directory. The last call he made. You spun him some tale and got him to meet you over here and that was goodbye Mr Hills.'

'I've got witnesses I never left the building that morning. So you're not so smart.'

'OK. You get a knife man at short notice. No shortage around here. What did he tell you when he phoned?'

Katawi laughed.

'The fool still didn't catch on. He was frightened I'd recognised him. Wanted to give me some story. I realised it would click with him sooner or later. Why I'd turned back when I saw him and left my car there. So I fixed to meet him.'

Odhiambo saw ahead of him the turn on to the footbridge. On his right was a path with a sign. Probably the path to the memorial where Hills was killed. He came to a halt. He needed to be face to face if he was to have a chance. It was suddenly very quiet; he could hear the old decaying trees creaking in the breeze off the river and in the marshy undergrowth on his left he heard the slither and plop as a small denizen of the island slipped into the water. He felt the circumference of pressure on his back.

'Go on. The bridge is on the left.'

Odhiambo started to turn but Katawi's voice became a snarl.

'Walk or you're the second body on this island.'

Odhiambo moved forward again. The bridge was in sight with some form of barrier at the far end indicating the island was closed. The trees ended here with grass sloping down to the water. There was only a thin strip of water dividing the island from the mainland, Odhiambo remembered. Across the water the lights of the large tower blocks in Rosslyn dominated the sky and the sound of traffic suddenly invaded and suppressed the island sounds. Katawi started to speak again.

'Musoke arranged Sam Bito's kidnap. The Jamaicans did the job for him. I reckon they heard of me from the man who did the Hills job. I hadn't time to organise it without him knowing who I was. So Musoke was about to tell you and that *mzungu* in Nairobi. But he was as foolish as Hills. He called me, said friends of his had got my name as the guy who hired Hills' killer. Said Kenya didn't need scandal so I'd better get to the Embassy and see my friend Kasanga. He was meeting you at the Visa building, then he'd call the *mzungu* in Nairobi. No chance the Jamaicans will go to the police. That's when I realised I was unlucky. One *shauri* after another. Hills, Musoke, then that woman. I told her at the party Omuto was shot at the station. Shot in the body and the head, I said. I forgot the official report never mentioned the bullet in the body. The *Post* reporter told her no one knew that. Got her thinking. She was a smart woman, nearly as smart as my boss. Lucky I was there when the report of her call to your wife came in.'

Ah yes, thought Odhiambo, and Cari had told Sally his theory that the killer disposed of his outer clothes. She had worked things out too. Wondered how Katawi remembered such an unknown detail from so many years ago. Unless it was much in his mind because of Bito and Chivers.

'What put you on to me, Odhiambo? A lot of people could have changed their clothes.'

'Not many with access through the back basement door. Plus knowledge that the skip was about to be emptied. Most would have to go past the guard at the desk. But, since you ask, it was your help with the project files. I know I played the fellow citizen card but the more I thought about it the more unlikely it was that the chief of security would hand out files to someone he hardly knew and leave them with him in a bar. You were too easy to convince. So I wondered why. Could it be you were steering me in that direction?'

Odhiambo was now at the bridge. He felt in his bones that if they reached the other side he was doomed. His heart accelerated painfully at the sound of a voice behind him. It wasn't Katawi.

'Took you a long time to get here.'

Gun in his back or no, nothing could have stopped Odhiambo's involuntary turn. He was in time to see Katawi crumple to the path, struck from behind by a figure who pointed a gun at Odhiambo. The gun was aimed at Odhiambo but the voice was directed at Katawi slumped on the ground.

'You got no business icing friends of ours, man. Don't make us look good, you read?'

The gun switched from Odhiambo, there was a double muffled cough and Katawi's body stretched in a rictus of agony and then became still. Odhiambo made an involuntary movement towards the killer, but the second man struck the second blow and it was Odhiambo's turn to fall.

23

Odhiambo found himself in a swirling forest: as he tried to look around, the vaguely formed branches swirled through giant arcs and then swung back. Through the swinging branches light penetrated, flickering from blinding brightness to darkness like the sun shining through a rotating propeller. The light hurt his eyes, but his real discomfort was the screaming of an animal hidden in the trees – the wail of an animal in its death throes. Odhiambo wanted to be sick.

Slowly the imaginary forest stopped rotating and Odhiambo managed to open his eyes. He shut them again as once more nausea threatened to engulf his system, and waited. He tried once more and this time managed to keep them at least half-open. Thanks be, the screaming animal had stopped, only to start again – faintly at first but growing in volume. Slowly recognition came; it was another police vehicle arriving at the scene.

Odhiambo cautiously went to move his arms only to find they were constrained. Suddenly his world heaved as if an earthquake had struck and Odhiambo let out an involuntary cry. The cry echoed and his world steadied as the stretcher bearers lowered him back to the ground.

'It's OK, fella. Just take it easy. Can you hear me?'

Odhiambo opened his eyes once more: he was getting better at it. He nodded.

'I'd hear better if they cut off those damn sirens.'

There was a short laugh.

'He'll do. Look, fella, you've had a bit of a crack on the head. Just lie easy and we'll get you some treatment, OK?'

'Katawi. Where's Katawi?'

'Don't worry 'bout nothin' right now. OK? Mal, let's get him over the bridge.'

'Hang on. I've a message for Bolling. Lieutenant Bolling. It's urgent.'

'Bolling? Who's the guy here? Hey, Lieutenant, victim here wants to say somethin'.'

Odhiambo heard the exclamation and then the familiar voice. He opened his eyes yet one more time, this time with a hope of permanency, and saw the outline of Bolling's head framed against some form of floodlight.

'Odhiambo. Can you hear me?'

'Everyone keeps asking me that. I can hear you and I can see you and I'm bloody pleased at that.'

'Yeah, well, you keep from getting excited. We'll have time to talk.'

'Katawi?'

'He's dead. Shot. You didn't know?'

'I remember. He got the jump on me. Was making me go with him. Then there was a voice. Talking to Katawi. Then he shot him.'

'Who, Odhiambo? Did you recognise him?'

'And Eves – Sally Eves. He killed her. Went to the apartment with Cari. Where's Cari?'

'Take it easy, just relax. Don't struggle on that thing. You're supposed to be quiet. We know about the Eves woman. The DC boys are dealing with it. Your wife got a message to me so I came looking for you. Got a report of cars up on the bridge and people jumping over so I thought you couldn't be far away.'

'Yeah. I stopped my car up there.'

'So I saw. But there was another behind yours. Unfortunately, by the time I arrived it had moved on, probably to the car-park here so that they could wait for Katawi at the bridge. We're looking for it now. Did you see the guy?'

'No. Too dark. He said something to Katawi, something about business with his friends. Oww!'

A searing pain shot through Odhiambo's skull as feeling returned.

Bolling touched one of the ambulance men on the shoulder and gestured.

'Get him to the hospital. I'll see him there. I'll send a man with him to keep an eye on him, OK?'

'No. Bolling, get a message to Cari. Tell her . . . tell her to tell the . . . the . . . *mzungu* in Nairobi that he must look after Sam . . . Sam Bito 'cos I got Omuto's killer.'

'OK. OK. I'll do it. Now quiet.' Bolling added *sotto voce* to the medic, 'Give him a shot otherwise he's going to get too excited.'

The movement of the stretcher as they crossed the bridge sent the rods of pain stabbing through his head but as they loaded him into an ambulance he fell back into a uneasy unconsciousness.

Cari Odhiambo waited at Sally Eves' apartment in accordance with the message relayed by one of the DC policemen on the scene. She did not have to wait long before Bolling arrived, spoke briefly with his counterpart in charge of the crime scene and came over to where she was sitting in Sally's dining-room.

Bolling gave her a quick synopsis of events on Roosevelt Island, assuring her that her husband was not seriously injured and in good hands.

'I'll take you over to the Arlington Hospital, but first your husband asked me to give you a message. He was very anxious you call a certain individual in Nairobi without delay.'

Cari, once apprised of the message, understood what James had in mind – and nobody better than Price-Allen, she thought, to know how to put the squeeze on. She called her mother both to reassure her that all was well, despite certain matters to be explained later on, and to get her to find Price-Allen's number in her notepad. She had to battle with impatience for nearly an hour, but at last the familiar voice was on the line. Cari gave him a suitably edited version of events.

'. . . and James is in hospital yet again. But he's got a confession including admitting to murdering Omuto on you know who's orders. He won't hold a press conference here as long as I'm able to tell him that Sam Bito is safe.'

There was only the briefest of pauses, followed by a dry chuckle. 'He is a character, your husband. And possessing a priceless ability to blunder about yet still arrive at the centre of the maze. The government would not welcome too much press speculation over there. I am now able to tell you, my dear lady, that your father is safe and well in the hands of government officials.'

'I don't call that much of an assurance.'

'I was about to say that this is but a step to his full freedom. He is being looked after while his health is checked, that's all. If you would care to speak to him I can arrange it. It would be helpful if you told him you would soon be here. And that you and your husband hope he will help to bring the right man to justice.'

'You have seen him? My father? Where is he?'

'I give you my word he is in Nairobi and in good health.'

'Your word is worth nothing to me, Mr Price-Allen. I'm going now to see my husband. He or I will ring you in say eight hours – that's morning here. I expect to speak to my father.'

Suddenly, there was a marked bite to the tone of the reply and Cari was reminded that she was dealing with a very dangerous man whom she could not afford to alienate.

'My word may mean little to you, but it has saved you and your husband before. You would do well to remember that. Give me your home number. I will call you at 10 a.m. your time and I will have Dr Bito with me.'

With that, Cari had to agree. On arrival with Bolling at the hospital they were quickly allowed access to the stricken Odhiambo, bedded alone in a small room with one of Bolling's men outside the door. Cari looked at her husband across the length of the bed. Bandaged around his head, he greeted her with a raised hand and a wink. She crossed to his side and kissed him on the mouth.

'Oh, James. What will I ever do with you?'

'This is nothing, Cari. Flesh wound. My head's too thick, they tell me. Hello, Bolling. Sorry if I was a bit vague earlier. Concussion, I guess. Now, Cari, love you and all, but first – did you get my message?'

He was reassured by his wife's quick account of her conversation with Price-Allen. Bolling listened with a sardonic grin.

'So I take it your father is back in Kenya, Mrs Odhiambo?'

'Yes. Although how he got there I don't know.'

James Odhiambo shot a glance at the Virginian policeman.

'The Jamaicans you think took him. I was thinking back to that bloody island.'

Bolling intervened.

'A Jamaican gang was probably hired to snatch Dr Bito and hand him over somewhere to another contractor, probably in South America, who would spirit him back to your people. The man or men who hired them wanted Dr Bito in Kenya alive not dead at Katawi's hand here. Chivers' death triggered it off.'

'Yes. Musoke was the middleman, and an intelligence man in Kenya called Price-Allen almost certainly was the one who called the shots. I'll get even with him one day for this. Chivers knew Katawi as a political assassin but he didn't tell Sam Bito. Katawi got that out of him before he killed him. Still, he couldn't be sure. He came to the party having killed Chivers to see how the land lay. Took nerve, I grant him that. Unfortunately, word about his role started getting about. Hills, Musoke, Eves. Katawi started on an orgy of killing. I don't know what he expected to happen in the end. I guess he became deranged. But it's Katawi's death that puzzles me. Was it –?'

Once again Bolling intervened, speaking while placing a friendly but restraining arm on the woman beside him who looked as if she was about to explode with frustration.

'I've spoken to the DC boys. It's likely Musoke was the Jamaicans' client. The police in DC have found the body of a young thug who works or worked with a knife. Looks as if he was executed. Looks like the Jamaicans got upset at Katawi going solo, and when he rubbed out their client they felt their status was at stake. The DC boys figure it's a man called Michael at the top. Arrogant guy and vicious. Can you remember what the goon who shot Katawi said? His precise words?'

'Yeah, it's come back to me. It was something about not making them look good when their friends were killed.'

'That's it. Michael sent a hit squad to get Katawi. They followed him to the woman's place, trailed you and him and waited for him at the exit.'

'Why didn't he shoot me?'

' 'Cos they're shit scared of their boss. If Michael says get A, he doesn't like them getting A and B. For all the shooter knew, you might be one of the "friends". So he hit you hard enough to get away, but no more. You're a lucky man.'

Cari finally got a word in.

'I'm not sure I get all this. But if you know who it was, will you pick them up?'

Bolling shrugged.

'Knowing and proving is the difference between a base hit and a home run, ma'am. Michael will have covered his tracks. Still, that's DC's problem – not Virginia.'

'So, James, what's going to happen with Price-Allen?'

Odhiambo put his hand to his bandaged temple and sighed.

'He's got your Dad and will need him for the government enquiry to bring down Kiwonka. Or more likely, knowing Price-Allen, he'll use the threat of your Dad's evidence to get Kiwonka to scarper. Price-Allen doesn't believe in judicial enquiries. I've got to get home, Cari, and look after your Dad.'

And so it was, thought Cari. James was right, of course. But what hammered inside her mind was the word "home". For him Kenya was still home. She knew he believed his destiny lay there, but she was frightened as to what that destiny would be. She hesitated, but only for a moment.

'*We*, you mean, big guy. *We*'ve got to get . . . home. I'm with you, although at times you drive me nuts.'

She bent over him, a tear splashing on to his face. Bolling smiled and then softly turned and left them to their future.